BLUE WATER
DREAMS

Visit us at www.boldstrokesbooks.com

BLUE WATER DREAMS

by

Dena Hankins

2014

BLUE WATER DREAMS

© 2014 BY DENA HANKINS. ALL RIGHTS RESERVED.

ISBN 13: 978-1-62639-192-5

THIS TRADE PAPERBACK ORIGINAL IS PUBLISHED BY
BOLD STROKES BOOKS, INC.
P.O. BOX 249
VALLEY FALLS, NY 12185

FIRST EDITION: SEPTEMBER 2014

CREDITS
EDITOR: CINDY CRESAP
PRODUCTION DESIGN: SUSAN RAMUNDO
COVER DESIGN BY SHERI (GRAPHICARTIST2020@HOTMAIL.COM)

Acknowledgments

This book benefited tremendously, as I have more generally, from close contact with Kate Bishop. Your gift of giving positive feedback buoyed my confidence enough to send this manuscript in and your insightful input helped make it good enough to be accepted. Thanks, darlin'. James Lane gave me the crucial twist and the courage to write my friends instead of more "acceptable" people. Marilyn Azevedo-Rhodes's support has been unflagging (thanks, Mom). Dean Hankins gave me so much more than a name—you taught me to be a thinker, Dad, and what's a writer but a thinker who scribbles? I hope I've made you both proud.

Dedication

Because of you, James, "write what you know"
means romance and sailing to me.
Thank you for making life inspiring.

Chapter One

Lania sailed northeast into a cobalt sky unseen in Seattle since the previous spring. She slipped over the little wind waves, the lapstrake planks of the boat's hull amplifying the whispered flirtation between wood and water. The jib's clew floated above the green water of Lake Union.

Alone in a responsive boat, Lania raced across the north end of the lake, every gust an opportunity and every calm a test of her judgment on sail trim. Fingertips alive to the precise tension on the jib sheet, she milked each patch of moving air by hauling in or slacking the line a half-inch at a time. She scanned for the ruffled water that indicated air currents and slipped from pocket to pocket.

The engagement of mind and body in each moment filled her with energy. This was the most fun she'd had in weeks. Puff chasing in a long ellipse around Lake Union.

She squinted at some rougher water ahead. The varnished teak tiller rested along her hip, transmitting the Morse code of the water's motions from the rudder into her listening flesh. She tugged the main sheet free of the fiddle block's cam cleat. The line sizzed through a block and tackle system that quadrupled her strength and made short work of bringing the boom lower and closer to the centerline.

She firmed her hands on the tiller and jib sheet as the green waters lifted, the peaks lightening to celadon and then growing frothy white beards behind each wind wave. She braced a foot on the opposite side of the cockpit as the small wooden boat began to heel and flexed her forearm and wrist in slow counterpoint to the growing force building behind the sails.

A tangled curl whipped across her cheek and lips, but she ignored the tickle. She pushed the tiller harder to port and fed the jib just enough slack to spill a little wind. This rebalancing of forces brought her up to an exhilarating six knots. She sailed the knife's edge where sail shape and heel combined for the best possible speed.

A young girl, eight or nine, zigged and zagged toward her on a tiny sailboat called a Laser. The child bounced from rail to rail on each tack as another child might walk along kicking a pinecone—casually, comfortably, and absorbed in enjoying herself.

Envy nipped at Lania, whose first sailing lesson was only one year past. She thought of all the reading she'd done—books of salty nomenclature, aero- and hydrodynamic theory, and the rules of the road. She'd done what she could to prepare, but the water, the sensory feedback of current, hull shape, and sail trim, had taught her what she really needed to know. Her inner ear judged balance faster than her brain. She could tack based on a feeling and justify it later with fact.

The envy dissipated in the pride of knowing that she had a knack for this.

As the girl drew close, Lania waved as sailors do. A small hand raised in her direction before another tack took the child and her Laser behind Lania's borrowed boat.

If she'd started sailing as a child, she could have set out right after high school. Or at least right after college. Sailing offered her a great deal of pleasure, but it was, for her, a means to an end.

I could be anywhere. Electricity pulsed through her body. *Not just if I'd learned earlier, but right now. Right now, I can travel anywhere I want.* Lania's hand tightened on the teak tiller.

A year's worth of study, work, and fun came into focus against the restlessness she'd always felt and the stagnation that had begun to permeate her life. She needed to explore, to savor the shiver of nerves that came along with the unknown. She was a good sailor—getting better all the time. She could launch herself into the world and sail it. A boat could get her from place to place, be her home base around the world, and provide the adventure she craved.

Lania eased out of the wind's path. The mast rose again toward the sky as she fed the jib some line in the softening breeze and tugged the mainsheet out of the fiddle block's cam cleat. As she knew it would, inertia slid the dinghy toward the Center for Wooden Boats with all sail slacked.

Joy warmed her in the cool air of spring. Underpinning the simple happiness of the moment, a deeper satisfaction and brighter excitement flowed from her newfound conviction.

She, Lania Marchiol, was going to buy a boat and set sail for parts unknown.

Lania stood in the cockpit as the boat approached the dock head-on. Her lashes filtered the sun's glare as she squinted, assessing the perfect moment to spin the boat parallel to the wooden float. She looped a dock line on her hand and saw a backlit figure wave from the float.

"Toss me your stern line!" A man's voice, unfamiliar and unwelcome at this moment.

Annoyed to have her concentration broken, Lania shouted her reply. "No, thanks."

The bow loomed over the rough plank on the edge of the float before she pushed the tiller hard to port in the final turn upwind. The stern slewed, rotating the boat into dock and bringing Lania within an easy step of the float. She dropped the tiller and hopped off the boat to snug the stern line to a handy cleat. With calm competence, she walked forward and pulled the bow line off the deck to finish making fast the boat.

She stepped back onto the deck to lower the sails, but the same voice disturbed her solitary peace once again. "Want a hand with the sails?"

Lania turned from the halyards at the main mast to look up at the persistent helper. Haloed by the mid-afternoon sun, his face was faded in shadow, and Lania could only see the general shape of him. He looked lean but strong in baggy shorts and a T-shirt. A brush of short pale hair glowed in the light, and Lania could just make out his sharp, youthful features.

Some of these boat nuts would do anything to get aboard. Lania sympathized, but she liked settling the boat herself. "No, thank you. I'm fine."

"Okay." His graceful shrug matched his easy tone, but he shifted his weight without leaving. Lania brought down the main sail, flaking it in neat, even folds. Self-conscious, she glanced at the man again. The brief look must have communicated her discomfort to him, as he gave a little wave and turned to walk away.

He sauntered down the bobbing float, and she watched him leave before turning to bring down the jib. As she let the sail drop to the deck and then unhanked it from the forestay, the image of a fit, graceful walk slipped into her thoughts. A very attractive man.

A half hour later, she'd stowed and scrubbed and made all secure. After pampering the small boat she'd borrowed, she shrugged her backpack on and made the rounds of the docks to check on her other favorites. Each boat was a carefully maintained work of art, from a red-painted seven-foot-long skiff to the forty-three-foot gaff-rigged teak schooner glowing with deep layers of old varnish. Of the twenty-seven boats owned by the Center, Lania spotted almost a dozen missing. A busy Sunday at the beloved but usually quiet non-profit.

Seattle knew how to take advantage of a sunny day.

On her way out, she glanced into the busy workshop beside the bottom of the gangplank. She waved to the slight old man pulling fragrant curls of wood from a teak board with a hand plane. He raised his bristly chin in quiet acknowledgement. His hands matched the grain and shade of the teak on which he often worked, and his calm, strength, and pride warmed her heart.

The Center for Wooden Boats floated by a lakeshore park that Lania enjoyed using as an office. A rich aroma of sawn wood, pine needles, and grass underpinned the living smell of freshwater plants. An oyster shell path split the Center's park, connecting the gangplank to the parking lot. The path curved under a pavilion displaying Coast Salish and Nootkan-style canoes and kayaks built by summer camp kids. Lania's bike was locked to a large-linked old anchor chain that ran around the park in a semicircle from the parking lot to the gangplank. A thorny tangle of blackberry vines draped the land's edge beyond the chain.

Lania slid into the park's picnic table with the sun behind her and fished her notebook from her backpack. The most recent submission she'd accepted for her magazine needed extensive editing. She pulled out the typed pages and began reading. Only a sentence into the piece, she started writing editing points in her notebook.

"Mind if I join you?"

Lania recognized the voice but spoke without hesitation. "Of course."

"You do mind?" Humor shook the smooth tenor.

She frowned up at the man who'd tried to help her dock the boat. "I meant of course you may sit here. I don't mind."

"Thanks." He sat, placing a backpack and bicycle helmet on the seat next to him. His short golden hair extended down his angled jaw in the form of light stubble. Eyes the green of tender, newly unfurled leaves echoed the humor she'd heard in his voice. They compelled her to share the joke, and Lania responded with an unbidden smile. A quirk in his thin lips stretched into a wide grin in response.

"Oly Rasmussen."

He certainly looked Scandinavian. Trapped by politeness, Lania grasped Oly's hand. "Lania Marchiol." The warm length of his fingers curled around her hand.

"Tanya?"

"No, Lawn-ya. With an L. Italian."

Her clipped tone didn't have the desired effect. He squeezed her fingers. "Beautiful park, isn't it?"

She slid her hand free. "Yes." Okay, so he was sexy. Half-sleeves in bold designs peeked from under his shirt, the lines complimenting his well-developed biceps and triceps. Still, she had work to do.

"Don't talk much, do you?"

"I'm trying to focus on this essay." She tapped her pen against the printout that lay beside her open notebook.

"You're a student?"

"No, an editor."

"Of essays?" Persistent bugger.

She tucked a lock of hair behind one ear. "Yes, of essays."

"What's it about?"

Was he flirting with her? It had been a few years since she'd been attracted to a guy. Ginger, her best friend, claimed credit for introducing her to so many sexy women. But this guy…

Pretty eyes aside, she didn't have time for flirtation. She needed to get this essay sent back for revision right away. Also, if she was going to buy a boat and sail away, dating ranked low on her list of priorities.

Lania drew on her obfuscatory powers, sure he'd crumble under the onslaught. "It's an essay on gender roles in activist communities and vestigial gendered forms of protest. It discusses the virilization of honor and how activists both subvert and replicate normative gender ideologies."

"Wow." She returned her attention to the paper in front of her, but, to her surprise, he continued. "I'm filming a documentary of the Seattle General Strike of 1919, so I've been studying up on labor history and the ways that even men and women in gender-normal jobs would step outside their roles during strikes. Is that the sort of thing discussed in the essay?"

Much less annoyed, she studied him closely and volleyed back. "Many people expect activist communities to be models of equality, but they're constituted of people just like any others, with a significant number of sexist, racist, homophobic, and otherwise discriminatory problems cropping up. Not to mention coercion, abuse of power, and other bad behavior. This piece is specifically about gender norms and how otherwise transgressive people fight or fulfill these norms."

She stopped to check his comprehension and his lips quirked again. "Don't worry about losing me. I can hold my own." Lania tried to resist the thread of interest winding through her. Oly

Rasmussen wasn't the only sexy academic she'd known, quite the contrary. But in this park, looking like a skater or bike messenger, he was unexpected.

"What do you do with these essays?"

"I publish a magazine called *Literate Life*."

"A magazine of essays? Is there a market for that kind of thing?"

"No, not really. I make the magazine myself. It's dedicated to exploring ideas that languish in academia. Sort of off-center highbrow." She never could do justice to her magazine when she tried to boil it down. She picked at the peeling red paint of the picnic table with a short fingernail.

"What is involved in making a magazine?" Oly spoke in a coaxing manner that seemed genuine, pulling the words out of her.

"In my case, I choose the essays and edit them, lay out the magazine, set the type, print, and bind it."

"Wait, did you say setting type?"

"Yes, indeed." Lania felt her shoulders loosen. "I use an old manual printing press that was built in 1872. Her name is Esmeralda because I lurch like Quasimodo when I'm printing." Lania mimed the motions of loading and removing the paper on each swing of the paper-holding platen against the inked type. Oly laughed. "I touch every bit of each magazine, and I'm completely independent. I set my own deadlines, and I'm the only one who even notices if I miss them. And I get the most amazing submissions, from pop culture analyses to dense interpersonal theories." Lania wrinkled her nose and tapped the papers in front of her.

"Independence is a different matter when it comes to film. I couldn't do it without the crew."

"How many people work on the film with you?"

"Oh, twelve to twenty people on and off, for different things. Most people wear more than one hat, and all of them except Jeremy, my main partner, have other paying jobs. We get some funding, but it's not like working with a major studio."

"What's your plan for the movie?" A breeze blew off the water and Lania's disordered hair drifted forward around her shoulders. She gathered it and twisted it into a thick rope over one shoulder.

"Major distribution, I hope. There are indie theaters across the country that would screen this if I can get the right distribution company involved."

"It sounds like you depend on a dozen other people, plus a distribution company. And if other people fund it, you're dependent on them too, right?"

"Making a film by myself would be impossible. We're independent as a group, and anybody who wants input on the film in return for monetary support is refused. I guess it's like how unions combine the individual skills of its members to be independent, as a group, from the bosses."

"Independent as a group. Maybe writing is so solitary that I've never been forced to depend on other people like that."

Oly tipped his head sideways and ran his palm over his hair. "You're looking at my situation as dependent. I feel like there has to be another way of phrasing it. I'll have to do some thinking about that."

Lania saw the sunlight fade and brighten in Oly's eyes as a cloud blew across the sun. Analytical conversation fascinated her, but she couldn't deny that physical attraction provided spice.

"Independence is a big deal for you. Is that why you refused my help on the dock?"

"To a certain extent. I'm planning to sail around the world, singlehanded, so I will have to be able to do everything myself." She relished saying the words aloud for the first time. A panicky thrill traveled down her spine, and she tapped her pen on the table.

"By yourself?" Oly's shock was funny, but not particularly flattering. Not the reaction she'd hoped for. "I've done some long-distance sailing, but I wouldn't want to do it alone."

"It's right up my alley." Lania spoke with firm conviction. "Where've you been?"

"Gulf of Mexico, Caribbean, and down to Rio de Janeiro."

"It'll be a long time until I get there if I head west around the world."

"I'd rather see the Marquesas." He paused. "Do you have a boat?"

"Not yet. I'm about to start on that part." Defensive tension drew her shoulders higher.

"I'm in awe." He shrugged gracefully. "Best of luck."

Her brave words suddenly felt like outrageous boasts. She cast about for another subject. "What a day off! A big bike ride and good conversation." Lightening the mood, she sat back. "Do you ride often?"

Oly nodded toward his bike, tension fading. "That there is my trusty steed. I ride everywhere."

"Me too. I bet I rode farther than you today."

Oly tipped his head back and considered Lania. He looked at her bike and then back at her. "Yeah?"

"Yeah."

"Wanna bet?

"What should we bet?" Lania wasn't sure what she wanted to hear. A date? Her phone number?

"Well, if I had the harder ride, you have to come to a party next Friday. It's a show for local artists at my friend's loft on the north edge of Georgetown. Cheap liquor and smart company." Oly's wicked smile put Lania on guard. "And if you had the harder ride, I'll fix your flat tire."

"What?" Lania turned toward the bikes. Just as Oly had said, her back wheel's rim rested on the ground while the tire bulged, flat, on either side. "I hate flat tires!"

"Well, you'd better hope you win, then. I'm not going to fix that if I don't have to…"

"Well, then. Let's play. You first."

Oly buffed his fingernails on his shirt. "I rode from Belltown down to the Ferry Terminal, over to Seattle Center, and thence here."

"Well, I'm not sure how you want to judge this thing, but here goes. I rode from the CD down Madison to the Ferry Terminal— funny we didn't see each other there—then to Shilshole via Fremont, back through Fremont, and thence, as you so eloquently put it, here."

Oly stood and sighed. "I'll get right on that flat." Lania looked for signs of resentment or irritation, but Oly got out his bike tools. "Will you unlock your bike so I can get the wheel off?"

She removed the lock and flipped the bike over. She started to reach for the quick-lock release for the wheel, but Oly stopped her with a shake of a finger. He reached down and began.

Minutes later, Oly stood Lania's bike back on its patched and fully inflated tires.

"Totally weird."

He turned to her, one eyebrow raised.

"Oh, the gender shit. You know. The girl, standing by, fluttering her hands while the big strong man changes her tire."

"Well, I'm trans, so that queers it up a bit, right?" Oly's tone stayed light, but he kept his eyes on her.

"It does, indeed." Lania shook her head. She couldn't help it; her eyes flickered down his body, looking for clues she'd missed. "So much easier to take, knowing that. Different power imbalance?"

"On a structural level, perhaps, but personally, I think we're pretty well matched." He bounced his eyebrows theatrically. "At least for wrestling."

"My weight versus your muscle?"

"Or your strength versus my speed..." Oly stretched his long body in the fading sunlight and Lania watched the flattering gold of sunset glisten on his fair skin. She cleared her throat, shaken by the clench in her belly at the sight. "It's getting late." She wondered how he'd smell. What kinds of hormones raced through his body, scenting his sweat?

"What time is it?" He looked at his watch. "Shit! I have to go! I have this thing, my assistant director, shit!"

Oly unlocked his bike in a flurry. He spoke over his shoulder as he tossed the lock in his backpack. "I'm late, but I want to see you again. Consider the party even though I lost fair and square?" He got on his bike, already moving. "Call me, okay?"

Lania stood, dumbfounded. She watched him moving away with increasing speed. "But you didn't give me your number..."

CHAPTER TWO

Lania picked her dad from the contacts in her cell phone and hit dial.

"This's Adam."

"Hi, Dad, it's me."

"Hey, Lania. Cool. Are you heading over the pass to see me?" His voice rose at the end, hopeful.

"No, no, I'm not planning a trip this month. Too much work to do. Is that the only time I ever call you?"

"Well, you know—neither one of us is big on phones. So what are you calling about, if not a visit?"

She paused. "I love you."

"I love you too. Uh oh, this must be a big one."

"Dad! I'm not trying to butter you up!"

"Sorry, sorry. I'm always happy to hear from you. Well, do we have to shoot the shit, or can you tell me what's happening?"

Lania took a deep breath and started pacing her bedroom. "I'm going to buy a boat and sail around the world."

After a moment of silence, her dad's cautious response reached her. "Okay. When?"

"Oh, Dad. You're great." She tucked her hair behind her ear. "I didn't know how you were going to take it."

"Well, you haven't given it to me yet. Tell me more about this. You liked your sailing lessons that much?"

"You know how much I want to travel. I have to keep learning, Dad, and I want the exposure to fresh ideas and ways of living. And I'm too lazy to want to hitchhike across Asia."

Her dad's voice dropped. "Too sensible as well. I knew that the move to Seattle wouldn't satisfy you for much longer, but I thought you might still join the Peace Corps."

"I was tempted, but all of the volunteer organizations I researched are so constrained. They're responsible for you, and that puts too many barriers on possibility." She sat on her futon bed and crossed her legs. "Voyaging under sail is the perfect mix of the planned and the unknown. On a boat, I'll always have a safe place to sleep. I'll buy strange vegetables in village markets, but I'll cook them on my very own stove. I'll be able to really absorb my experiences, rather than being overwhelmed by them. Making my own water and electricity, using wind power to get from place to place. It's an environmental dream. You've talked about getting the farm to a carbon-neutral standing. "

She coaxed her silent father with his own words. "Besides, paying rent month after month is just throwing money away. You brought me up with the idea that I should buy a house so that I can earn equity with my monthly payments, but buying a boat is very similar. Any money I put into it adds to its value. It's an investment. Plus, I can move it anytime I want, which will satisfy my love of new surroundings."

"I know that you're not happy selling eyeglasses for a living, but I always thought you'd make the magazine a paying concern and devote yourself to that. What are you going to do with the press?"

Lania swallowed. "I'm going to sell it for the down payment."

"That's a huge step. How do you feel about that?"

"It's painful, of course. I can't let that stand in the way of going."

"Sorry, but…I'm sure you've given this a lot of thought, but it sounds like you'll be giving up so much to make this happen. The magazine, your friends, even the kind of normal comfort most people take for granted. I've read some sea stories. Adventurers spend a lot of time cold or wet or both."

"I can't tell you how much thought I've put into this." Lania's throat felt tight. "I'll miss you and Ginger and Hoss and the others, though I can keep up with you and my friends by e-mail or Skype when I'm near shore. I'm torn up about letting the magazine disappear. But I'm not giving up more than I'm getting. I can't let my dreams fade and turn into stories I once told myself so I could get through the day."

"You're an amazing woman, as well as my favorite daughter." He sounded proud, if a bit worried.

"Only daughter," Lania said, supplying her line in the routine.

"Not many people would want to set out by themselves to sail around the world. Have your sailing lessons prepared you for this sort of thing?"

"I have certificates in everything up to coastal cruising. I finished the last course yesterday. I've learned more than I ever dreamed existed about halyards and sheets and seacocks and through-hulls. I want to do my offshore passages aboard my own boat. I'm certain I have enough background knowledge to work out the rest myself. Until I get my own boat, I can keep my chops on the small boats at the Center for Wooden Boats." Lania cast about in her mind for the other arguments she'd prepared.

Her dad cleared his throat. "I can't wait to see what you come up with. Do you have any boats in mind?"

Lania took a deep breath and told him all about her dream boat.

❖

Jeremy Noor huffed as he tossed lighting soft boxes into the van. "What do you mean, we're not independent filmmakers?"

"No, no—in that labeling kind of way, we are independent filmmakers. But you know what that means nowadays. Most of the other so-called independent films being made today get half their funding from subsidiaries of the large studios." Oly leaned on the van door. "It's not really about that, though."

"What is it about, then?" Ordinarily a mobile-faced clown, Jeremy was still. At rest, his body tended to slump into a long, skinny question mark, head drooping forward.

"I met this woman yesterday at the Center for Wooden Boats. She got me thinking."

"About whether you're an independent filmmaker?"

"About being independent in general. She publishes a magazine all by herself. She edits the articles and prints them on an old-fashioned printing press. Isn't that cool?"

"You mean, she sets type and does the ink thing and all that?"

"Yeah. All that. And she has this bug up her butt. We got into it over the meaning of dependence."

"You met a woman and got in a fight with her? You're the smooth one!"

"It wasn't like that. It was…It was like the late night philosophical discussions you only have with your best friend. Like the way you and I talked in the shared housing our freshman year. I was trying to flirt with her, but she got me talking about real things instead."

Jeremy dropped his jaw in exaggerated awe. "You mean you treated a strange woman like an actual person? You? The quickest pickup artist in Seattle and fastest to leave when a girl falls for you?"

"I hate it when you call me a pickup artist. I'm no predator."

"Granted." Jeremy flourished a bow. "The women you fuck are just as motivated as you are. Even more motivated, the morning after."

"Yeah. Unless my gender is too much for them." Oly shook off the old banter. "Well, anyway, we got to talking about being an independent filmmaker, and I've been thinking about it ever since. It's really an inaccurate description. We're not independent—we're interdependent."

Jeremy cocked his head to the side.

"What do I do myself? I plan things, I tell people what to do, and sometimes I hold a camera myself. But you, of all people, know how much I don't do. If I tried to do the lighting, sound, and camera work myself, I'd go insane. Every film is a complex set of interdependencies."

Jeremy nodded. "It's true. We've got to have the technicians who can get what we want. And the actors, of course. They are a big part of the end result. I see what you're saying. But what's wrong with that?"

"Doesn't it ever get to you that we put heart and soul into getting the images we want on film, then hand that over to some tech who develops the film and may or may not do it right?"

Jeremy's brows lowered. "It's a gamble, every time. I know that. But when I see a final shot that is perfect, that was created by the cooperation of a dozen people or more…when it all comes together and it's right…that's a communal kind of art."

"You really are a poet, Jeremy." Oly sighed. "It's an art form we both love. I'm just thinking what it might mean to try something on my own. For now, it's enough to know that we're a set of independent-minded people, negotiating and sweating our way through the making of this film."

"So, what is a no-strings guy like you doing obsessing on a philosophically inclined girl?"

"You make it sound like I've never dated a woman with brains."

"I can't imagine how you'd find out whether the women you date have brains. You never stick around long enough to talk."

"You're so full of shit, Jeremy." Oly tried to dismiss his words and the whole conversation.

"I'm glad you've met someone who turns you on in more than one way. Is it serious?"

"Come on, Jeremy. I'm not talking about marrying this woman."

"I'm just saying. There's this new girl and you've already had more conversation with her than any other woman you're not working with. You're thinking about her, and I think it's a good sign."

"Yeah, it's a sign that I was dehydrated when I met her. Look, I doubt I'll ever see her again. I don't know anything about her and, in case you haven't noticed, Seattle is a big city. I kind-of, almost invited her to the loft party on Friday, but I didn't even give her any information about it."

"Oh man, you were so freaked out that you lost your head? I can't believe it."

Oly gave up on the conversation. "Get back to work. We have to get all this gear loaded and get out of here."

"Oh, this is going to be fun to watch."

Lania chewed over the fact that she was dressing up for a party that she ordinarily wouldn't be going to, for a guy who might or might not have invited her to it. And wasn't she supposed to be focusing on boating anyway? What good would it do to start dating a new guy right now?

On the other hand, it had been a while since she'd gotten laid.

After the sudden way Oly had departed, Lania had returned to the picnic table and tried to focus on her editing, but there was no room in her thoughts for commas, semicolons, and deciding between that and which. She left soon after Oly did.

Ginger Curadero, her best friend and an excellent writer of niche pornography and speculative fiction, had invited her to a party a few days afterward. Lania's first instinct had been to turn down the invitation as she usually did, but Ginger wouldn't let her say no without telling her about the event. As Lania listened, she had realized that it sounded like the party Oly had used for his wager. Lania had accepted the invitation and agreed to be picked up at eight. Her desire to see Oly again made her skin twitch, but she refused to think about it.

Now, almost a week after meeting him, Lania studied herself in the mirror. She gave her dress a little shake to make the gathers fall evenly. The flowing material with its amorphous pattern in brown and blue flared around her wide hips and gathered under her breasts to enhance their rounded undersides. Lania tugged the scoop neckline upward.

Ginger was a few minutes late. Lania shook her hair out of her face and resisted the urge to try something fancy with the heavy mass that waved past her shoulders. Her distant great-great-grandfather's Italian bequests had been a last name, a Roman nose, and a thick, untamable mane with curls at the bottom, impervious to elegance. The doorbell rang just in time to drive the idea from her head, and Lania grabbed her soft linen handbag. She stepped to the door with amazing restraint, but when she saw Ginger filling out jeans and a Sex Pistols T-shirt with her big curves, Lania began to chuckle. Ginger looked on in good-natured confusion as Lania sat in the chair near the door and released her built-up tension.

"Did I do something?" Ginger asked, her head cocked to the side.

"Oh no, Ginger, I'm not laughing at you. I just put so much time and effort into getting ready for this. I never asked you whether it was going to be a fancy party, and I wanted to look nice. I was thinking art opening…" Lania gulped and stepped into the kitchen for a glass of water. "Sorry for the rude welcome."

Ginger followed. "I'm tough and you'll be fine in that dress. Art parties are notorious for the eclectic attire of the guests. We set each other off quite nicely if I do say so myself." Ginger dropped into one of the two dining chairs by the little table in the ambitiously named breakfast nook. "As long as I don't have an ear of corn sticking out of my hat or something silly like that."

"Nothing like that, though there is…" Ginger sat up at attention. "That adorable gleam in your eye. You look like you have something up your sleeve."

Ginger smirked. "I also invited my cousin's new co-worker. She's cute and I've got a crush."

Lania lifted an eyebrow. "Should I make secondary plans on getting home?"

Ginger looked away. "If it wouldn't put you out, I think that might be nice. You don't have to, of course. I'd never leave you stranded. If you meet up with someone, though, let me know, okay?"

This time, Lania was the one who looked away, blushing a bit. She didn't say anything right away, and Ginger looked her over again. "What are you all dressed up for? Are you meeting someone? I should have known when you said you'd come to the party. You never come to parties! I should have known. Tell me all about it!" Ginger grabbed Lania's hand and pulled her down into the other chair.

Lania ducked her head. "It seems so silly. Last Sunday, I met a guy at the Center for Wooden Boats and we hit it off. He had to leave suddenly and we didn't have time to exchange phone numbers, but he mentioned that he'd like me to go to some party. He told me a little about it, and I thought this might be the party he was talking about."

"Is he cute?" asked Ginger, cutting right to the chase.

"Yes. He's a bike rider, slender but strong legs. His eyes are green—a bright, light springtime green." Lania gave in and started in on the long version of their day together. At the end, Ginger sat back with a considering look on her face. Lania came out of her daydream enough to realize that Ginger was staring at her. "What?"

Ginger shook her head. "Lania, he sounds perfect for you. That's a little weird, but good, I think." Ginger pursed her lips. "You have a great dress on, but those shoes are unacceptable."

"Don't start in on me. You know I can't wear high heels. I don't understand how people do it, and it certainly wouldn't be impressive if I fell down right in front of him."

"Wear those blue ballet-type slippers you bought the last time I tricked you into shopping."

Lania jumped up and kissed Ginger on the forehead. "I totally forgot those," she sang as she ran back to her bedroom and kicked off her boat moccasins. She rummaged around and came out victorious. She danced back into the kitchen and did a pirouette in the middle of the room.

"I'm so glad you're here to help me, Ginger! I wouldn't even have these if you hadn't convinced me to buy them…" Lania danced out toward the door and Ginger stood to follow her out.

Lania jangled her keys in rhythm to the song in her head and enjoyed her buoyant excitement.

❖

An hour later, Lania held a watery mixture of vanilla vodka and ginger ale in a plastic cup. Her ice had melted and so had her mood. She didn't know anyone but Ginger, who was intent on the new girl she'd met through her cousin. The party hadn't picked up yet, and the room felt barren. Concrete walls and wooden plank floor, plus a tall ceiling of bare beams, made for a large open space with a rabbit's warren of smaller rooms at one end.

Too self-conscious to dance in the near-empty space, Lania stood near a wall showcasing large abstract works of art. She was relieved that Ginger had been right—in the wild mix of clothing already being displayed, Lania's classy but relaxed dress didn't warrant a second look. No Oly, but he seemed like the type to come late to parties.

A middle-aged man in sweatpants and a paint-splattered tunic wandered up to her. "Hey, there." She nodded agreeably. "I'm Robbie. Some of this is my work."

Lania perked up. "Oh, yeah? Which pieces are yours?"

Robbie stepped closer and touched her shoulder to turn her attention behind her. "Those are a few of them." He eyed his work with a satisfied mien.

Lania studied the group of paintings. "You like Jackson Pollack?"

Robbie stepped back and pantomimed slashing his wrists. "These aren't copies. This comes from the deepest parts of me." He moved closer again. "Do you see the emotion?"

Lania flashed him a placating smile and then looked back at the paintings. She stepped closer to see the texture of the paint on the canvas and then back, feeling like an impostor. Robbie seemed to have taken her remark as a challenge. "There are such deep cuts in the paint on this one. It looks very frustrated, or maybe it's about exorcising frustration." Maybe that would satisfy him. She turned all the way around, looking at the other art and scanning the growing crowd for Oly. "It's all very wonderful."

Robbie stepped right up next to Lania's shoulder. "What's your name?"

Lania started to look at him and then realized how close he had gotten. She turned, flustered. "Oh, my friend is waving. I'll talk to you later." She tossed the words over her shoulder as she walked away.

Lania wandered around the room and wrestled with the feeling that she was doomed to be a wallflower at this party. Her pride wouldn't let her go hide in a back room, so she meandered around the room, feeling lonely.

❖

Lania was still carrying the same drink another hour later. The lights had gone down, and the room was filling up. She studied a large acrylic painting and cheered herself up with bad poetry comparing the painting to the drink in her hand, flat and lacking in taste.

A tall, skinny man in a red shirt with silver snaps and black leather pants walked up next to her and gave her a companionable nod. He held a plastic cup and took a sip as he scanned the expressionist painting in front of them. She nodded back and he caught her attempt to look serious. "What's that all about?"

"I was making up a poem that was so horrible I had to give it up for dead."

The man nodded with mock seriousness. "Want to try it out on me?"

"Oh, no, it was far too bad to share. I've laughed at myself enough. You'll have to wait for another opportunity."

"I'm Hideo."

"Lania. Nice to meet you, Hideo." They shook hands.

"Lania's a pretty name. So, what do you write that's any good, Lania?"

"I don't write much at all, but I edit a ton of great writing. I edit and print a magazine called *Literate Life*. It's a monthly."

"That's your magazine? You're Lania Mar…hey, how do you say your last name?

Lania answered the question that had stalked her throughout her school years. "Mar-key-all."

"You're Lania Marchiol? I can't believe this! Hey, can I introduce you to some friends?" Hideo dragged Lania along to the next room over. "They're not going to believe that you're here tonight! I can't believe it myself!"

Lania followed as Hideo blazed a trail through the big room and into a small, dimly lighted room, empty of furnishings except a grand piano with a natural walnut finish. He broke into a circle of seven people talking near the gorgeous instrument. "Hey, you guys, guess who I found?"

Amused, annoyed, and questioning gazes all fell on Lania. She tucked a heavy curl behind her ear and scanned the group through her lashes. Not a single person in the group was dressed like Hideo, in his rockabilly gear. As a matter of fact, no two people were dressed alike, and Lania was drowning in the mixed social cues.

Hideo didn't hesitate. "This is Lania Marchiol, everyone." The group seemed taken aback, and Hideo started throwing names out and pointing at people. Lania didn't catch a single name but was laughing by the end.

With the ice broken, talk resumed and she began to meet the people in the group. Hideo, it turned out, was a huge fan of her magazine. Lania didn't even know she had fans, so she was all the more surprised to find out that everyone in the group knew and respected *Literate Life*.

A tall, skinny woman named Mitzi, her hair pinned tight to her head, wanted to talk about the revolution delineated in William Blake's poems and how it could be put into action. "When's the last time you read his major works?" Mitzi asked. Lania had to admit that she hadn't made it past his poetry, mostly the pieces in *Songs of Innocence and Experience*. Mitzi began to lay out, with copious citations, the bare bones of the Blake Paradigm, as she called it.

Interested but overwhelmed, Lania ended her conversation with Mitzi by promising to read the essay and consider it for the magazine. Though excited by the idea of some fresh blood, she was a bit bemused by the idea of veering so far from her more usual works.

A tiny woman in her sixties tapped Lania's arm. "How do you do, my dear? I'm Ms. Most, or Gillian—whichever you like best." Gillian chattered on without waiting for a response. "I love your magazine, dear. But do you have the ability to print images as well as words?" Lania nodded, the only response Gillian allowed her. "Because I have the most wonderful cartoon! A Ford Galaxy 500, covered with bumper stickers that criticize cars. Sayings like 'No Blood for Oil,' 'Subvert the Dominant Paradigm—Earth First,' and 'Stop Global Warming.' And the car is clattering away, blowing a huge cloud of exhaust and dripping oil on the ground." Gillian beamed. "Get it?"

Before she could get a word in edgewise, Gillian prattled on. "I have more cartoons in my car." She leered at Lania. "Want to see my etchings, little girl?"

"As a matter of fact, I do." With a fresh contact in her cell phone, Lania moved on. She mingled like a pro, far more comfortable than she'd expected.

Drinks were refilled; conversation got more raucous and impassioned. Ginger stopped by and joined a debate on the subject of depression medication, a dazed-looking dark-skinned girl in a sleek white ball gown tucked under her arm. Realizing that this must be the cousin's co-worker, Lania disengaged her from Ginger and brought her into a conversation about the difficulty of writing poetry about ugly subjects like politics.

"...and Shakespeare couldn't have gotten laid as much as she did using that line!"

The spontaneous pickup line contest rolled on while Lania checked out a commotion at the freight elevator. An entire crew swept in, yelling and grabbing people, with Oly in the middle. Lania shivered all over and tried to catch up with the conversation that had gotten away from her. Ginger caught the byplay and looked at her with a raised brow. Lania shook her head at her, mouthing "Later."

From a room away, Oly's presence caused her uncomfortable waves of anticipation. It wasn't hard to keep track of him— everywhere he went, people yelled his name and the names of the people with him. Hugs and jokes and boisterous behavior followed

Oly like a wake as he circled the room. Lania rejoiced that she had become a part of a conversation. To be found by Oly hiding in a corner would have been intolerable.

Some minutes later, a tipsy woman offered to get Lania a fresh drink. She looked at the warm, flat soda with a start and decided to get her own. She left the music room and started across the dance floor to the bar. Maybe she should try to find Oly. Lania reached the bar and leaned forward to signal the bartender.

Lania's neck hair prickled and, from behind, a warm voice murmured in her ear. "Hey, sailor."

CHAPTER THREE

O ly watched Lania's shoulders ease before she turned. "Hey, yourself."

He bent his head close to hers, hunting her light scent. "You made it."

"Yes."

"I'm glad."

"I…I wasn't sure this was the party."

"I haven't done such a bad job of asking a woman out on a date since I was in high school."

"Hey, you want something?" Tommy, the surly bartender, demanded their attention.

"Yes, Tommy. A rum and cola and…"

"Vanilla vodka and ginger ale."

Drinks appeared and Tommy disappeared, leaving them alone among the hundreds of people at the party. "Hey—let's find somewhere we can sit down and talk."

Oly turned, looking back to make sure Lania was following. He led the way behind the bar, waving at Tommy, and opened a doorway hidden by a tapestry. He held the tapestry away from the wall so that Lania could follow and dropped the covering back into place behind her. In the sudden darkness, he reached out and took her hand, guiding her through a succession of echoing rooms. He brought them to a quiet, dark room from which he could hear, muffled, the music from the main room.

Paintings leaned ten and fifteen deep against one wall. Reflected light peeked through the doorway, and neon blinked from outside the windows spanning one wall of the room. He led her to an opulent red velvet chaise lounge nestled in an inset in a side wall and motioned for her to sit at the head. The niche hid the doorway from them and gave a warm sense of privacy. The red and yellow city lights outside the window flowed over Lania's shoulder and glowed in her hair.

Oly watched Lania sip from her drink and look around the room. She'd flirted, unselfconscious, minutes ago, but now she looked stiff.

"Hey." The breathiness in her voice revealed excitement.

"Hey." He should set her at ease, but her tension brought a lick of heat to his belly.

"Um." Lania turned the cup in her hands. "I met a whole bunch of great people here. There's a guy named Hideo who asked about the magazine, and it turns out that he and his friends read it. They can never find more than a couple copies since I spread them so thinly, so they share the copies they find. They said they read every bit. It's so amazing. I thought only my family and friends read it. I keep putting the magazine out there, but I don't hear back much, and I was afraid that no one really liked it." She stumbled to an end, her amazement endearing.

Oly reached for her hand and toyed with her fingers. "Is that why I couldn't find a copy myself? I drove myself nuts this week, going into every bookstore I could find, trying to figure out how to contact you."

The tension in her fingers grew. "I've never tried to get the magazine into bookstores. I leave them in coffee shops with the pamphlets and flyers."

"Why do you do that?"

"I don't want the magazine to have to fit anyone's criteria but mine. If I tried to sell it instead of giving it away, I'd feel constrained to publish what the purchasers want to read."

"You don't have to give your work away to keep creative control." Oly stroked her fingers from palm to tip, one at a time. He didn't want her completely relaxed with him, but that didn't mean he couldn't soothe.

"I have a few subscribers. It's pretty much impossible to turn down your dad. The others are random people who have never explained why they wanted it. I figured they were friends of people I'd published, but I don't know."

Oly studied her outline in the dimness. He gripped her hand and tugged on it. "Maybe they like it," he said. "Why doesn't it occur to you that they might be into your work?"

Lania withdrew her hand and he stopped himself from grabbing it back. She leaned away from him on the high arm of the chaise lounge, and propped her chin on the back of her wrist. She looked off into the distance and Oly caught his breath at her strong profile, backlit by the city's neon and fluorescent lights. Lania's straight brows and soft chin framed a mouth so full it looked like she'd been biting her lips.

He thought about skipping the rest of the conversation, delving into their physical attraction and leaving her low self-esteem for someone else to ameliorate. She would warm for him. He was sure of it. He wasn't nearly as sure why he pursued the thorny subject. "Why don't you sell the magazine?"

"I don't know. I believe in the writers and the ideas, but I don't know how to put them out there. I feel guilty sometimes, knowing that I'm not doing enough to get them heard."

Oly took Lania's hand back to gauge her state of mind. "That's not what I meant. What about you? Your ideas, your values. That's what the magazine is about, right? You pick writers who need to be heard and give them a venue. But it's your baby, and you need to believe that it's worth whatever people try to give you for it."

Lania's hand relaxed in his. "You wouldn't believe some of the things people offer me. One guy offered me this huge collection of free coffee cards all stamped and ready to be redeemed. This other person and I have traded magazines for vibrators. I got the best of that deal."

Oly shot Lania a warm look. "You'll have to tell me more about that sometime." Fine. Let her lighten the mood.

"Sure, sailor, you just let me know when you're feeling brave."

"Maybe there's a little bravery welling up right about..." Oly leaned forward and closed the distance between them. "Now."

His lips met hers, retreated. Lania dropped her mouth open the tiniest bit and he couldn't resist kissing her again. When his mouth met hers, she nipped at his lower lip and licked away the sting before allowing him to match their lips and press them together. He hummed, enjoying her style, excited by her boldness. She lifted her hand and cupped his cheek, laying her thumb at the corner of his eye and tipping his head to the side. He let her take control and heated at her hungry shiver.

Oly inhaled deeply, soaking her up. He slid his cheek along hers and then leaned back. Lania's first words did nothing to calm him. "I like that."

"I liked it too." He turned sideways against the back of the lounge. "So, back to your magazine..."

Lania shook her head. "Oh, no—we're not going back to that subject. You'll have to read it before we talk about it more. I just finished printing the new issue, and I'll be putting it out this weekend. Who knows? You might decide that it's not worth the paper it's printed on."

"Yeah, right."

Lania tucked her feet up under her skirt and leaned sideways against the back of the lounge. They faced each other from opposite ends, each with an arm draped across the back. Their fingertips almost touched.

"So—what were you up to tonight? I heard you and the others show up at the party, and it sounded like filming was a big deal today."

"That batch of people was mostly crew. Jeremy, who does pretty much everything with me, is officially the production manager. Verona, our aesthetics person, does set design and decoration and is the prop master, wardrobe master, and makeup artist. We couldn't do anything without her. Roshan Gita should be along soon. She's the director of photography, and she had to put the cameras to bed."

He sighed. "I'm glad there was a party tonight. We all need to relax. Today, I got nothing but stiffs. People who are used to being behind a camera don't always like to be filmed. Like I was telling you, the film is about the Seattle General Strike in 1919. It only lasted five days, but working people flexed their muscles and felt their power. The strikers kept the daily life of Seattle moving in a time when no one had large stores of food, milk, and other necessities. They created a short-term communal system that made sure that people were supplied with the necessities of life. Seattle is a great union town, and that's partly because the union members have known since 1919 that they could stop everything and run the city more fairly than the politicians."

The summary was getting smoother. He'd have to keep working on it. Elevator pitches and party summaries—so much funding was born in casual conversation. "So my bright idea for showing what we've inherited from those strikers was to make the filmmakers part of the story. Workers are workers, and I figured that, by showing the production workers respectfully and with honor, I could honor all workers. What I didn't realize is that not everyone who loves being involved behind the scenes wants to be filmed."

"Does someone need to love being filmed for you to be able to get good footage?"

"Not necessarily. They can hate it brilliantly or love it brilliantly, but they can't freeze up and give me good footage. We're shooting at Sixth and Union, where the office of the labor newspaper, the *Seattle Union Record*, used to be. It was also one of the two places where police started teargasing protesters during the stonewalled WTO conference in 1999. Union battles at the beginning and the end of the century plus new glossy buildings to contrast the old photos of how it looked during the Strike. I tried interviewing some of the crew members who were at the protests, but they all froze up when the camera was on. I've never had such a hard time getting someone to talk to me on camera."

Lania stretched toward him and hooked her fingertips around his. "I'd probably freeze up too. It's a great idea, though, and I hope you can work the crew into the film. They need appreciation as much as the rest of us. Do you have ideas on how to help them relax?"

Oly shook his head. "Right now, I'm thinking tranqs. Valium can work wonders."

"Well, I'll let you know if I think of something. In the meantime, I'm feeling pretty distracted." She rose to her knees and Oly felt a clench inside. His concerns about the film faded. She leaned over.

Their tongues met and slid in slow corkscrews around each other. He slid one arm around her waist and the other behind her neck. She sank into his arms and he gripped her tightly, feeling a contradictory tensing and softening throughout his body. He pulled her hip down as he turned to lean against the back of the chaise lounge. They settled facing each other, Oly seated forward on the couch and Lania next to him with her legs curled against the back.

He pulled her close with firm hands on her waist.

The shock of the sudden full torso contact stopped everything but his breathing, which rasped in and out of his throat. Lania's eyes were wide, dark pools of heat. Hints of surprise and skittishness drowned in hunger. Oly groaned at the sudden revelation of her desire. She put a hand on his chest and rested her forehead on her hand.

He held her waist, his hands riveted there at her narrowest point as he looked down on the wild disorder of her hair. He pulled her up onto his lap and hugged her. She put an arm around his neck, and he resisted the urge to rock his hips. He wanted her, but not on the couch at a party.

She stroked his hair and he closed his eyes against the movement of her breasts under her dress. He couldn't block her scent, though, and indulged himself with a deep breath.

She pulled away, slid off his lap and into a graceful crouch beside the lounge. With her hair wild in her eyes and the big skirt spread out around her, Oly thought she looked like a fiery courtesan from days gone by. His eyes followed the line of her cleavage, pressed against the low front of the dress, and then down to her curved waist. This wasn't the nice girl in the park. He was surprised and fascinated by the passion pumping off her. Lania looked up at him through her hair and reached out to his thigh.

Lania couldn't resist touching the soft corduroy, squeezing the large muscle that jumped as she moved her hand. Tempted, she put both hands on his knees.

She loved sex, and the whole getting to know each other phase was part of it. The coiled heat of sexual tension thrived when she drew it out. She wanted him, but it was the wrong moment to press. She rose and took a cross-legged seat at the foot of the lounge, holding herself tall and proud. She considered him, still propped against the head of the chaise lounge.

Someone called Oly's name and she looked toward the door. Four people burst into the room, still calling him. When they turned the lights on in the room, Oly stood. "Yeah? What do you want?"

"You have got to see this, man! It's amazing! This guy has movie footage from the Strike. You're not going to believe your eyes…" They clamored for Oly to come with them right away. Oly looked at Lania.

Lania mocked him gently. "You have to go see it, man! It's amazing!" She shooed him out and stayed behind to pull herself together.

"I'll be back soon." Oly cried this over his shoulder, borne along on the enthusiasm of the others.

Lania gazed after him, considering. This was becoming a habit. What was so alluring about this guy? He was rough and moved so fast. He was also graceful and intent, and it was nice to have someone's full attention. She supposed it was a healthy flirtation.

She made a vain attempt to smooth her hair. She'd become so absorbed in him. He could be dangerous to her peace of mind. Just when she was getting her life into motion…

Lania left the empty room, heading toward the beat of hip-hop music. After negotiating the much-increased crowd, she leaned over the bar. "Hey, Tommy!"

A swaying woman pushed in beside Lania and leaned in front of her. "Bartender! Get my friend and me some drinks!" Lania recoiled from the stench of liquor and overmuch perfume. The drunken woman raked her bleary eyes up and down Lania, and Lania glanced over the woman in turn. Her proportions were similar to Lania's but presented in quite a different fashion. This boozy, blowsy person wore a form-fitting satin dress that hiked her bust up under her chin and drew the eye to her waist—which was lovely,

Lania had to admit. Lania decided to let this lady take her bad night out on someone else and turned away.

"You're not going to find him. He's better at disappearing than he is at cinemat…cinematography. I'm Cynthia, Oly's last fling." The woman tossed the words like a gauntlet, steadying herself on Lania's arm. "Are you some kind of…of tranny chaser? I saw you disappear with him. Come back all diss…disheveled. The bastard won't return my calls." As Lania stood, frozen and horrified, Cynthia gave a mighty sniff, tears welling.

Lania felt something akin to vertigo as her vision of the whole evening shifted. Taking a deep breath, Lania tried to reorient herself. She and Cynthia were nearly body doubles. Was Oly running on some sort of type he liked, not really interested in the rest of her? She had chased him down by coming to the party. No, he'd been into talking too. Surely it wasn't all a come-on.

Lania felt a headache build as she tried to avoid listening.

"I met him at a party about three weeks ago and we went back to my place. I didn't even know he wasn't a guy-guy until I was three or-orgasms in. When I woke up, he was gone, and I've been trying to track him down ever since." She sniffed noisily. "It's how he is, you know? He's a love 'em and leave 'em kind of guy. He's fucked half the women here, and I'm sure they're all still in love with him. He moves on, sooner rather than later."

Lania couldn't stay and listen to any more of Cynthia's booze-sodden babble. She stumbled over an excuse and darted back to the piano room. Hideo saw her enter. "Lania, you have to meet Tim. He's writing an essay and needs help on a title."

Lania tried to shake off her funk. She, Tim, and Hideo ended up talking for twenty minutes before Ginger snagged her. "I gotta leave. Do you have a ride or do you need one?"

Lania frowned. "Wait a minute. Let me find out." She scouted through the party, but she couldn't find Oly. She didn't want to be left without a ride if Oly had been whisked away from the party or if he didn't want to spend the rest of the evening with her.

Lania exchanged contacts with a handful of the people she'd met that evening, inviting them all over on Sunday for a magazine benefit party. She followed Ginger out the door, looking back at the last minute with regret.

"Shit!" Oly realized that he'd been in the sound room for a half hour and spoke to the film editor, Edouard. "I want it, but I have to go. Call me."

Edouard nodded and pushed the stop button. Oly rushed out of the room calling good night to his friends and wandered around the party, checking each room several times before he began to believe that Lania wasn't there. It was late, but why didn't she wait for him? He remembered that she didn't have a car and cursed when he realized that her ride must have been leaving.

Oly had seen Lania with some people earlier, and he hunted down that group. He tapped a man in a dark red rockabilly shirt and black leather pants. "Do you remember a woman named Lania?"

"Remember her? I idolize her!" said Hideo. "Lania Marchiol edits and prints an excellent independent magazine. She's gone, though. I think you missed your chance."

Oly committed Lania's last name to memory. "I hope it's not my last chance." He turned away and strolled back to the bar for another drink.

Disappointed but determined to find her again, Oly retreated to the sound room. A raucous cheer welcomed him back, and he dove into the excited mass.

Oly sat down to do some good old-fashioned research—on the Internet. He got comfortable on the rickety old wooden chair and pulled himself close to the laptop on his bedside table.

He searched on "Lania Marquial." The only result was a suggestion that he might have misspelled "martial." He tried "Lania Markiol" and got nothing once again.

Oly wished Lania's last name was Smith or Baker—something he could have an easier time spelling. He decided to go the other way around and searched on *"Literate Life,"* with results ranging from articles on life expectancy to storytelling. There was a website of that name, but it wasn't for the magazine.

About six pages into the hundreds of matches, Oly saw a promising entry. It looked like a site that reviewed magazines, and he clicked on the link. He was right; the link took him to an article about Lania's magazine. It didn't have any contact information for the magazine, but he got caught up in the complimentary review. He hadn't realized how highly regarded she was by that community. Lania hadn't said anything that gave him the idea the magazine was so popular. The review said that *Literate Life* was required reading for anyone who wanted a cosmopolitan range of subjects, printed and bound like art.

Back to the search results, Oly found a handful of citations and reviews along the lines of the one he'd read, but no one listed any contact information for the magazine or linked to a website for it.

Oly stood and stretched his back, which was cramped from crouching over the small computer. He paced around his room for a minute before moving to the warm, wood-paneled living room of the loft he shared. He threw himself down on an ancient, sagging couch and then stood back up and stalked out into the huge main room that was used for musical recording, filming interviews, or just plain partying. He stepped up to the bank of floor-to-ceiling windows that faced the Belltown alley between Second and Third Streets and dropped his hands in his roomy pants pockets. In normal Seattle fashion, a gray day had devolved into a fitful misty rain. Fine drops beaded the windows. The asphalt alleyway and parking lot gleamed in the streetlamps and oil rainbowed the puddles.

Lania had an unselfconscious and enthusiastic way of scrunching her eyes when she smiled. Her skin was a rich olive, setting off her dark brown, almost black hair and deep blue eyes. He wanted to see her in a cool winter sunrise, dressed all in white. Her long, strong nose gave her a classic profile, but it was the only straight or firm part of her. Everything else was soft and rounded, from her cheeks down to her lovely bottom. She had a plump pad of flesh under her chin, reminding Oly of a Bollywood movie goddess.

His cell phone rang; the caller was Jeremy. "What's up?" he asked in an even tone, controlling his irritability.

"Just wanted to tell you that we're on for filming in Ruby's storage building," Jeremy said.

"You never told me how you found that place."

"Book people are packrats. When I heard that the oldest bookstore in the city had lost its founder, I figured someone inherited a huge headache. I can't believe that it turned out to be the second floor of an insurance building." Jeremy's tinny voice rang. "The people working downstairs had no clue they were working under a book collection bigger than a library's!"

"So we'll be opening it up first?" Oly asked.

"No. The guy who inherited the stuff looked around a little, but he beat a quick retreat when he realized how much moldy paper was in the place. I can't wait to see it."

Oly loved the seriousness and sense of excitement in Jeremy's voice. He was lucky to have him as a best friend and partner. "Want to pick me up around ten tomorrow morning? We can go scope it out and do the background filming."

"Actually, we'll probably want to start sooner than that." Oly waited for an explanation, the realization dawning that Jeremy had made another of his infamous agreements. "You know how close to broke we are."

"As usual."

"The guy who inherited the books will pay us five hundred dollars to clear the place out. He's having a Dumpster delivered tomorrow. After we film, we're going to have to throw all that stuff away. He did say that we could keep anything we liked."

Oly leaned his head against the glass. "How many books is this?" he asked, with the beginnings of a headache.

"I don't know, actually. We'll see tomorrow, I guess."

Oly winced and reminded himself that Jeremy's creative financing was part of his undeniable value. Still lucky, though it was harder to appreciate in moments like this. "Great. See you at seven, then?"

"Sounds great, Oly," Jeremy said. "This'll be great. You'll see!"

"Great."

He put the phone away in his pocket. He looked at his watch and sighed. He should get to bed early.

His mind drifted back to Lania, and frustration billowed up in him once again. He'd met her twice and failed to exchange even the most basic of contact info. For a man who could get a phone number off a girl in the time it took a bus to pause at a stop, this was a new, embarrassing low. The phone number didn't always lead to a hookup, but that was more about coming out as trans. When he even bothered to do so.

Whatever.

He strode back toward his room. One last look at the search results. He'd read a couple more reviews and then go to bed.

He pulled up an article about Lania having a benefit party. Excitement prickled along his arms. The party was scheduled for tomorrow, and he now had the address.

He wrote down the party information and realized that he was in for a long day. He would be working early and perhaps working hard. He called Jeremy back. Jeremy answered, "Hay-low," and Oly said, "If we're going to work all day, let's party all night. I want to go to a benefit party tomorrow night, and you're coming with me, capice?"

Jeremy agreed with obvious resignation and mumbled, "I'm sleeping now. Good-bye."

Oly decided to match that and meandered back toward his room, whistling "As Time Goes By."

"How much are we making for this?" Oly stretched his shoulders and groaned.

"Quit messing around." Jeremy shoveled another pile of moldy paper through the room's door and into an old, red-and-rust wheelbarrow. His mobile face was as grim as it ever got. "We got some great shots in here and you know it. The whole disrespect-of-the-past thing will work well, and we'll just come back tomorrow for the other rooms."

Oly hefted the arms of the wheelbarrow and staggered down the dingy hall with the load. The wheelbarrow's one creaky wheel wobbled, and he tried to avoid adding any new scrapes to the ancient wallpaper that flaked down the hall. What was that print? Cabbage roses? His grandma had similar wallpaper in her front room.

When he reached the large window at the end, he levered the wheelbarrow back a little on its braces to get the lip onto the battered windowsill. He heaved up on the handles and tipped the wheelbarrow's contents out the window, listening with grim satisfaction to the sound of the heavy, damp paper sliding down the tarp into the Dumpster. Brilliant, if he did say so himself. They'd built a garbage chute using twine and tarps, saving them hundreds of trips up and down the stairs with thousands of pounds of moldy books and magazines. The windowsill was getting badly treated, but he couldn't tell their marks from the decades of older splinters and cracks.

Oly turned around and hauled the wheelbarrow backward like a horse cart. He stopped by the keeper pile to see if Jeremy had added anything. He stood in silence for a moment, awed, before yelping and picking up the top magazine. It was an undated copy of *Playboy* with Marilyn Monroe on the cover and in the centerfold. Oly obeyed a sudden urge to put the magazine down, afraid that he'd dirty or tear the valuable copy of the very first issue of that famous magazine.

Oly picked up another magazine in the pile and blinked, amazed at the *Cosmopolitan* from 1900. It looked like a literary magazine, and the featured articles were written by Rudyard Kipling, Jack London, and H.G. Wells. Oly thought of Lania and couldn't wait to show her the popular magazine's literary roots.

He started to realize that he and Jeremy were standing in a treasure house. He thought about the businessman who owned all this and remembered that he'd told Jeremy they could keep anything they wanted. He refigured in his head, tripling the amount of time they should spend clearing out the many rooms packed with books and magazines so that they could look through the stock while they moved it out. He grabbed the wheelbarrow's handles and started down the hall with new energy.

When he reached the room Jeremy was working in, he heard Jeremy groan. Oly walked through the door to share his new idea of how they should clear out the space.

Oly stopped short and stared. Jeremy quailed before a door that had been hidden by a rickety bookshelf. The door opened onto a pile of books, stuffed floor to ceiling, with no space to step into the room. Judging by the fact that none of the books fell out of the doorway, they were packed tight.

Oly dragged his feet to stand beside Jeremy and began scanning the paperback spines. "Oh, man," he whispered. The room was full of paperback romances from the sixties.

Oly and Jeremy looked at each other with horror. "It's a closet, right?" Jeremy cackled with a hint of hysteria. "It has to be a closet." They both sputtered.

Oly sobered. "I doubt it."

"Well, let's get to it." Jeremy pulled a single book from the packed pile and dislodged a small avalanche. "Oh, boy."

Oly picked up his shovel. "On the count of three."

Jeremy raised his shovel over his head.

"One. Two." Oly shifted into attack position. "Three," he hollered, and they both whooped and hacked at the pile in the doorway, flinging old books left and right.

Aching, unenthusiastic, but cleaned up, Oly and Jeremy tried to follow the driving directions they'd printed from the Internet. Jeremy was driving the film van through one of the confusing areas of Seattle's Capitol Hill where streets ended and started back up again, circled roundabouts, and generally made life difficult.

He'd thought he knew a shortcut. It had become a long-cut instead, as they crossed the blurry line between the Capitol Hill and Central District neighborhoods, but they weren't worried about being late. It had been ages since they'd been on time to a party, and they joked about losing themselves again to let things get going.

"Who's playing this party?" Jeremy asked again.

"The Train Track Pennies. I've never heard of them, but I like the name," Oly said, watching the house numbers get closer to the party address through rain-speckled windows. "I think the party's going to be in one of these houses."

Sure enough, they slowed and parked near an old, renovated house, split into flats like so many of Seattle's old homes. Odd to find parking so close to the party. Oly strolled up the driveway during a fortuitous break in the rain.

Jeremy scoffed. "I knew we were going to be too early. It doesn't sound like there's anything going on in there!"

Oly stopped on the sidewalk and cocked his head to the side with an odd feeling. "Actually, I think there is a party going on, but this might not be what we thought it was."

They looked up at the front of the house and realized that all the windows on the second floor were shining with light. They could hear soft music and occasional laughter.

Oly squared his shoulders and let go of his expectations for this party. He spent a couple of nights each week at some party or another, but most of them were warehouse or large loft parties. He'd assumed that a popular magazine would have a roaring party, but as he reached the red front door, he remembered that *Literate Life* wasn't popular, really. It was well respected within a small group of intellectuals, but not in a way that would fill a warehouse. He went to knock on the door and realized that it was open.

Oly shot Jeremy an "are these people crazy?" look, then ducked under the dripping awning and poked his head through the entrance. A thin mosaic of colored beans snaked up worn wooden stairs, pointing the way to another open door through which they could hear, closer, the same sounds they had heard from the sidewalk. Oly stepped through the red door and then felt uneasy at the idea that this might be a fancy dress event. He turned and surveyed Jeremy's damp clothing and then his own. They were dressed casually but in Seattle chic, so they could handle anything except a black-tie event.

Jeremy sent Oly a questioning look and Oly turned away, flushing. *No way am I nervous*. No way. He did this all the time. He climbed the stairs, careful not to muss the beautiful looping arrow of beans.

As Oly led the way through the door at the top and glanced left, the music stopped. People kept chattering, and the first person Oly spotted was a man in what looked like a punk rock business suit—arms torn off the pinstriped jacket, safety pins holding the front together over a sleeveless Butthole Surfers T-shirt, matching pinstriped pants torn off just below the knees, and, of all things, knee-high argyle socks inside loafers. Well, he thought, I don't need to worry about my clothing.

Oly looked around, taking in the apartment. He stood in an entryway lighted by an electric candelabrum stocked with multicolored lights. Oly entered the main room of the apartment. Jeremy stepped up beside him and then nodded with a wink in the direction of the snack table along one wall. Oly followed Jeremy to the table, taking in the polished wooden floors and small groups of strangers, then stepped on past to pick up a drink. He felt a little grim as he realized that his choices were wine, fruit juice, and water. Bottles ranged along a pass-through window from the kitchen, and Oly looked around the large, modernized kitchen, impressed by the size and hominess. He poured himself a small glass of cheap red and wandered to a doorway across the room. As far as he could tell, he was in a large one-bedroom apartment, but much of the bedroom seemed to be filled with a printing press and stacks of paper, bottles of ink, and trays of type. Excitement quickened in him with the belated realization that he was in Lania's home.

The press must be "Esmeralda," the love of Lania's life. All the printing paraphernalia had been stacked so people could congregate in that room as well as the main room. Oly eyed the futon couch tucked beside the press and wondered if Lania slept there. He didn't see any other bed.

Oly scanned the crowd, if a group of thirty or so people in a living room could be called a crowd. People seemed involved in vigorous discussions rather than the usual party chat. Beside

Jeremy, two silent people focused on the food at the snack table. Jeremy finished piling finger food on a little plate and stepped over to a small group of chairs facing the room. He settled in and started munching, and Oly turned back to the people gathered in the living room and kitchen.

He wandered around the room but didn't engage. The party chatter he'd grown used to was largely meaningless, but these folks talked like they were going to figure out the meaning of life. He gravitated toward the largest group. As he got close, a short, dark-haired young woman eyed him and broke away from the group.

She reached him in two steps and challenged, "Hey, did you donate on the way in?"

Oly felt an unfamiliar awkwardness. He had forgotten that this was a benefit. He looked toward the door, and, sure enough, a decorated, woven basket sported a sign reading "Keep Life Literate—Donate for Paper, Ink, Etc., Etc."

"Sorry." He cleared his throat. "I missed the basket. I'll take care of that right now." He'd brought money for the cover, but had forgotten about that in his distraction over the party being different from what he expected. And who expected people to put money in a basket anyway? That's no way to finance a magazine, he thought, exasperated. Oly turned away, and his self-appointed party guide followed.

After he dropped twenty dollars in the basket, Oly turned and asked, "And who might you be?"

The woman broke into a stunning smile and Oly blinked. "I'm Ginger Curadero, the resident critical eye on the medical field. And you are?"

Oly swept Ginger a small bow and replied, "Oly Rasmussen, at your service. I am a non-resident inexpert eye looking for Lania Marchiol." He caught a flash of impish excitement before Ginger dropped her eyes and shook her head with mock sadness.

"I'm sorry, but she has stepped out," she said with a quick look up through her bangs.

Oly searched her ripe, round features for hints on why this stranger was having such fun teasing him. It didn't feel like flirting, but he could tell she enjoyed something about this odd conversation. "Now why would Lania leave a party she is throwing, a benefit for her own magazine, early in the evening?"

Ginger tipped her head at the groups of people filling the apartment. "We didn't expect so many people, so she had to go get more snacks and drinks. We've never had more than twenty or so at one of these little gatherings. Every few issues, I talk her into throwing a party. It's one of the few ways we can all pitch in and help her out."

Oly hid his shock to hear this described as "so many people" and looked over the people around them. He started to discern a pattern—a few core groups of people who seemed very close, and a scattering of people who floated around the rest. She continued, "Well, come along and meet some people!"

Music started, something New Wave sounding, as they stepped back toward the large group Ginger had left. The man in the punk suit caught Oly's eye again, and he realized that he'd seen the guy last in a rockabilly outfit. He glanced around again and found most of the people from the last party.

Oly said, "Actually, I have met that man over there. I'd like to say hello."

To Oly's surprise, Ginger stuck close to him, trailing him across the room, and exclaimed, "Hideo, you didn't tell me you knew Oly!"

Hideo gaped at her. "I don't! I mean, we met, but I didn't even get his name!"

Oly spoke up. "We met very briefly. I was looking for Lania at the loft party last weekend, and I knew that Hideo had been talking to her. He didn't tell me about this benefit, though."

Ginger performed the introductions.

"How do you know Lania?" Oly asked.

"Just met her by chance at the loft party, but I've been reading her magazine for ages. There's a group of us that picks up a copy or two and shares it. There are never enough copies. I'm a bigger fan than ever, now that I'm in love with Lania," Hideo declared with a flamboyant sigh.

"Sure," Ginger said. "You've been panting around every woman here with a polysyllabic vocabulary."

"I'm a sucker for a smart woman, what can I say?" said Hideo. "That's why I want to be yours, Ginger!"

As Ginger rolled her eyes, a new commotion started in the far corner of the main room. Two women had entered, carrying musical instruments, and a large, tattooed man spread what seemed to be a rack of trash in the corner. Ginger grabbed Oly's arm. "They're getting started!"

Oly put his hand over hers and leaned down to ask as the noise level rose, "What's this?"

Ginger smirked. "You don't know them? You're in for a treat tonight."

"They're playing here, in her living room?"

"What of it? They're the Train Track Pennies. The guy in back is Hoss. He plays percussion and lives down the hall." Oly craned his neck and blinked at the spectacle of a man in dirty overalls with no shirt, no shoes, and tattoos covering his arms and chest. "The woman with the banjo is Carla. She's the lead singer. She's a wild performer." Oly eyed the skinny alley cat of a singer in her handmade, pioneer woman dress and had the feeling that Ginger wasn't exaggerating in the least.

Ginger sighed with hopeless desire. "Last but never least, the hottie setting up the marimbas is Melody Memzelle. I can never decide whether I want to be her or do her. She sings backup and plays harmonica, along with the marimbas."

Melody was a big woman, hourglass in the old-fashioned way of abundant breasts, thick hips, and round, soft arms. Even in such a small room, she drew the crowd's attention with a hot, sweeping glance. "Imposing."

"You don't know the half of it," Ginger said. "She scares the shit out of me, for the most part, but come on. There's no denying she's hot as fuck."

Melody stepped forward and announced in a commanding contralto, "We're going to get started now. If anyone wants to sing along, make it loud and fuck the neighbors! Just don't break Lania's stuff and we'll get along fine." She stepped back, even with the jittery Carla, and picked up her mallets.

The man in the back—Oly had a hard time believing the guy's name was Hoss—started to move the strips of metal hanging on his rack of random stuff. They clanged together louder when Hoss picked up a set of mallets and hit them in rhythm. He kept them ringing while he worked up the dynamic by adding cowbell, pots, and, finally, a five-gallon water bottle attached in front of him on its side. He picked up speed and moved faster, hitting the odd assortment with the mallets and bumping the whole rack with his knee to create the main beat. Oly watched, amazed, as the rhythms became more and more complex and then settled into a fast shuffle.

A low rumble rose among the percussive sounds, and Oly realized that Melody had begun to play the marimba. She rolled the low notes along with the shuffling beat and then rushed her mallets up and down the keys, creating a sound that reminded Oly of a train. He caught the thought. Train Track Pennies, indeed.

Melody leaned forward and blew a long note on the harmonica, holding it and then bending it downward, just like a train's whistle. Oly shouted along with most of the room, an involuntary response to the anticipation they were building.

Carla had been facing Hoss this whole time and getting more and more jumpy as the beat built and drove forward. Just as the whistle died away, Carla jumped to face the room and started to play her banjo.

Her hands stretched and contorted as she picked out a complicated, unending melody that moved on and on, never repeating a phrase, until all three players reached a frenzied crescendo. As one, they stopped and played three huge, descending, coordinated beats and then started again at the beginning of Carla's long banjo solo, simplified and at background volume. Over the first phrase, Carla began to sing.

Her rich, husky voice ached in a deep contralto. Oly shivered in dreamy realization as he recognized the song they played. Carla's voice strained and shook with the plaintive cry of a laid-off worker. She plumbed the low notes with astonishing grace and brought the melody back up to the chorus. Her flat chest heaved under the long line of buttons down the front of her sprigged cotton dress.

Oly found himself singing along as Carla began the second verse.

"Which will you pick when you get turned away,
Laid off from the factory floor?
Laid off by the bosses that sit 'round all day.
Do you take their sanctimonious charity
Or do you break down the door?"

People joined in and the chorus became a mixture of drinking song and marching song. Jeremy appeared at Oly's side and they grinned at each other while singing along:

"I'm an image in an old photograph,
Faded and wrinkled and gray.
An outlaw to you,
May as well make it true.
You'll blame me; I'll just ride away."

At the emotional high moment of the song, the music stopped and Carla's voice rose, alone, "This train car will take me away." The opening train-like sequence crashed back in and the band played another couple minutes of mad, chugging music for the jumping, packed-in crowd, then faded out with another long whistle on the harmonica.

The band dove into a song that sounded like an old spiritual while Oly and Jeremy looked at each other in excitement. "What are we going to do?" Jeremy asked.

"Hire 'em."

They listened to four early twentieth century union songs, one after another. They'd been missing this in their movie—the background music that would enhance the photos and brief movies they'd collected. Their oldest, silent footage required music that would represent the vigor of the old unionists. Carla's vigor and precision epitomized the spirit that brought the workers together in those days.

Melody stepped up and blew a long, ululating note on her harmonica, letting it fade into silence. In the quiet that remained, she announced, "We're moving down the hall now, back to Hoss's apartment. Come on over if you'd like to hear more! If you didn't give at the door on the way in, make sure you give on the way out."

Hoss folded his kit up and rolled it away while Melody put her marimba in its case and stood with it. She gazed at the marimba and harmonica stand for only a second before a humble fan begged permission to carry it for her. Melody nodded gracious permission and led the way out the door.

Carla vibrated with tense shyness, the neck of her banjo in one hand and the case over her shoulder in the other. She put her head down and bulled through the crowd. A stream of people followed, leaving the apartment for the show's continuation down the hall.

The atmosphere metamorphosed back into cocktail party, though sweaty and with a higher energy level. Jeremy went with the bulk of the people to Hoss's apartment, and Oly found himself alone in a room of tight-knit groups of friends. He walked back to the snack table for something to do with his hands, doing his best to project cool confidence.

As Oly turned back toward the room, napkin filled with pretzels, Lania materialized next to him. She stepped into his path and said, "I didn't expect to see you here!"

Chapter Four

O ly's pulse stuttered and his mind froze as he absorbed the woman in front of him. How could a person radiate happiness so freely? She wore jeans and a T-shirt and had no makeup on. Her unconfined hair spread across her shoulders in dark, unruly cables and soft frizz. The honest excitement in her expression broke something in him, the sophisticated mask that had become his habitual social face.

Oly swept Lania an elaborate, old-fashioned bow and addressed her comment. "I wasn't invited. I tried to find you online, and this party seemed like my chance to see you again. I also read that you're respected, brilliant, and motivated." Lania waved his words away. "I wonder why no one mentioned how beautiful you are."

Rather than the modest but pleased response she had before, Lania faded at the compliment on her looks. Oly was disappointed to see her lose even a bit of her joyous glow. She cast a pained glance at herself and shrugged. Sensitive about her looks. He would have to compliment her carefully or run the risk of having her discount his words. He shifted the pretzels into one hand and touched her cheek softly with the other. "This soft curve along your cheekbone makes me wish for a camera." She swallowed. He changed the subject. "Have you enjoyed the party so far?"

"Isn't that my line?" She raised an eyebrow. "I love getting these people together. Everyone's so smart and funny—it can't help but be a good party! And now there's some fresh blood with the people I met at the loft party on Friday."

Oly munched on a pretzel as he scanned the room. Even the shy or gawky guests had opened up. People were having fun. "You do have amazing friends. And that band!"

"I love them dearly. It took a while, though," Lania confessed. "I lived down the hall from the drummer, Hoss, for months before I got up the nerve to introduce myself."

Oly shook his head. "That's brave." He pictured an apprehensive Lania gearing herself up to talk to the enormous, rough-edged Hoss.

"He was totally sweet and told me about some of the other tenants, too. I mentioned the thumping I heard sometimes, and he admitted that he was always hitting something or another." Her direct gaze mesmerized him. "Can you imagine? Here I was, deciding he wasn't scary, when he says that he hits things all the time! I was completely confused, but then he told me about being the percussionist in a band and I busted out laughing.

"So of course I had to tell him why, and instead of getting annoyed about the whole thing, he was tickled at the idea that I had screwed up my courage to introduce myself. He showed me his metal and the rest of his percussion kit, and then showed me pictures of his boyfriend. You think Hoss is big? His boyfriend is a chief petty officer in the navy so he's gone a lot and I haven't met him, but he's huge."

"There's someone in this world bigger than Hoss?"

Lania wrinkled her nose at him. "Hoss and I go out to coffee or have tea now and then, and he asked if they could play for the benefit. I said yes, of course, but I didn't realize that would mean that their die-hard fans would come to the party." She circled her head as though dizzy.

"Did they break anything?"

"No. I checked," Lania admitted. She tucked a heavy curl behind her ear.

"Did you? Did you check the basket too? There were a lot of people in and out of here. I'd hate to hear your money had been taken."

Lania frowned a little. "I don't see that happening here." But she moved off toward the door nonetheless and Oly followed her. She reached up into the basket, and her eyes flew to his in shock. Her hand emerged filled with bills, and she reached in with the other hand, pulling out another handful. She looked at the money, seeing ten- and twenty-dollar bills.

He took the basket off the shelf. She let the money she held drop back into the basket and goggled at the full take for the evening. Oly looked at her. "Will this help?"

"This will print two or three full issues. I won't have to pay for the supplies myself. God, the pressure!"

She shoved her hair back, squared her shoulders, and took the basket from him. "Let's get back to the party and make sure everyone enjoys themselves!" Lania took his hand and led him away from the door.

Lania was more than satisfied with the party. Ginger would call it a raging success.

After introducing Oly to everyone in the room and dipping into a dozen conversations, Lania asked, "Are you here alone?"

"No way. I didn't know what I was getting myself into, so I strong-armed my best friend into coming along. He went to watch the band, but I think he slipped back in for more snacks." Oly looked around and then pointed at a thin man in a quiet seat on the sidelines.

"I'd like to meet him."

"Of course." Oly led her to stand in front of his friend.

He looked up and jumped to his feet. "Hi!"

"Lania, please allow me to introduce my long-time friend, the production manager, location manager, transportation captain, and generally useful fellow, Jeremy Noor. Jeremy, this is Lania Marchiol, publisher of the venerable magazine *Literate Life* and the person who lives in this apartment." Lania shook hands with Jeremy. His friendliness negated the impression of reserve his lonely seat had made.

"It sounds like you have a lot of work to do on this film," Lania said.

Jeremy blushed. He tossed a pleading look at Oly, who said, "Jeremy is the make-it-happen guy. I wander around trying to be artistic, but Jeremy ensures that we actually make a film."

Redder than before, Jeremy said, "You and Joyner build everything, and Roshan does the filming—I never touch a camera…"

Oly waved in dismissal. "You know nothing would get done without you. I'm going to refill our drinks."

He left with Lania's glass, and Lania and Jeremy looked at each other with surprise. Ginger appeared, towing a woman wearing thick glasses and a conservative tweed skirt suit. "Jeremy, I couldn't help but overhear that you're working on Oly's film. I'm Ginger Curadero." She offered him the hand that wasn't dragging the other woman and then joined their hands forcibly. "And I don't believe you've met Joyce Blockcolski. She is writing an article titled 'Unions vs. Cooperatives—the Us/Them Experience,' and I think you two should talk."

Ginger pushed them closer and shoved them off to walk away together. She said, "It's hard work bringing the geeks together. Joyce wanted to meet Jeremy, but do you think she could simply walk over and introduce herself? No, no, no—she needed a push."

Ginger watched Joyce and Jeremy walk toward the snack table, and Lania watched Ginger view her handiwork with satisfaction. Ginger said, "She has so little self-confidence. She doesn't even know how lovely her eyes are. She'll slay him in no time if they can get to talking about unions. She gets so passionate."

"I hadn't thought about bringing them together."

"I don't know if they ever would have spoken without my help. I want the whole world mixed up and shaken back out again. It makes life more exciting when the people around you are feeling the flush of first love. Speaking of which…"

"Not now! He'll be back any second."

Ginger looked over Lania's shoulder and squinted up. "Trying to get my girl drunk?"

Lania's jaw dropped at this parental tone from Ginger. She turned to take the cup and Oly put a hand on her shoulder. "I'm sure Lania can speak for herself, Ginger. She'll stop drinking when she doesn't want any more wine."

"Be good." With that message for Oly, Ginger leaned close and whispered in Lania's ear, "Be bad."

Lania shook her head and allowed Ginger to fade off into the crowd with a last significant look at Oly's hand on her shoulder.

She looked at him. "What did you say to Ginger? I've never seen her go all mama cat like that!"

He chuckled. "It may be that I missed the donation basket on the way in. Or it could be the way I was looking at you just now from behind."

Lania pulled her shirt lower in back, flushing again. He looked down and she followed suit. The way her breasts pushed against the neckline in front, she was glad they hadn't popped right out. She released her clothing and shot him a sharp look. Oly leaned close and growled in her ear, "Don't worry, I don't eat up little girls at benefit parties."

She melted, her whole body going lax and falling into a hipshot stance. She shot him a warm, teasing look from under her hair. "That's too bad. Am I wasting my time?"

He dipped his head closer to hers, but she took his hand and turned away. She wasn't ready to get hot and heavy with him. She was bringing her best game to the flirting, but it left her as volatile as dry kindling. Soon, but not now.

He gave her hand a hard squeeze and followed her lead. She took him across the room to meet Joyce and so she could see how Ginger's fix-up was working out.

Joyce blinked at Jeremy as they came close enough to hear the conversation. "Don't you see that unions place workers and bosses in opposition and foster antagonistic work environments? Why not eliminate bosses and organize cooperative structures?"

Jeremy gulped but stepped up to the challenge. "That's exactly where the evolution of the Wobbly ideals ends up! Workers owning the means of production! Aren't we saying the same thing?" Jeremy sent Oly a silent "Help!" but Joyce jumped right on top of his statement without looking at Lania or Oly.

"No! No, no, no! Haven't you been listening?" Joyce bulldogged him, leaning close enough to wipe her glasses on his shirtfront.

Still holding Lania's hand, Oly broke in. "Listening to what?"

"Unions are adversarial organizations while cooperatives are cooperative organizations." Joyce stopped short, seeming to lose her train of thought. "Jeremy, attend me in my apartment. I must transcribe this argument."

Jeremy was towed away by the much smaller woman. Lania turned to Oly and laughed out loud at the consternation on his face. "Don't worry about them. Joyce lives on the third floor. She'll take him to her apartment, suck him dry of ideas, and walk around muttering about unions and co-ops for the next week."

Oly raised an eyebrow at her. "That doesn't sound like much fun for Jeremy. That woman seems too geeky to know when to stop."

"She's just excited to talk about her pet subject." Lania withdrew her hand.

Oly mocked the gravel in Joyce's voice. "Come with me so I can strip your brain and toss you out in the cold."

"Don't be mean, Oly. She's a little socially backward, but she's a good person and a friend of mine. Not all of us can be smooth like you. Joyce and I have more in common than you think."

"You've got to be kidding. You're beautiful, fascinating, and talented, and she's just about the geekiest, funniest looking woman I've met in years. And socially backward? You think? She never even let you introduce me. And what had she done to her hair?"

"Stop it!" Lania cut Oly off before he could dig himself any deeper. "Why are you being so cruel? She's a nice person and a brilliant theorist!"

Lania was gratified when his face turned a bit red with embarrassment. "I'm sorry," he said. "I wasn't thinking. I imagine she is all that and more."

Through a painfully long moment of silence, they looked at each other. Oly repeated, "I'm sorry."

Lania considered his penitent expression. "You know, most of my friends are like that. Too deep into their own heads to worry about hairstyles and sometimes too wrapped up to worry about polite manners."

Oly took Lania's hand back. "I'm not usually so judgmental, I promise. I like your friends so far. I'm sorry I went off like that. It's…I may be a bit protective of Jeremy."

"Maybe you'll tell me about that some time."

"It's not that complicated a story. I don't want him to be hurt."

"But he has been?"

Oly sent Lania a sharp look and tugged on her hand. "There you go, being all perspicacious and shit."

She let the subject drop and released his hand. "I'm going to check on the snacks."

When she got back to him, Oly had wandered into a conversation about technology and science fiction. She watched him hold his own in a heated discussion on a topic that seemed outside his field. He listened carefully while Clark explained his argument, then asked pointed and demanding questions. The prickly scientist started making notes on a new train of thought revealed through Oly's questions, and Lania tipped her head in a hint that they should leave him alone.

"Well done. Clark seemed really fired up by whatever you asked him."

"A major requirement for a documentarian—interview skills. That was fun, though. He has some great insights about the relationship between imagination and invention."

"This group has a lot of those—great insights, I mean."

Lania wasn't kidding, and she was proud to show off her friends. She pulled Oly into conversations on environmental activism, gender and queer theory, Shakespeare and William Blake, and more, plus got him talking about his film.

❖

Meanwhile, Oly kept an eye out for Jeremy. When he returned with his hair and clothing rumpled, Oly took in the mussed appearance of him and thought, make-out city, eh?

The Train Track Pennies could no longer be heard down the hall, and Oly saw Jeremy talking to Carla. He turned to Lania. "Will you excuse me for a few minutes? I'd really like to talk to Carla about using the Train Track Pennies in our film."

Lania put her hand on his bicep. He couldn't resist flexing a little under her grip. "You don't know what that would mean to them. Carla has had a terrible time finding a job over the last couple of years, and she keeps threatening to move to San Francisco, where she thinks she'll have less trouble."

"What's her field?"

"She's an audio tech. She's done studio work, sound for clubs, and a few tours with bands. Most people stopped hiring her when she transitioned."

Oly nodded with grim sympathy. "I bet she had trouble. Most sound techs aren't known for their highly developed sense of feminism. It's easier for me, but in a creepy way. My masculinity reinforces the sexist sense of superiority. Like, of course I'd rather be a dude. I'm picky about who I work with, because I hate it when my transition is used to prop up fucked up ideas about manly being better." He took Lania's hand. "I'll be right back."

Oly joined Jeremy and Carla, who'd retreated to a corner to talk. Jeremy said, "The post-production sound mixing will need to wait until most of the editing has been finalized, since we're doing so much of this on the fly and we won't know what sound effects we'll need until we've cropped out the parts that don't work. I'd hate to put you to work on sections we'll end up cutting out of the final. We just don't have the money to pay for work we won't need in the end."

Oly caught on. Jeremy wanted Carla for more than a couple of recordings to play over stock footage. Jeremy's ability to make snap decisions about people was second only to his ability to get them on board before they could resist. His verbal mode swung from tongue-tied to bulldozer in those moments. Watching him work never got boring.

"I'm happy to have the work," said Carla. "I'm even more excited about the project." She turned to include Oly in the conversation. "When can I get a look at the script so I can pick out some good music?"

Oly asked, "E-mail?" Carla nodded and the three of them had a cell phone moment programming each other's contact information. "You'll get the script tomorrow. When can I expect to see your first list of suggestions?"

"We know this music forward and backward. Melody, Hoss, and I can have a preliminary list to you by the end of the week, but you and I are going to need to talk before I can be sure I understand your requirements."

Oly nodded. "I have very particular ideas on what mood I want. I wrote the script, and a lot of my needs are described in the notes, but we should arrange a meeting." Oly asked Jeremy, "When do we have an afternoon or evening free?"

Jeremy checked the calendar on his phone. "What if we have dinner together next Thursday? That way, we get the artistic and production details out of the way and chow down at the same time. If you don't think Melody and Hoss would be bored, maybe we can all meet?"

Carla gripped her own elbows. "God, this is really going to happen, isn't it?"

Oly looked her straight in the eye. "This film needs you and the Train Track Pennies."

Carla sighed and the corners of her mouth lifted.

"Will you make sure to get the script to Carla tomorrow?" He gave Jeremy a significant look that meant, I want you to babysit this one, and Jeremy nodded in understanding. Jeremy guided Carla over to Joyce and the three of them started another conversation about labor history.

Oly left them to it. He refilled his wine and couldn't keep himself from seeking Lania out among the small groups left. She walked through the room, exchanging a word here or there. Oly wondered if Lania knew that her shy smiles left ripples of good will behind.

Watching her hips move in her loose jeans, Oly's mind turned to more carnal questions. He stepped into her bedroom, which looked more like an office. Her futon couch would make a damned uncomfortable bed for two people. Could he get her to the loft after the party?

Oly sensed a presence at the door and turned to see Lania leaning against the doorstop as though it were holding her up. She lowered her dark lashes, but he got a glimpse of the tumult inside her. He took a sip from his drink and stayed his ground, inviting her to be alone with him in her bedroom.

CHAPTER FIVE

That rascal, thought Lania, half-amused, half-agonized by the throbbing she could feel throughout her body. She took a calming breath and stepped closer to him. She looked up with as much composure as she could summon and then melted in the gentle heat of his gaze.

He was alone in the bedroom. She wanted to sit him down on the old, tired comforter and straddle him while holding on to the back of the futon. Her temperature rose and her body swayed with her imaginary rise and fall on his lap. She thought he was packing, from the fall of his pants, but she wondered if he had a fucking cock with him as well. Would offering her dildo be a breach of etiquette? It could go both ways with the butch dykes she'd fucked. Of the guys who'd been assigned male at birth, few had any interest in using anything but their own cocks, unless it was for pegging.

The thought of a whole new sexual realm added an edge of nervousness to her overall tension. What did a sexual relationship with Oly have in store for her? Lania could only wonder and hope she had the chance to find out.

She knew that Oly was playing a game, daring her to join him. He maintained a gentle manner as he took one last step backward to the folded bed and sat.

Lania's chest rose and fell as she worked to control her breathing. Not having been privy to her fantasies of a moment ago, she suspected he was surprised that his ploy to bring her closer had such a strong effect. She moved closer, but sideways, sliding over to stroke the flywheel of her printing press, prolonging the tense moment.

"That's a funny toy to have in a bedroom."

"Yes, but I really wanted to keep some sort of living space." She looked at the press with reverence. "This is Esmeralda. She was made in 1872 by George Phineas Gordon. He developed this design in 1851, after a dream in which Benjamin Franklin described it to him."

Lania let the sexual tension simmer on a back burner. "This was the absolute best small press in the country. You work this treadle with your foot, feed the paper with one hand, and remove it with the other. Keeping things moving without smearing ink all over the place is tricky. That's why she's Esmeralda—because I'm Quasimodo when I'm printing."

"You said that when we met, but now I can really picture it."

"This was one of the first presses to be made after he improved the design in a few small particulars, and it was special ordered by a couple—George and Mary Jane Washington."

"You even know who commissioned it?"

"The short version of the story is that they were trying to get a town started. George was the son of a slave. He moved to the Oregon Territory with the family that had owned his father. Racist laws kept him from owning property himself, but the family finagled it so that he ended up with six hundred and forty acres where the Skookumchuck River meets the Chehalis River. He farmed that land for years. When the Washington Territory was formed, without the requirement that a person be white to own land, they turned it over to him legally." Lania paused. "Did I say this was going to be the short version?"

Oly laid an arm across the back of the futon. "Don't worry about me. I'm fascinated."

"When the railroad came through in 1872, George and his wife decided they'd like company, and he platted out a town that he called Centerville. They took out ads to draw settlers. A friend lived on the land and operated a little general store, so that was one selling point. They decided that a newspaper would make the town more official and ordered the best press they could afford." Lania stroked the platen arm and moved to sit next to Oly.

"Eight years later, there were seventy-eight residents, so he must have been right. They didn't like his name for the place, though, and in 1883 they changed it to Centralia." Oly sat up and refocused at this information.

"Have you heard of the Centralia Massacre?" Oly asked.

Lania tipped her head to the side. "No. What happened?"

"The Industrial Workers of the World was formed in reaction against the AFL's mobster leanings, dealings with the bosses, racism, and failure to organize women. They created a more radical organization and called themselves Wobblies. Their aim was abolition of the wage system, not the more conservative fair day's wage for a fair day's work. Talk about scaring the businessmen."

Lania nodded but gave Oly a puzzled look.

"This does come around to Centralia," he assured her. "Across the country, Wobbly leaders were tried and executed without evidence. They were bad-mouthed by regular unions and demonized by company bosses. They upset the peace, didn't support the U.S. presence in World War I, and resisted towns that tried to get rid of them.

"In 1919, Centralia celebrated Armistice Day with a parade. Lumber company people agitated the returned soldiers against the Wobbly organizers, painting them as communists who endangered democracy and the American way of life. In the middle of the parade, the marching American Legionnaires turned off the route and attacked the Wobbly union hall."

Lania sat, stunned, while Oly continued. "During a Red Cross march the year before, the union hall had been destroyed and the Wobblies had been beaten in a real, old-fashioned gauntlet of local businessmen. A year later, when the police refused to guard the union hall during the parade, they armed themselves.

"When the Legionnaires attacked the hall, Wobblies opened fire from several points. In the end, four Legionnaires died. All of the Wobblies were arrested, as was their lawyer. The hall was destroyed and the membership list was given to the town prosecutor. One man was taken from jail that very night and lynched. Seven others were convicted of second-degree murder. Their sentences ranged between twenty-five and forty years."

Lania shook her head. "Centralia's George Washington was known for being a kind and lenient man. He forgave debts and gave people food when times were tough. Even the town plots were basically a gift. He charged ten dollars per plot, but it was free if you built a house on it. There's no way he would have allowed a lynching in his town. He died in 1905. It only took fourteen years for the red scare to overpower the values he built that town on."

Oly sat in silence for a moment. "How did the press end up with you?"

"In 1974, Matt Tomlin built a bank on the old newspaper's land. He found her in an old outbuilding, rusted but not ruined. He had her refurbished and set in the bank lobby. When he retired, he decided that she deserved to be used and put out notices that she was to be sold or donated.

"I was in college and having mixed feelings about the whole thing. I loved the classes and the reading and writing, but I couldn't help but see that I was being pushed into a mold along with everyone else there. The people who couldn't fit did poorly and resigned themselves to stopping at a BA, even though some of them were coming up with gorgeous theories that we all loved exploring. I decided to start a magazine that would publish the essays I loved, even when they weren't academically viable."

"Cool idea. Seems like desktop publishing would have been easier, though."

"Of course, Seattle is all about computers, and I was all for it. And then I saw the notice about the printing press and realized that I wanted more than control-x and control-v." She rubbed her fingertips against each other. "It's amazing what a close relationship you have to the words when you've set the type, physically touching every single letter. It can be infuriating—it is another place where typos can be introduced—but more often than not, it's just plain old beautiful. And Esmeralda has turned into my most prized possession.

Whenever someone asks me my life story, I always end up telling them about the history of this press instead. I'm boring, but this— this is real and important."

Oly raised an eyebrow. "I'd argue the boring part, but we can get into that later."

"I got my bachelor's degree in English literature and Esmeralda in the same week. That funny old man gave me the press, all the old type, and the small collection of books he had on the subject—for free. He was well off, didn't need the money. He was looking for a tax write-off, I'm sure."

"It sounds to me like you must have set him on fire, at least a little bit. He could have donated it to a museum for a write-off, but you were going to use it. Besides, you're not a non-profit organization, so he didn't get a write-off." Lania blinked in surprise. Oly changed the subject. "It looks like you need a bigger place, though. Have you ever thought about moving?"

"I like being on the Hill but not right in the busy Capitol Hill area itself. I like being close to work and riding my bike everywhere. I could move even closer to work, but I like my neighborhood." Oly just looked at her with one eyebrow raised, and she returned his look with a cool, defensive one. "What, you don't like this neighborhood?"

"Well, it doesn't have a great reputation. Aren't there gunfights and gangs and such?"

Lania had been over this subject many times with her extended family. They wanted her to move into a safer—to them, that meant richer and whiter—neighborhood.

"Most of the reputation is exaggerated. I'm more worried about being part of a first wave of gentrification. I used to avoid letting people see my apartment. I felt that it should be kept secret so that I wouldn't bring more people to the neighborhood and drive out the residents who'd been there for decades. I gave up on that recently. Lots of people have been moving out as the prices have gone up."

"You're serious? You were trying to hold back gentrification all by yourself?"

"I may not recognize all the problems or know what I can do to make things better, but when I see an opportunity to do the right thing, I have to try."

Oly found the simplicity of her attitude almost frightening. She didn't seem to realize that most people rationalized participating in racism and gentrification. Did she expect that sort of automatic commitment from the people around her? Oly could feel every time he'd ever compromised one of his beliefs to make life easier.

There would be no chance of a casual relationship here. Lania hand-printed a magazine so she could be that intimate with it. She made a home in a neighborhood with a reputation for racial tension and violence and tried to protect the neighbors from a force that, it could be argued, she was a part of. If she expected so much of herself, what would she want from him?

Now it was Oly's turn to change the subject. "What do you work at? You mentioned that this is close to work…"

Lania shrugged and tucked a lock of hair behind her ear. "Nothing exciting. I make eyeglasses. I've been an apprentice optician since I was seventeen years old."

Oly's pale eyebrows flew up. "I wouldn't have pegged you as a slow learner. Why are you still an apprentice?"

"I don't really care about becoming a licensed optician. The pay's not that much better, and this way I don't have to pay to take the test. This was supposed to be the job that paid my living expenses through college, and I've never been very attached to it. I guess I've been focusing on the magazine, and letting my work life float on by."

Oly reassessed his earlier thoughts about her unflinching commitment to living by her own rules. "Do you think it is right that the magazine gets treated like a hobby?"

Lania looked taken aback. "I have to support myself and the magazine somehow. I can't be dependent on other people to pay my way in the world. How do you finance your filming?"

Oly spread his hands. "However I can. Jeremy and I get donations, throw benefit parties, work some, and find supporters wherever we can. There are about a dozen people who get a share of this film if it sells. It's the only way we can focus on getting the film made."

"Do friends and family help you out?"

"I'm not a burden on anyone. I keep myself fed just fine."

Lania pulled her heels up on the daybed and wrapped loose arms around them. "I'm sorry. I'm not trying to insult you. I just have it in my head that my first order of business is working to feed, house, and clothe myself. Anything else I do is bonus. Artistic expression of any kind is bonus. I play several instruments and sing, but I could never imagine a career in music. I guess I see this magazine as being like that. I've always felt lucky that anyone would entrust their writing to me and allow me to print it."

"Oh, Lania. I can tell you for sure that you are more respected than that. I did some Internet research and found out that much. You aren't valuing *Literate Life* the way the literary and theoretical community is. You could be getting grants for this publication, Lania. You could get any of dozens of organizations to sponsor issues. Why don't you see that as an option?"

"It's not the same as doing it myself! Once other people have a stake in the magazine, there would be all these expectations, and you're right. Anything that would improve the magazine would mean spending a lot more time on it. I've thought about growth, and I certainly have enough submissions to increase the size. That means a lot more work and no time for a real job. I can't imagine counting on other people to pay my bills."

"What's the difference between depending on grantors or sponsors to pay you for the work you do and depending on a paycheck from your boss at the eyeglasses place?"

Lania shook her head. "I guess it's not about the paycheck this week. It's about rent four months from now. I guess I have to know I'm working toward keeping things under control."

Oly stroked the satiny fall of hair across her shoulder. "I feel like I've gotten off the treadmill of regular jobs and focused on what I love."

"I feel like I do my regular job so well that I have energy left over for the things I care about."

"Wow. How do you square that with wanting to sail away?"

"Fuck. I don't know. I'm hoping that simplifying will take care of a lot of it. I won't need so much money if I'm sailing. Before I go, I'll have to pay off the boat I buy and save up enough money to feel confident I'll have time to find work wherever I go.

"The thing is, I can't stand even this kind of life. Where I live in someone else's building, plugging into electricity I have no control over, washing myself with water from who-knows-where, and sending my wastes into a system I don't understand. Just when social liberation started sweeping through, the whole human race tied itself to technologies most of us don't understand. If I'm going to rely on something, I want to know exactly how it works. If something catastrophic happens, do you know where to go for clean drinking water?"

The naked intensity in Lania's gaze made Oly uncomfortable, but in a way that stimulated him. He'd never heard anyone talk about being dependent on such basics. He struggled to formulate a picture of life without such things.

"I want electricity, but I want to know that it came from solar panels and that it will continue to work as long as the sun keeps my batteries charged. I want access to water, but I want to know that it will keep coming from the faucet as long as I keep the watermaker in good repair, which requires parts, which require money." She shrugged.

"Sailing away. It's not just the adventure you're after, then?"

Lania bit her tender lower lip and hesitated. "I want to learn and grow through travel, but I also want to live my life in a truly self-contained fashion. I want to run my whole life by the hiking motto—leave nothing but footprints, take nothing but pictures."

"Making your own power and water? You'd still have to buy food, right? It's not like a cabin up in the mountains where you can plant a kitchen garden. When my uncle and I sailed the Caribbean, we traded for or bought food at every stop."

"True. Because of that, even on a boat, I'd need to work. It's not just food, either. There will be parts and tools for maintenance, clothes, and moorage when I'm in a marina." Her lips quirked. "And people do seem to want money for those things."

"You're talking about a need to work in order to support yourself."

"Can you see where I'm coming from?"

"I think I do. I can respect that you have a strong work ethic and that work to you means something that results in a paycheck. I just have a wider definition of work. I'd say that making films is worthwhile simply as art but also a long-term investment if you can get it distributed."

Lania tipped her head to one side, sending her hair cascading across her arm. "So, it's not just our definitions of independence that differ. It's also how we think of work. The magazine isn't work; it's a labor of love. I guess I define work as something regular, something I get a paycheck for every couple weeks. I'm really talking about a job. I'll have to think about that.

"Hideo would kill me if he knew I thought that way about jobs. His essay posits that joblessness and homelessness are poor indicators of if people are willing and able to work. He talks about the struggle to survive on the street and claims that it's less work to have a regular job, so the structure around jobs is the problem, rather than the motivation of the jobless person." Lania took Oly's hand and stood. "Let's go talk to him about this. We'll have a debate."

Oly followed Lania out of her room, impressed once again, this time by her ability to release her vanity and reexamine her beliefs. How many people would put themselves into a debate with two people who disagreed with her? Especially for the purpose of broadening her own ideas?

As the party wrapped up, the music caught Oly's attention. "Mozart?"

"Yes, indeed. Do you enjoy his piano concertos?" They moved to her computer to check out her collection. After discussing music for a while, Lania pulled the keyboard closer to her and brought up her e-mail program. She wrote an e-mail with her phone number in it. She asked for his e-mail address and sent the message to him right that moment, then jumped at the buzz in his pocket. He pulled out his smart phone and said, "Don't look." Thumbs flying, he found the Web page he wanted and pasted the link into his reply.

Lania craned her neck to look at his screen and he gave her a severe look. Finally, he nodded.

She turned back toward the computer and brought her e-mail program back up. His message appeared.

> To: Lania Marchiol
> From: Oly the Holey
> Subject: Let's roll!
> I sure do like you, and though I've enjoyed spending time with you at parties, I'd like to have you to myself. How about we go to Silverwood?

The word "Silverwood" was a hyperlink, and she clicked on it. Oly fidgeted as the Web page loaded. Silverwood wasn't a spa, or a club, or a campground. It was an amusement park with dozens of rollercoasters and other rides.

Lania stood and faked a sappy swoon. "Yes! Yes, my prince, take me away and rollercoaster me until we can't rollercoaster anymore!"

Oly caught her in his arms. "Oh, dearest, I will rollercoaster you like you've never been rollercoastered before!"

He placed a soft kiss on her soft lips. He firmed his lips on hers and tightened his hold for a moment. He backed up by mere inches and his voice dropped to a lower register. "So you'll come?"

With a dirty, teasing grin, Lania stepped out of his arms. "Well, that will be partly up to you." She couldn't possibly know what vivid images she started in his mind with that unexpected double entendre. "Let's start with Silverwood and see who comes where later."

CHAPTER SIX

O ly held a foot-high stack of yellowed paper in the doorway of a small side room. "Jeremy, you have to see this." Oly stepped around the wheelbarrow and its pile of near misses.

Jeremy scratched his skinny belly and leaned on his shovel, focusing on Oly's load of magazines. "Whatcha got there?"

Oly started in on his finds. "They're *Fortune Magazines* from the 1930s and '40s. Check this out." Oly handed the stack to Jeremy and opened the top magazine to a page he'd marked with a bit of a stained *Mad Magazine*.

Jeremy whistled. "What year was this?"

"This one is from 1943. See how this map shows the progress of the war? It's a two-page spread, in perfect condition. I know that there are collectors who'll pay good money for this magazine, just for the advertisements and this map here."

Jeremy breathed deep. "If I'm right about the value of these things, you and I will be able to focus on filming from here until this thing is done. No more day jobs."

"I know."

❖

In the big room of his loft, Oly answered his cell phone.

"Who are you, and how did you meet Carla?" demanded a clear soprano voice.

Taken aback, Oly adjusted the phone a little way from his ear. "Who are you and why are you attacking me?"

"Whoa. I'm not attacking you, buddy. I just want to know who you are. Carla says she has work for herself and a gig for us, and she's so excited she can't even tell me about it. She keeps crowing that it's her big chance." A worried undertone floated to the surface.

"Is this Melody?"

"How did you know that?" Melody sounded suspicious.

"Okay. Let's start over." Oly paced in front of the loft's bank of windows. "I'm Oly Rasmussen, writer and director of a film about the Seattle General Strike of 1919. My production manager, Jeremy, and I saw the Train Track Pennies play at Lania Marchiol's *Literate Life* benefit last night and spoke to Carla about using you in the score. Jeremy and Carla also made plans for her to do our postproduction sound mixing."

A moment of silence dripped through the phone. The next thing Oly heard was a muffled "damn" and a couple of deep breaths, then Melody came back to the phone. "I apologize for the way I started this conversation. Carla's pretty cynical for the most part, and seeing her thrown for such a loop really freaked me out."

"Is she okay?"

Melody's voice was sour. "Yeah. Apparently, I'm the one who's not okay." Oly heard an unladylike snort through the phone. "So do you accept my apology? I am sorry I attacked you like that. Carla's been wanting so badly to get back into sound, and I was afraid you were dicking her around."

"I accept and only partly because I want you guys on this soundtrack. I also liked Carla right off the bat, and I'm glad she has you on her side."

Melody laughed, openly and fully, and the roll of it over the phone reminded Oly of her tremendously sexual presence. He shifted on his feet, shaking his head at her power. Oly couldn't deny that Melody was a big bundle of hotness, but she was also a natural top, and he wasn't looking for that anymore. Back in his puppy dog phase, though, she would have been his dream come true.

Melody said, "Just so you know, I usually set up our gigs. This is two in a row that haven't been mine—Hoss with the party last night and now Carla with this film. Maybe I feel funny about that."

"Do we need to deal with you from here on out?"

"We're not formal about it. It's just always worked out that way because they're both so shy. I'm usually the only one who can make the phone calls and shake down the club owners for our money afterward. Speaking of which, what kind of agreement did Carla make with you?"

"She didn't make any firm agreements about the score. She said we'd need to talk to all three of you." He could hear Melody shifting into gear. "As for her mixing work, she'll get guild rates."

"Good. Very good."

"Do you guys have enough material to score the whole movie? Or can you hook us up with bands like you to flesh it out?"

"No, honey, we'll make sure you have all the songs you need. We have the *Little Red Songbook*. We can deliver those Wobbly songs like it's 1899."

❖

Lania had a notebook dedicated to listing the features of her ideal boat. The boat needed to be small enough to sail single-handedly, large enough to hold all the supplies she'd need for long crossings, and fast enough not to drag out those crossings. She wanted to be as independent as possible, having enough technology that she'd be safe and sure of where she was but not so much that she started depending on anything that would leave her in dangerous conditions were it to fail.

Lania lay belly-down on her flat futon bed and flipped to the back of the local sailing magazine, *48° North*. As far as she could tell, there was no better way to find a used boat than through the *48° North* classifieds. Though she'd gone online after deciding to buy a boat, she'd found few that sounded right to her. Most people didn't seem to think of small boats as world travelers—and for good reason. Most of these small boats were built for lake or Puget Sound sailing, not for ocean rollers. She had printed out a few listings, but preferred thumbing through the magazine.

Lania scanned the boats in the twenty- to thirty-two-foot range, circling a few for later follow-up and filling notebook pages with her impressions of each one. Her shoulders swayed to the Afro-Portuguese music of Mabulu as she read every boat ad in her size range.

Printouts and *48° North* in hand, she turned the music down, danced to her little dining nook, and curled up on a hard wooden chair. She grabbed her phone and started calling.

After twenty minutes, Lania had left almost a dozen messages and only reached one person, arranging to see that boat the next day. It was early; surely the others would get back to her.

Lania felt a flutter of nervous excitement at the idea of checking out her first boat. What if she liked it? What if it happened just like that—she called, she saw, she wanted? She'd been thinking of the purchasing process as something that would take a long time, but suddenly she wanted to get a boat right now! She turned the music back up and danced around her apartment, dressing and cleaning up at the same time.

No reason to waste all this energy—she was going to look at boats! She grabbed her backpack and stuffed it with her phone, her notebook, the *48° North*, and the printouts, along with an energy bar and a bottle of water. She strapped the backpack on and wheeled her bike out the door. She had to get down to the water.

Outside with her bike, she eyeballed the sky and thought it looked like the rain might hold off until night. The fast, exciting ride down Capitol Hill brought her to the Center for Wooden Boats in no time flat. Rather than stopping, she kept riding around to the west side of Lake Union, heading toward the boat sales docks. She didn't slow at the first two—both featured new boats with prices in the hundreds of thousands of dollars.

A little farther down, in an area away from the bustle of Seattle Center, Lania slowed and then stopped at a rickety dock. Many of the boats had for sale signs on them and the front gate was wide open. She locked her bike and walked down the planked gangway.

At the bottom was an office and she could see a bald head through the open top of the Dutch doors. The head lifted as she came nearer. A short, stout man stood and walked over to lean on the door.

"Can I help you find something?"

"Maybe. I'm looking for a small single-hander that is solid enough to travel the world."

He squinted toward the boats. "Weeellll…" He scratched his head, then turned and stepped to the back of the little office. He rummaged about for a moment then turned back with a big ring of keys and a couple pieces of paper. He handed one to Lania and led the way onto the dock. She glanced down the sheet as she walked and realized that it was a list of specifications for one of the boats.

"I'm Charles. See here—this is a twenty-eight-foot Hunter with some nice features." He pointed at the sad looking boat in front of them.

She stood on the swaying planks of the finger pier and shook her head. The boat was half covered with moss, telling a story of long neglect. She could also see on the sales sheet that it had a fin keel. Boats with that underwater shape turned more easily in close quarters but didn't track as well through the water, especially when the current or the wind tried to shove the boat sideways. A full keel had a continuous curve from the front of the boat all the way to the back and would keep her safe and comfortable in ocean rollers.

"I'd rather go with something a bit less run-down, and I think I'll need a full keel. If I planned to spend most of my time getting into and out of marinas, a fin keel would be fine. That's not what I have in mind, though. I want to spend quite a bit of my time in open waters," she said.

Charles looked at her more closely. "What's your name?"

Lania offered her hand. "I'm Lania Marchiol. Nice to meet you."

"Nice to meet you, Lania." Charles cocked his head to the side. "So you're serious about the traveling part, eh?" He handed her the second sales sheet and led her back to the head of the dock and down a different pier.

Charles stopped and gazed a moment at a boat, then turned to Lania. "Full keel. What else do you want in a boat?"

"Well, I have a list here." She had never shared her notebook with anyone. She had started cataloging qualities she liked in boats when she was in sailing class, but she had also scribbled ideas whenever one came to her. It was not organized or presentable, in her opinion. "I'll need to be able to cook aboard, and I'd prefer a propane stove to kerosene or alcohol. I'll want to be able to sleep on deck or in the cockpit if the weather permits so that I can keep an eye on the sails, but I'll want to have a comfortable single berth inside. And storage—I'll need enough for food on long journeys and for books, although I'm considering going to an e-reader. I don't need much space for clothing, but somewhere to hang wet foul weather gear would be nice."

Charles held up a hand to stop the flood of information. "I think I get the idea." He heaved himself aboard a tidy little boat with round sides like a big belly and unlocked the companionway. "I'll start to write up your needs assessment while you take a look at this boat here, and you can fill out the name and contact information when you're done looking at it. You can give me the full list then. I'll keep an eye out and try to match you up with the right boat. Sound good?"

Lania was surprised but pleased at his desire to help. "Sure thing. I'll just stop back by your office on the way out. Should I lock this one up?"

Charles inspected the sky. "No, leave it open. It'll be good for it to air out some, and I don't think it'll rain before nightfall." This confirmed her weather opinion and, more secure than ever in the knowledge that she was doing the right thing, she stepped aboard the little boat.

Every move she made sent the boat swinging on its dock lines. The motion, far from making her seasick, made her yearn to untie the boat and get it out of the dock. Shivering with excitement, Lania stepped forward, swinging around the wires that steadied the mast from the sides—the shrouds. She walked to the bow, turned around, and inspected the boat from that vantage point. It looked to be solid and true, with a few rust spots showing that the boat hadn't been cared for recently. Otherwise, it looked as though someone had loved the boat very much. She estimated that the owner had neglected it for about six months. Nothing much seemed worn, just dirty.

At the bow, forestay in her hand, Lania was overtaken with the realization that she would need to look at every square inch of the boat if she was going to know for sure that it was ready to go.

Lania tore through the boat, turning winches, testing the motion of the lines through the blocks. She tried everything on the exterior, including the rudder, before going below. She stepped down the steep companionway ladder and struggled to adjust to the sudden gloom. Her first impression of the interior was one of smell—salt water, mustiness from being closed up, and a slight tang of gasoline.

She looked around and found a light. Teak slats and rounded cream surfaces gave the interior a feeling of warmth and cleanliness. Lania sat on a cushion and absorbed the feeling of being aboard the boat.

As she studied her surroundings, everything came into focus. That nook was the galley, the cooking area for the boat. That niche was the navigation area. It was crowded with electrical panels and instruments. She realized that she was sitting on the sleeping berth and that the small seat across from her was the only other seating area. The mast didn't extend down into the boat, so it felt more open than some boats she'd seen pictures of, though it was very, very small.

Lania realized that the boat was a bit smaller even than she'd been thinking. Twenty feet wasn't all that much space, though she wasn't sure that mattered. It was so cozy and warm below decks that she wanted to hang out for a while.

Lania started at the front of the interior and made her way back. Her first uneasiness came from the discovery of a tiny closet that held a portable toilet. She wanted a plumbed-in toilet and a holding tank for waste.

She sat and looked at the sales sheet again. Outboard engine, fuel gasoline, said the sheet. A removable engine clamped on the back of the boat. She thought that seemed a very easy engine to steal, and gas burned a lot faster than diesel.

Lania sat back down on the berth and looked around with regret. She spoke to herself. "Necessities—a plumbed in toilet, an inboard engine." What else was she going to learn in the process of looking for a boat? Lania clambered off the boat and walked up to Charles's office to work on her list of requirements.

Ginger sat across the little table at the café. Lania turned her mocha in circles, the china of the oversized cup smooth in her hands. "Guess what I did today. You'll never guess, so don't bother trying. I looked at sailboats. I'm going to buy a boat, live on it, and get it ready to sail around the world. Isn't that amazing? I can't wait to tell you all about the boats I saw. I'm glad I started at a sales dock. I was able to really narrow down my list of requirements. This nice guy named Charles helped me. I started out with a hundred different things I'd seen and liked on boats and he helped me decide into which category they fell. There are the things I must have, the ones I'd like to have but can add myself, the ones that I dream of having, and the ones to avoid. He's really good at his job! Too bad he doesn't have any boats that fit my needs right now." She stopped, aware that she was chattering from nervousness.

"Are you serious? I've never known you to joke about something so big, but…sailing? On your own boat? I thought that's what the Center was for."

"It's great to use their boats, but it's frustrating to leave the dock knowing I have to get back by a certain time."

"So get a membership where you can stay out later."

"No, though you're pretty damn cute for coming up with that idea. It's not about a curfew; it's about setting sail and heading into the unknown, into waters I've never seen and ports I've never visited. All the possibilities without any limitations."

"You are crazy, girl." Ginger tapped Lania's notebook. "But if I know you, this notebook holds all the information you need to make it happen."

"You know me well. I have lists of boat features, lists of marinas, lists of everything."

"What does Oly think of all this?"

Lania shrugged. "He thinks I'm weird, but he's fascinated. Just talking about it makes me feel like an adventurer and he seems to like the idea of me being that person."

"You have a reputation for being precise and careful and I know you think of yourself as slightly boring, but Lania?" Ginger took her hand. "I've never known anyone more prepared for or meant for adventure than you. You'll plan enough to stay safe and strike out enough to be happy."

"Hell, Ginger, you're going to make me cry." Affection and hope swelled in her. "I love you."

"I love you too, Lania. I'm going to miss you like fire."

"I haven't even gotten to the part where I think about missing people. I have so much preparation to go through before I can set off. I have to buy a boat, outfit it, and work at the optometrist's to pay for all that and save up a ton of money. I don't know when I'd be leaving—not soon—but getting on the boat will be the beginning. Moorage is cheaper than rent and my other bills will drop too."

"You'll have to take me sailing, let me see if I like this new life you're dedicating yourself to."

"Love to. Seriously."

Ginger drained her latte and stood. "Time to go to work. Keep me up on how it's going."

"Of course." Lania opened her notebook and went back over her lists for the sheer pleasure of it.

Chapter Seven

Oly and Jeremy enjoyed celebratory burritos at Mama's Mexican Kitchen. They were spending far more time than they had planned on clearing out the stash of books and magazines in the building they'd started calling "Shit Palace," but it promised to be worthwhile. They kept finding items that, though without value when they had been shelved, were now worth good money to collectors. Though Jeremy felt a little shifty about it, he had confirmed with the owner that they could take everything they wanted to keep.

"I didn't exactly tell him what this stuff is worth." Jeremy squirmed.

"We'll just consider him our latest supporter, eh?"

"We can put him on the thanks list in the credits."

They took a couple more bites of burrito in companionable silence.

"What do you know about boats?"

"I guess I know the general stuff. That's how people got around for thousands of years. Most exploration has been done by boat."

"I was thinking in terms of today's boats. Have you ever been sailing?"

"There wasn't much opportunity to sail back home in Santa Fe. And I haven't known anyone here who had a boat."

"I've been thinking a lot about boating." Oly hesitated. "Remember the summer I sailed on my uncle's schooner?"

"Before we met, right?"

"Yeah, the summer between my junior and senior years in high school. My uncle worked on that boat for so long that I didn't believe he would ever finish it. He had it out of the water in Galveston, Texas, but he launched it in Corpus Christi when I was seventeen. He made a real showpiece out of it." Oly shoveled more burrito into his mouth.

"And you went sailing on it? Where all did you go?"

"We hit most of the settled islands in the Caribbean. We were delivering mail, so we got a hero's welcome everywhere. I went all the way to Rio de Janeiro with him. I had some great times, but it was when I was getting into film...strange I didn't talk about it more."

"Not really. The first few months I knew you, you hardly talked about anything but movies. Making them or watching them. Then you started hormones and hardly talked about anything but girls. Testosterone angst. And film, of course. That was pretty consistent." Jeremy slid a neat forkful of burrito into his mouth and chewed slowly. "What's got you thinking about boats?"

"Sailing is Lania's big plan for beating her addiction to society. God, Jeremy, you wouldn't believe how intense she is on the subject. She was even going off about public utilities. Like where would we get clean water in an emergency and where does our waste go?"

"Whoa—she is serious." Jeremy munched a chip while Oly demolished another huge section of his burrito. "So what's that got to do with boats?"

"We didn't get into it too much, but she was talking about solar power and watermakers as alternatives to power grids and such. She brought up boating then. The first time I saw her, she was sailing into the dock at the Center for Wooden Boats. Sailing off into the sunset. Sounds like a dream, right?"

"But how would you fit all your gear on a boat? Doesn't seem like it would work for you."

Oly stared at the statue of Guadalupe behind Jeremy's shoulder. "All that junk. Piles and piles of junk that breaks and gets in the way. We're always paying for something new or replacing something old. I'm tired of carrying a ton of shit around everywhere I go."

"What do you mean?" Jeremy stopped eating.

"What if…what if I went digital? What if I could get a camera, lenses, lights, and mics that would fit on a boat?"

"But what about me? Would we still work together?"

"It doesn't matter what I do. You'll keep working, Jeremy. I know that people keep trying to seduce you away. Your talent is obvious, and people want to work with you."

"But we're partners. I like what we have."

"I'm not saying I'm out of here right this minute. I'm just thinking about simplifying. Running through possibilities."

"I think this one sucks."

"The way we make films, it takes a hundred people to get everything done. I want to do something by myself for a while."

"It's not a hundred strangers you're talking about. A good partnership is being stronger together."

"It's like Lania said—"

"You are freaking out, man. What is this woman doing to you? I thought she might be good for you, but this, this is too much."

Oly scrubbed his hand across the top of his head. Jeremy might be right. He was quoting a woman he'd just met to a friend he'd had for years, and it was strange. "It feels like she's identifying dreams and ideas that I've buried inside myself. She mentions something and it feels like my own idea. Does that sound creepy?"

"Sounds like brainwashing."

"Lania, of all people, is too straightforward to be a brainwasher." He couldn't help but laugh at the idea that Lania was leading him to these thoughts for some nefarious purpose.

Jeremy struggled to speak. "You…I…hope you find another answer. We're doing good work."

"I know. Jeremy, I know. But what Lania is doing sounds perfect. What could be better than simplifying my life and traveling the world?"

"Well, then it sounds like you're well matched. Maybe you're soul mates."

"I wouldn't go that far. I'm just tossing ideas around."

"Keep in mind how well we do together. I'm sure you could do without me, but do you really want to?"

The thought burned. "No. You're right. We're too good together to let these fantasies change things."

Lania bought two little boxes of chocolate milk and a roll of packaged doughnuts from the tiny airport's vending machines and strolled out with her treats. She twisted her hips while she walked, willing her legs to regain feeling after the two-hour plane trip that had landed her at a small airport in Moses Lake, Washington. Oly must still be in the men's room. He had walked straight in there without hesitating and she wondered how long he had been able to use the gender appropriate restroom without being challenged or feeling out of place. There was so much she didn't know about him, but the specifics of his trans history seemed like the smallest part of what she looked forward to learning.

She leaned against a hot concrete wall and watched three burly men toss bags of potatoes into the last of the empty cargo space of the small two-propeller airplane. She sighed, wondering if sitting on the produce would be more comfortable than the floor had been. Couldn't be any colder, though now she was broiling in the hot sun. The end of May in Seattle was still spring, but the middle of the state was high desert and summer reigned.

The plane would be leaving again in a few minutes, and Lania was not thrilled that she was going to be on it. When Oly had taken over the computer and showed her around the Silverwood website, Lania had been excited by the idea of going to an amusement park, and Oly had seemed like the perfect person to enjoy it with.

Though she'd agreed to let him run the show, Lania had worried about backup plans in case something unexpected happened. She couldn't work out alternatives, since she didn't know the main plan. As her workdays passed, Lania had mused on how Oly intended to get them both to Silverwood and back. It was hours away by car. She wasted more time wondering than she would have spent planning the whole operation.

Now, thinking about her off-the-mark guesses as to how Oly was going to take care of things, Lania was more awed by him than ever. Lania had assumed that Oly's cavalier attitude toward money meant he was a trust fund baby or had a big grant or some such thing. The clues were adding up to no such thing.

Their trip had begun at five in the morning, when she rode up to his loft apartment in the rain and lugged her bike up the two flights of stairs to the loft. He wedged the dirty mountain bike next to his in a bike rack. He kept checking his watch, jittery and excited. Lania brushed off the seat of her multi-pocketed, denim carpenter pants and checked the scooped neck of the shirt Ginger had given her, which left her more exposed than she was used to. Oly chivvied her back downstairs and they exited the building.

A van with an open door waited and Oly hustled Lania into the backseat before she could ask what was happening. He joined her on the bench seat, scooting close.

The driver turned in his seat and introduced himself. "I'm your pilot for the day. You can call me Rafe." Lania blinked at the, yes, raffish grin of the thick-eyebrowed man who leered at her. He chattered in half sentences to Oly, who seemed to take this incomprehensible wordiness in stride and responded with random noises of interest.

Oly leaned closer to Lania. "Rafe is an old friend who wants to be an actor. He keeps me around even though he thinks my films are too serious, in case I can introduce him to other filmmakers. He's our transportation to Silverwood." He leaned forward and started talking to Rafe before Lania could question him on that. This was going to be a very long drive.

On the freeway, Rafe followed I-5 south instead of exiting onto I-90, and Lania was confused again. They were headed toward Portland and away from the park, which was in Idaho. She tapped Oly's thigh and sent him another quizzical look, but he just winked and leaned back in his seat. When "Money for Nothing" by Dire Straits came on the oldies rock radio station, Rafe turned it up and the three of them continued on, wordless but for Rafe's tuneful and soulful singing.

Rafe clicked on the turn signal, and Lania realized they were exiting the freeway near the airport. Oh—he'd said he was the pilot! She had never approached the airport from the direction Rafe was taking them, and she was surprised to see a bunch of small planes. They pulled into a parking spot and both Rafe and Oly jumped out of the van in a hurry, so Lania grabbed her backpack and chased them. She followed their quick steps to the entrance of one of the hangars and then slowed when she saw the bustle inside. Even at five thirty in the morning, there were delivery trucks and passenger vehicles and airplanes starting their engines, creating an echoing cacophony that stunned the ears.

Rafe gestured to her from the open hatch of a small propeller driven airplane, and he hauled her in by the hand when she gave it to him at the bottom of the strange little ladder. He rushed into the cockpit while a random overall-clad man closed the hatch behind her. Oly gestured to her and shouted over the noise as the engine started. "You might want to hold on to something. I'll put down a blanket."

He pulled a small blanket out of his backpack and tossed it onto the floor in a small empty space in the cargo hold. He pulled her down onto the blanket and showed her the nearest handgrip. The plane started moving. They were surrounded by pallets of printed materials looking like promotional materials for Silverwood. Obviously, they were flying to the park. She settled on the blanket and gave Oly a game "what now?" look.

Oly sat on the floor also and leaned close. "If you want, you can lean on me and get comfortable." He opened his arms wide and leaned back on the bulkhead between the cockpit and the cargo space. He seemed satisfied with his new throne, like a cat with a mouse. The plane had gained speed and was taking off.

Lania raised one eyebrow and decided to have a little fun of her own. She tapped one of his knees, directing him to separate his legs, and reclined against his chest between them. She felt him stiffen before he groaned into her hair and put his arms around her ribs, under her breasts. He squeezed her and she put her hands over his, settling against him. She could feel the heat of his chest against her back, and she gave a little wiggle to tease him further. They were closer together than they'd been since the loft party, though the metal floor of the plane was far less comfortable than the chaise lounge had been. He breathed a sigh that she felt in her hair, and she leaned her head back on his shoulder.

The plane banked sharply, and his arms tightened around her as they both swayed with the motion. When he squeezed his arms around her ribs, her breasts plumped above the round neckline of the blouse. She looked down, feeling warm-faced and self-conscious.

Oly scooted his hips closer to her, and Lania realized that her bold move was getting her all worked up too. She was heating up, but the air was getting colder and colder around them. The metal under the blanket held a chill that was soaking through her clothing and numbing her bottom, but she didn't want to move.

Now, two hours later, she did a few toe-touches and deep knee bends, trying to work the kinks out of her hips and back. She almost laughed at Oly's walk when they exited the plane until she realized that Oly wasn't playing around; he had hobbled to the men's room. She bought the treats as an apology after she realized that what little comfort she had during the ride was at his expense—pressed up against the cold bulkhead, taking most of the stress of the plane's maneuvers.

She sighted Oly crouched beside a stack of pallets, stretching his knees and back. He creaked to an upright position. He tried to stroll toward her, giving up when one of his knees almost buckled. "Don't mind me; my leg fell asleep." His voice was warm despite his discomfort as he looked her over.

Lania stepped around piles of potatoes and sat on the pallets next to him, handing him one box of chocolate milk and offering the doughnuts. Oly grabbed both with enthusiasm and then had to hand the doughnuts back in order to shake and open the milk.

Lania sipped her own milk and then set it down to open the doughnuts. She handed one to Oly and looked around the busy loading zone. "I wasn't expecting to see anything like this today."

Oly licked powdered sugar from his lips. "I know. I wasn't sure I could pull it off, but Rafe was great. It takes too long by bus, and I didn't have the money to rent a car." He looked around with a mixture of satisfaction and triumph.

"Is this how you make your films, too? Friends, acquaintances, and fortuitous circumstances?"

"Yeah, mostly." Oly's pride straightened his shoulders.

Lania shook her head. "I had no idea. You seem resourceful, but when you said you didn't have a regular job, I assumed you came from money." She was embarrassed to have misjudged him, but Oly nodded.

"My parents are great, but they don't have money like that." He took another great swig of chocolate milk, finishing off the little box. "My mom and dad own a drugstore. Mom's a pharmacist, and they do okay. Well enough to live on. But my older brother, also a pharmacist, is taking over the shop as they get older, and it can't support more than my parents and my brother's family. I moved to Seattle for the opportunity to do what I love, and the city has taken good care of me. I work on this or that, day jobs for enough money to keep eating. My rent's cheap, and my friends don't mind that I don't throw parties myself. If it weren't for free parties, I'd never go out."

"Do you have any other brothers or sisters?" Lania realized that she was curious about Oly in a way that she wasn't used to. In their world, she took people as they came, as though the histories that made them were less important than the people they made out of themselves. It seemed to be an unwritten rule of the young city folk to let the past go and focus on the now.

"I have one brother and one sister. My brother, Thomas, is older and, like I said, he has his life all mapped out for him." Oly grimaced. "If it weren't for my younger sister, Sibyl, I'd be the black sheep of the family. She horrified my feminist mother by getting pregnant the summer after high school, marrying the father, and devoting herself to safeguarding the future of our genetic line. She has three kids now and doesn't seem inclined to stop. She's a housewife with no aspirations beyond getting through each day without a major childhood injury."

Lania blinked but refrained from commenting.

"Don't get me wrong. I love her and I want her to be happy, but I don't see how it can work out in the long run. She looks ten years older than me, though she's younger. Her husband supports them as best he can, but he was right out of high school too, and he works for the city. He'll get regular raises over the years, but their path is just so constrained."

Lania nodded. "Sounds about opposite of you."

Oly's lips twisted. "Yeah, and though my mom is disappointed with Sybil, still she understands that more than she understands me. I'm so far outside their Nebraska experience that they really can't imagine what my life is like. It's not even me being trans so much, though they're still a little careful, like they're afraid to say the wrong thing. Mostly it's that they have no frame of reference for the whole thing—making movies, the loft, friends. All of it."

"I've had that feeling about my parents too—that there's no way to show them what my life is like on a daily basis. My dad's not very far from here, but he's an old retired hippie. He got chickens a while back, and all I can say is I'm glad he waited until I moved out. My mom's in Florida, soaking up the sun every day. She's happiest when she's on a beach or in the water. Both are great, but wow, does my life ever sound strange to them." She sipped the last of her milk and made an "ick" face. "I don't usually drink milk, but it seemed like the right thing for the doughnuts."

"It was perfect. Just what I needed. I think my legs have even come back to life."

Lania blushed and made a wry face. Before she could make the apology she felt was in order, Oly put his arm around her waist and pulled her around to face him from a few inches away. He kept his arms loose around her, ducked his head, and kissed her. His warm, firm lips touched hers for only a moment. He left his hands on her waist, but didn't move closer or pull her to him.

Lania felt hypnotized when he searched her features one by one, as though memorizing her. She put her hands on his tattooed biceps and then brought one palm to the line of his jaw. She leaned into him, kissing his satiny lips twice, and then stroking his curved lower lip with her thumb. She pondered the straight lines of his face, the angles and bones so different from her own. She parted his lips by pulling down with her thumb and kissed him again with more urgency, licking at the small gap between his lips. He stood, quiescent, allowing her to nibble at his lips and learn the feeling of him. She loved the way he gave in to her demand to control the kiss.

He smelled delicious. She brought her other hand to his hair. When she angled his head for better access, he groaned in response. He tightened his hold on her waist and began to kiss her back, slipping his tongue out to meet hers.

A loud clang sounded nearby, and they both jumped. Rafe was standing a few feet away, facing the plane, and he glanced back at them with an apologetic expression. "Sorry, guys, we got to get back in the air." He bowed them toward the open hatch.

Lania bit her lips, releasing Oly. Oly kept a hand on her back all the way to the plane. Lania sat cross-legged on the bags of potatoes. Oly shrugged and sat sideways to her so he could look at her and into the cockpit both. Rafe leaned out of his seat and hollered, "We're only going to be about forty-five minutes on this leg." He gave a thumbs-up, and Lania nodded her thanks for the information.

The rest of the trip passed in a fog. Lania was impressed by the strength of her reaction to Oly's kisses. She'd had plenty of kisses in the past, but nothing that had overwhelmed her, made her thoughtless. She tried to pull herself together, but she couldn't keep her mind off the length of Oly's leg stretched out in front of her. Or the rest of him, for that matter.

❖

The last box of flyers was stacked in the loading area behind the park before Oly took Lania's hand and said, "Enough work. Let's play!" Lania stretched her back covertly, not wanting to admit that she wasn't used to moving around such heavy boxes. She was satisfied with how she'd kept up with him. They worked together well, settling into a graceful dynamic. And having done their part, they were free to enjoy themselves.

After entering the park through a service door, they proceeded to ride rollercoaster after rollercoaster, eating cotton candy and drinking lemon ices. Since they'd shown up early in the day, they got to ride everything of interest before the lines got too long.

They were heading for a second go on a particularly exciting rollercoaster when a display for glider rides grabbed Oly's attention. He looked at Lania with dawning excitement.

"Let's find out what it costs."

He dragged her up to the booth from which the tickets were sold. Surely it was going to be too expensive! She couldn't help but get caught up in Oly's excitement, and she hoped that they'd be able to afford it.

Oly questioned the gray-haired ticket seller and reported back. "It's forty dollars per ride. I can cover one ticket, but not two."

"I can almost cover my own, but not quite." She looked at the ticket seller and spoke to him directly. "Is there anything you can do? Any coupons or, or anything?"

The man behind the counter harrumphed and waffled for a minute before admitting that he could, if the pilot didn't mind, give them one ride that they could share. "Lemme ask Rick. He'd be the glider pilot. I'm Leonard. We don't always let people know that the glider fits two. Cause sometimes it don't, see? You two are no twinkies, but you'll do."

Rick was as small as Leonard was large, and he had a tiny, rabbity face to complement his short, skinny frame. He seemed to have shrunk into his years while Leonard had never stopped growing. Neither one of them had much hair left, though, and the wispy balding patterns matched each other exactly. Lania blinked and realized the men must be related.

"Rick!" Leonard hollered, though they were within a few steps of him by then. "You willing to fly the glider this time? These two want a ride together."

"Sure thing," Rick answered in a soft voice. "Just let me finish cleaning up the mess from the last rider, okay?"

Lania felt queasy as she realized why Rick was cleaning the glider. He was wiping down the foot well, and the bucket next to his foot was mucky with half-digested stomach contents.

Just as she started to back up a step, Rick turned to her and held out his hand. He had such a kind look on his face that she couldn't refuse it. She reached out, wondering if the smell of vomit was going to set off motion sickness in her too. Rick said, "I cleaned up that glider just great. My brother shouldn't have brought you back here to see that. I'm sorry if you're disturbed."

Rick's old-fashioned manners relaxed her. "I'm sure it won't be a problem," she said, giving the eye to an unsure Oly.

"Fine." Oly put an arm across Lania's shoulders. "Let's just go on up and see how it goes!"

Rick smiled at them with affection. "Newlyweds? I can always tell the excited young couples from the boring old grumps."

Lania shook her head, but Oly nodded. He whispered in her ear, "Let the old man have his fun." Lania shook her head again. As Rick kept chattering, she realized she wasn't going to get two words in edgewise to correct him, so she rolled her eyes at Oly and tucked her arm around his waist.

Rick and Leonard ran through an incomprehensible set of double-checks, attaching the airplane-shaped glider to the prop plane and seeming to duplicate every duty in their desire to get things done their own way. Leonard turned the sign in front of the ticket booth around so that it read, "Flying now, back soon." He lumbered into the small prop plane and pulled on headphones.

Rick guided Oly and Lania into place in the single seat behind his place in the glider. She eyed Oly's slender build and thought it was a good thing that he was slim in the hips or they'd never fit. She ended up sitting half on, half off Oly's lap, wedged in and twisted so that she was glad she hadn't had a single bite more food that day. Oly laid his arm across the back of the cockpit, which eased the crush a bit, and murmured for her ears only, "It's a good thing we're in tight quarters; having you on my lap is making it difficult for me to behave myself." He shifted a little and she tossed him a smoldering look over her shoulder.

"I'd flirt back, but I'm afraid I'd break you on the edge of the seat."

"You're so kind."

Leonard got the lead plane running and they started to move. Rick yelled at them, something about achieving some height and disengaging, circling the park or lake. As they left the ground, Lania let go. There was nothing she could do now except enjoy herself.

The racket of the plane in front of them was hard to ignore. She tried to peer over the edge of the glider to see how high they were, but she couldn't see the ground below them. The only land she could see were hills out toward the horizon. As they gained altitude, awareness of Oly's thigh under hers obsessed her. The trip would be worthwhile for that alone, even if she couldn't see anything. She looked up and around, and the breath caught in her throat.

Glorious clouds, sunbeams, multi-hued blue sky. It was all so beautiful that her hand tightened on Oly's. He was also absorbed in the pageant of light and air before them.

Rick yelled something again, and Lania felt Oly shrug, not knowing what he was saying. They seemed to be gaining on the airplane, though, and Lania tensed in her seat. Rick leaned down and pulled a lever. With a clatter, the wire that had attached them to the airplane fell loose and tapped the bow of the glider a couple times before Leonard banked and headed back to the airfield.

In moments, the rumble and clank of the airplane turned into the rush and quiet of the glider. As the airplane receded, they looked around with wide-eyed amazement. The glider was flying, feeling out the air pockets and maintaining enough altitude that they couldn't see the park under them.

"It's like sailing." Lania could feel the air on the wings like feeling air in a sail.

Rick yelled, "How are you doing back there?"

Oly yelled back, "Just fine, sir. It's beautiful!"

Rick questioned them at the top of his thready voice. "Are you up for some banking maneuvers? It's easier to see the scenery like that."

Lania squeezed Oly's hand and yelled, "Yes, please!" She was startled by how loud her voice was and continued in a normal tone, "Why are we yelling?"

Oly whispered, "I think he's half deaf."

"Oh," whispered Lania. She didn't have the opportunity to comment further, because Rick began long, sweeping passes over Lake Coeur d'Alene and the park, tipping them for a better view and then balancing the wings again. For twenty minutes, they circled and swept the seam between Washington's high desert and Idaho's wooded hills. Oly lifted Lania's hand and kissed her knuckles. She leaned her head on his shoulder in response. Musing on the beautiful sky and land before her, Lania hardly noticed that they'd lost enough altitude to begin their landing approach.

Rick yelled back, "We're coming in. Conditions are perfect, so just relax against the padding."

Oly shifted his shoulders against the edge of the cockpit. He started to say something, but Lania lifted her hand and put one soft finger on his lips. "Shhh," she murmured. "Don't you think this is perfect?"

"You're perfect."

On the ground, Lania pulsed, overflowing with happiness. She helped Oly unfold to follow her to the dirt airfield. Oly grabbed her shoulders and then slid his hands along her shoulder blades, pulling her close. Lania stepped into his embrace and they shared a smashing, open-mouthed, tongue-tangled kiss.

Rick muttered, "Ah, newlyweds." They pulled apart for a second without letting go of each other's waists and then sank into a slower, groaning touching of swollen lips.

Leonard coughed behind Lania. "Well, um, just come by the booth before you go."

CHAPTER EIGHT

Lania woke with a stirring low in her belly. She could smell him. Oly was with her. She absorbed the warm, wonderful feeling of his arm on her waist and his body tucked close up behind hers.

They'd talked about the glider ride, about sailing, about the wind and the rush of moving to the dictates of the air. They'd caressed each other behind ticket booths and cracked up at the antics of the man who wanted Oly to try the strongman hammer. They'd clung, basking in the happiness of being together, on the plane ride back to Seattle. They'd arrived at his loft after midnight, exhausted and hungry. He'd handed Lania a peanut butter and jelly sandwich and, when she started to nod off, he made her take a couple more bites and then took off her shoes, socks, and jeans. He'd left her shirt and underwear on and stripped himself down to his underwear. She'd squirmed a bit, not quite asleep, and pulled her bra off and out from under her shirt. He'd lain with her, spooning his body behind hers.

Barely awake, Lania was abashed to have fallen asleep. She turned onto her back, and Oly snuffled and turned away from her to his other side. Her body followed his and they settled again, her front against his back. She could see the hairline at his neck, tender and vulnerable where the slight tan ended, and her gaze followed the muscles of his neck down to the spot where they disappeared into his shoulder.

She wrapped her arm under his, and longing stabbed her at the feeling of his belly against her hand. Light and longish hair tickled her fingers just below his belly button. She skated her hand to the spot just below his ribs where she could feel him breathe.

His breathing deepened, and Lania realized she'd been caught. She kissed his back. Oly groaned and turned onto his back, opening his eyes and struggling to focus on her face. She snuggled against his side and began slow, sweeping motions of her hand from his sternum to the waistband of his boxer briefs, petting him like a cat. Oly emerged from his half-sleep, stretching a bit under her hand.

Lania raised herself on one elbow, the better to see and touch him. Her breasts shifted, heavy under her low-necked shirt, and she felt him sigh to see her press them against his arm. His reaction warmed her, and the friction stiffened her nipples. The warm feeling low in her belly made her stretch her back, plumping her breasts higher on his tattooed bicep.

"May I?" She circled her hand an inch over Oly's chest and he nodded. She undertook to touch each square inch of his bared skin, starting at his pale collarbones and smoothing her hand down the bold lines embedded in his arm. She crossed the line between inked and virgin skin then caressed the inside of his elbow. He tensed as she drew her hand along the inside of his arm.

Lania glanced at his face and was gratified to see the heat gathering. Lania swept her hand across his pectoral muscles one at a time. He was strong, but his relaxed muscles gave at her touch when she pressed them. Slightly offset from his muscles, the top-surgery scars began in his wispy chest hair and spread under his arms. One showed evidence of a popped stitch, a little pucker, and Lania ran her fingers across it.

"I'm a sucker for scars," she said.

"I have more than those," Oly said, his voice still heavy from sleep. "Check lower."

Lania held his gaze and licked her lips. She scratched through the light hair that led from his sternum to just above his belly button, savoring the crisp feeling of the hair on her fingers. She caressed with her palm along the side of his belly and squirmed, unable to control her body's desire to get closer to Oly's warm, resilient flesh.

"Oh!" She found three tear-shaped scars, close together. They looked like punctures that had been torn as well.

"My brother's cat is half-wild. My dad pulled up in his truck one day while I was holding the cat, and his dog jumped from the bed. The cat tore me up, using me as a springboard for getting away."

"Seems like there's a pussy joke in there somewhere, but..." Lania swallowed. "I can hardly think right now."

"What would you rather do?"

Lania felt his gaze on her from under lowered lids, serious and quiescent, willing to let her have her way. He lifted his chin as though requesting a kiss and Lania took the hint. She rolled up onto her knees and straddled him, absorbing the exquisite shock of her bare thighs bracketing his hips. She nipped at his chin, scraping her teeth across the stubble there, and then brushed her lips across his once, twice, before flicking the end of her tongue across his lower lip. It was perfect—firm but with enough roundness to nibble. She nipped at it before licking along the seam of his lips and then settling her mouth on his. She felt herself clench inside at the feeling of his mouth and restrained a moan. She held her head still until he began to move his lips under hers, turning his head on the pillow just enough to create a warm friction between their mouths.

Oly's sleepy, slow responses gave her plenty of time to absorb every moment. She didn't feel skittish, as usually happened with a new lover. Fear of losing control often blocked Lania from the feelings of her body, but Oly's patience and the looseness in his muscles made her bold. Lania lowered her body onto Oly's, allowing her cotton-covered breasts and belly to touch him before she fitted her hips to his and pressed down. The cotton of his shorts felt damp, and he bucked a little at the pressure on the organ that strained up at her. She quivered at the sensation. Like warm caramel, she allowed herself to pour over him.

Pinned by her body, Oly jerked and panted into her mouth. She stared at him from kissing distance and he brought his hands around her back and to her shoulder blades.

Bracing her hands on either side of his head, Lania arched her back, keeping their lower bodies in contact, but bringing her breasts off his chest. Oly slid his hands down her shoulder blades and around front. He brought his thumbs together at her sternum and let the weight of her breasts rest on the backs of his hands as his long fingers settled on her ribs. Lania had a fleeting thought that no one had ever supported her like that. It made her shift her body on his and hardened her nipples. She could see Oly swallow at the sight of the distended cotton. He stroked down and then back up under her shirt. He supported a breast in each hand and reared his head up to taste her. Lania dragged her body upward to give him better access and sighed at the warmth of his breath on her hard nipple through her shirt.

She tried to breathe, but his mouth on her nipple was too much stimulation, and she tore herself away, sitting up on his belly. She hauled her shirt out of the way and bared her breasts for him. His groan was her reward. His hands once again cupped her breasts, and he tipped his hips, encouraging her to bring them closer. She allowed herself to fall onto him and kissed him mouth-to-mouth while rubbing her nipples in his chest hair.

She kissed her way down his neck and chest. She rolled off him and, before he could follow her, she pushed one hand against his chest. "Stay there," she said. "I want to drive you out of your mind. Tell me what you like. Be specific." He lay back with his hands behind his head, directing a smoldering look her way. Joy soared when he complied with her wishes, and she felt safer than she ever had with a lover.

After a deep breath, Oly said, "I like my cock jacked, rubbed from the base to the head. I like it sucked with a lot of tongue at the tip. My front hole gets really wet and can take a lot." The raspy tone in his voice and his detailed words pierced Lania, making her cunt pull and clit swell. "I don't usually start out letting someone touch me like that, though."

"You want to do something else?" The spear of disappointment struck Lania as oddly strong, but she would respect Oly's wishes.

"No." He stroked her cheek. "This is already different from most of my hookups. I'm usually packing and ready to show a girl what a stud I am." His smirk softened. "I want you to touch me."

She plastered herself against his side, tossed her hair over his chest, and reached deep between his legs to cradle his cock and the loose flesh below through his boxer-briefs. She squeezed and, to the sound of Oly's deep moan, ran her flat palm up from his ass over his cock. She stroked the tops of each thigh and hip before she reached under his waistband. Oly tried to breathe as she explored, pulling wetness up from below to spread on his cock. She tried to encircle the base of his cock with thumb and forefinger while cupping his fleshiness with the other fingers. The muscles corded and jumped in the exposed undersides of his arms as he clenched in the effort to remain still.

It was working, but she needed to see what she was doing.

After a moment, her legs and hips shifting, Lania shoved his waistband down to his thighs. "Oh," she whispered, and lifted her head to send him a heated look. A fleshy cock about the size of her thumb jutted toward her, draped in a hood that looked stretched tight. Her fingers damp with his juice, Lania traced the line of the hood and he shivered. She watched him jerk and knew that the head was tender. So tender.

She wanted her mouth on him and wanted to keep watching his face respond. She wanted to explore him and wanted to dive in without delay.

She wanted to please him.

She did as he'd asked and gripped his cock between her thumb and forefinger at the base. Pulling toward the head made his lips roll inward. She adjusted her grip so that her palm pressed the head of his cock when she slid her hand back down, sliding the hood along with her.

She experimented with stronger and looser grips until she found a tightness and an angle that had Oly gasping. Her other hand went to her own cunt and the heat there was no surprise.

She held his cock, pressed down against it, and leaned way forward, brushing her disordered hair and the tips of her breasts against his chest. "I'm going to fuck you." She didn't know exactly what she was going to do, but her confidence was strong.

"Please," he begged, bringing his hands to her hips.

Lania rose to her knees beside him. She slid the underwear past his feet, moved back to his side, and pulled off her own panties. She slid back on top of him, placing her nipple in reach of his mouth. He latched on, sucking, raking his teeth down the slope, and rolling the hardened tip on his tongue. She groaned and pulled away, only to give him her other breast.

His cock bumped against her pubic hair and the feeling drove her crazy. He thrust, uncontrolled, and Lania gasped, muscles clenching. Her legs were spread wide across his hips. She reached down and grasped him between her legs, stroking him a couple of times without squeezing. He was so wet! She turned the same hand to herself, slicking on his creamy natural lube and spreading her pussy lips so that he could thrust against the hot, wet satin between them. Her belly muscles quivered and she gasped when his cock slid between her lips and pressed her clit. He was hard, but more like cartilage than bone. Stiff but resilient. Without plan or thought, she squeezed her pussy lips around Oly's cock, trapping it where it jarred her clit.

She looked up at him and realized that Oly was watching her face as she engulfed him. A shock ran through her. Tenderness, surprise, and something nebulous passed between them. She slid her knees higher on his waist and began to move. She pressed her cunt down hard on his cock and wet folds, arched her back, and tightened her fingers. Her pussy lips became a tunnel of flesh that led Oly's cock directly to her clit.

Tiny quivers communicated that he wasn't going to be able to hold still for long. His hands were hard on her hips, and she raised an arm to toss her hair over her shoulders. His hands rose to her breasts and she settled deeper, leaning back. When her bottom reached his thighs, he bucked and couldn't seem to stop himself. A fierce and contrary pride filled her when he lost his staunch control. She met his short thrusts with her own. The pull of his cock raised and lowered her clit hood as they rocked, driving her crazy, making his hard hands feel so good on her hips. He set the pace, fucking her pussy with abrupt and fierce strokes until his face and chest were both bright red. Lania felt his cock as though it was the size of an oak tree, and she knew by the sudden, last minute swelling that Oly was going to come.

She slipped her thumb between her pussy lips and gave his cock head a little flick at the top of his strokes, just when it impacted with her clit. She wanted to drive him crazy, but wasn't surprised when the feeling started to tip her toward orgasm as well.

He groaned, long and low, shuddering and jerking, through an orgasm that seemed to rip him up over and over.

Lania watched, awed by his fierceness, until Oly flipped her onto her back and began to move. His cock was softer, but not by much. With greater control of the movement, Oly could focus on pleasing Lania. He pumped lube from a bottle over them both. Over and over, he rubbed her softness with his hard cock, angling to give her clit even more stimulation. When he added a twist at the apex of each thrust, flicking his cock head across her clit instead of directly into it, her eyes rolled back and closed.

Lania was beyond thinking, beyond fear. She was rushing down the current of a river, in the grip of the exact kind of loss of control that would have made her pull away from most people. Lania kept her hips moving and passed her hands along Oly's shoulders, gasping and moaning in time to his thrusts. She pushed her heat and intensity back at him, sharing the incredible energy they were creating.

Tighter and tighter, her muscles spasmed and her heels beat the bed. Oly raised her breast and bit her nipple. He smashed it against the roof of his mouth, sucking hard and chewing on the soft flesh. The pain and pleasure speared to Lania's cunt and she came, hard and suddenly, frozen in a bow of tension for uncounted moments before the shattering came, leaving wave after wave of shivering glory to wash over her.

They couldn't stop—they went on and on. Legs tangled, they caressed each other with their hands and mouths until it seemed that there was no time between orgasms.

After their breath had returned to normal and the sweat had dried on their bodies, Oly leaned up on one elbow. He nipped her shoulder. She raised her hand to cup his cheek. "Breakfast?" he said, and Lania stretched before nodding. "Well, let's get up then. I need my coffee."

❖

"Do you like eggs?" Lania asked, eyeing Oly's pancakes and then making a great show of studying the abstract paintings lining the walls of the little diner in Belltown.

"Well, yes. Why?"

Lania folded her napkin in her lap, elaborately casual. "You see, I like pancakes."

"Yeah?" Oly began to get the drift of the conversation.

"Yes. If you want, I'll trade you one egg and a piece of toast for some of your pancakes." A casual shrug accompanied her suggestion.

"Sure. Was I supposed to play coy?"

"I got my way. I'm not going to complain that you're too easy."

"Just wait until you really have to work for your pancake!"

Lania gave him a considering look and then nodded. "I have a feeling I know how that moment will go—the one where I want something that you have."

"Oh yeah? You think you'll get your way."

"It isn't that. I think I may enjoy the fight." She shot Oly a heated look. "I think you might enjoy it too…"

"If we don't enjoy the fight, we'll just have to make sure we enjoy making up."

Lania sopped up the last of her yolk with some toast. "Do you have a lot of fighting and making up with the people you date?"

Oly paused. "You done with your egg?"

"Yes—ready to switch?"

Oly handed Lania his plate and took hers. "Well, I guess I do argue some. At least, I tend to disagree with people a lot. And I'm not shy about saying what I think. You can either call me honest or insensitive." He gazed at Lania. "You seem pretty easygoing. Do you ever say something that you know will upset or insult someone?"

Lania's laugh rang in the small diner. "I thought you'd been paying attention this whole time. Remember about the part where I edit people's writing? I don't think there's a more insulting, upsetting experience in the whole world for people. You'd think I was killing some of these writers, the way they react to a little conversation about their clarity or the things they leave out." She shook her head. "But I know what you mean. I am a bit of a social peacemaker, so I try to steer conversations away from disagreements with people."

"Give me an example," Oly prompted her.

"Okay. Let me think." Lania took a syrupy bite of Oly's pancakes. "I was talking to this guy last weekend about boating. He is selling his sailboat because he has a bad back. I was super sympathetic until he started to talk about what he planned to buy to replace it." Lania grimaced and shook her head. "He's going to get one of those overgrown speedboats. It looks like a regular speedboat, but it's like fifty feet long. They are so disgusting. They burn something like thirty gallons of fuel an hour." Oly wrinkled his nose and shook his head. He dipped toast in egg yolk as Lania said, "Yeah. Gross. And so here I am. I don't care about this guy. I was just standing there, trying to figure out how to tell him that he's killing the earth without starting a fight." Lania added more syrup to the pancakes and took another bite.

Oly humphed, covering his mouth, and mumbled around his food. "That's more diplomacy than I'm capable of."

Lania shook her head. "Well, me too. I choked out something along the lines of, 'I have to go,' and ran away. I guess that wasn't such a good example after all."

Oly wiped his mouth and paused before his next bite. "I'd love to hear more about your boat buying."

"You sailed with your uncle, right?" Another thing they had in common. The buoyant feeling in her chest increased.

"Years ago. I've been thinking about it since you brought it up the other night, though."

She realized that Oly had finished her second egg and she offered his plate back to him. They swapped back.

"I like how you prepare your eggs. Just the right amount of salt and pepper…"

Lania stopped chewing and lowered her fork to her plate. She realized that she'd been acting as though they'd been sleeping together and having breakfast for years. The newness of their acquaintance hit her hard, and a flutter of panic passed through her. She had become comfortable with him so quickly. Oly shoveled down the last of his pancakes without noticing that the tone of the silence had changed. Lania watched the muscles in Oly's jaw work as he chewed, and she followed the bobbing of his throat as he swallowed.

She looked at his shoulders, picturing them bared to her as they had been that morning. She felt such a wave of hunger for his skin that she reeled. "Restroom." She ran to the bathroom and, once inside, stood in front of the mirror. Her cheeks were feverish and her eyes were glassy. Her hair was messy and huge around her head. She looked like she felt, scared and turned on.

Lania tried to calm herself. She stared, bewildered by the power exerted by the combination of physical passion and comfortable conversation. She'd never experienced the like. She'd explored physical pleasure with happiness and playfulness, but not with such driven feelings as she was experiencing in the dingy bathroom of a cheap, greasy-spoon café. She'd always held back some part of herself, treated sex with a bit of intellectual distance. She'd always known she'd be fine when the night or the relationship was over. The few outrageous passions she'd lived through had been momentary and fleeting.

Maybe she'd been running away from this all her life.

She felt like running at the moment. She didn't want to go back to that table and look Oly in the eye. What would he want? He was at the center of a whirlwind of partying and people, and he had tons of women to choose from. What if she didn't see him again? She tried to get a grip on herself, sensing that she was taking this too far, too fast for reality to keep up. They'd only met a couple weeks ago. They'd slept together once.

But wow, what a time they'd had.

With one last deep breath, Lania walked back to the table. Oly was staring out the window. As she sat down, she snatched at the first conversational gambit she could think of.

"Do you come here often?" she asked, realizing as she said it that she sounded like she was hitting on him in a bar. Oly blinked. "No, really, they have good food. I was just wondering…"

"I don't have breakfast very often. I like breakfast better when I'm eating with someone else."

Bells went off in Lania's head. "So you don't have people stay overnight very often?"

Oly leaned back in his chair and crossed his arms over his chest. "Not very often. Occasionally." He studied her face while she tried to keep her reaction to a non-committal nod, though she felt her spirits start to lift. "I'm more likely to stay at someone else's place overnight."

"Oh." So much for the mood lift. Lania tried to stay cool. "Do you date anyone regularly? You don't have a girlfriend, do you?"

Oly's mouth quirked. "Depends, and no. I don't have any exclusive girlfriends, but I do see a few women on and off." Lania's heart plummeted, and she tried to hide her response by draining her coffee cup.

"A woman named Cynthia warned me away from you at the loft party." Lania decided to jump in with both feet. "She said you slept around, and that you never called her back."

Oly cocked his head and frowned. "Was she about your height, with blond hair?"

Lania nodded. "She said some really bitter things about you." Lania chewed the inside of her bottom lip. "I don't even know why I'm bringing this up. She seemed like a bummer."

Oly leaned toward her, his elbows on the table. "She was a lot more interesting while I was drunk."

Lania felt lightheaded with nerves but she forged on. "I want to know if I'm going to hear from you again."

"I'm not in the habit of dropping people without communicating with them."

Lania nodded to acknowledge his response, but it was a distanced answer to her real question. "About the women you date. I'm not a very jealous person, but I am very proud and very private. If you and I end up dating, I'd need to know if you're seeing anyone else." She looked at Oly with a little frown, wanting him to understand. "I hate the feeling of everyone knowing something that I don't. Honesty is more important to me than monogamy."

Oly cleared his throat. "I hear you. I know that feeling, and it sucks. So are you saying you don't want to be exclusive?"

Lania shook her head. "I don't want to make promises to each other that we might have problems keeping. We both have big lives, and it sounds like you get around a bit. I want to know about it."

Oly rolled his water glass in his hands.

Lania waited a moment. "Do you want to continue to see other people?"

"I haven't thought about it. I'm caught up in you right now. I haven't wanted to go out with anyone else since your party." He frowned at her. "Is that enough for now?"

Lania glanced down at her hands, folded in her lap. "Since what I'm asking for is honesty, that certainly fits the bill. What I ask is that you let me know if you start seeing anyone else."

"Well, I can't promise you'll be the first to know, but you'll be no later than third." At her frown, Oly changed his tone. "I want to keep seeing you. I had a lot of fun yesterday, and we had some stupendous sex, if I do say so myself. And if that means I need to tell you about anyone else, I will. Do you want to know before, or is after okay?"

Lania gave a shrug, somewhat at sea. "It would be nice to know before, but I'd say at least before other people would hear about it." She thought a moment. "Seems like it would be enough if you told me you were going on the hunt or something like that. You know, if there's a party and you're feeling like getting lucky."

"Sure, I can do that. What about you? Will you do the same for me?"

Lania's face warmed. "I'm not huge on picking people up at parties, so I don't know if that'll come up."

"If you're more serious with the people you sleep with, I really want to know about it. As a matter of fact," Oly said with an uncomfortable frown, "I think I'd like to hear about it if you think it's heading toward some kind of relationship, whether or not you plan to have sex right away."

"Good point." Lania tipped her head to the side. "We'll just be open with each other about anyone else who sparks us sexually or romantically. Definitely we'll talk to each other before we act on anything like that."

"Sounds like a deal. Or like a plan. Or like a relationship."

She cleared her throat, but couldn't come up with any response to that.

Oly continued after a moment. "As far as my dating history goes, I've only had one serious relationship, and that was high school. I've been focusing on my filming projects."

"I get that. I haven't dated much recently, and my last real relationship was right after college." Lania thought about telling him that they couldn't get serious, though she couldn't remember ever feeling less casual. She planned to sail away. Oly had the sexual history of a rabbit. Surely it would be a race to see who broke it off first. She exhaled and thrust her worries away. Live a little. Right. "Are you all done? Let's get out of here."

Oly agreed and they both stood. On impulse, Lania grabbed Oly's hand, tugged him nearer, and kissed him on the cheek. She let go and stepped back, cheeks warm. "I like you. Let's do this again."

Oly's smile brought out the lines of his cheekbones. "Yeah—more is better. What are you doing today?"

"Working. I didn't realize we'd be together all night or I would have told you. I have to be at work at four to cover the evening shift."

"Drag."

They walked together to the cashier. Oly tried to insist on paying, but Lania demanded the check, arguing that the amusement park had been his treat and that breakfast should be on her.

After paying for the meal, they walked out the door and lingered a moment on the corner of First and Blanchard. Unlocking their bikes took all too short a time. They waited at the light and then swung onto their bikes to ride across First Street. Lania led the way back toward Oly's loft and then stopped on the corner at the alley leading to his door. Oly pulled up next to her and leaned over to take her chin in his hand. He kissed her lips and murmured, "E-mail or call me soon."

Oly let go of her, turned, and pedaled down the alley. Lania took off before she could moon over him too long and started the long ride up Capitol Hill. Though she ached from the short night's sleep, Lania looked forward to the uphill bike ride as an opportunity to exhaust some of the confusion roiling inside her. As she picked up speed, she thought, I'll e-mail him tomorrow…

❖

The smell of green surrounded Oly and Lania as they rolled along the Washington Park Arboretum path. Between her full time job and his filming schedule, it had been a week since they'd seen each other.

Lania tipped her head back as they passed under an enormous camellia and breathed the dense smell. With a lungful of pollen, she sneezed several times in a row. Oly called, "Are you okay?"

Lania blinked her watering eyes. "I believe so." She sniffled a moment and then shook her head.

Oly pulled ahead of her. "I'm going to stop here."

Lania looked around herself with new clarity. The beautiful, lush garden glowed with golden motes floating through the early summer air. She squinted at them and then glanced at Oly with chagrin. She fought with herself for a moment, not wanting to ruin this second real date but feeling more and more stuffed up by the second. "It's allergies." She forced a laugh. "I didn't realize the air would be quite so filled with pollen."

Oly laid his bike down and walked over to Lania. "Hey, let's get out of here if it's no good for you. I'm down to do something else."

Lania cast about in her mind for a good alternative. Frustrated by her thick head, she turned away to keep Oly from seeing how upset she was. Oly stepped to the side, following her face as she turned. Her physical misery was compounded by Oly witnessing this bout of weakness.

"I'd really love to get some food soon," he said. "How about we go to the U District for some falafel?"

Lania knew a line when she was thrown one, and she grabbed with both hands. "That sounds perfect! We'll cross the Montlake Drawbridge and head up Pacific Avenue."

Oly brightened and grabbed his bike. Lania took off as Oly mounted and then they both rode back along the Arboretum trail. By the time they reached the drawbridge, Lania was hot from exertion but breathing better.

The bridge was just beginning to rise. The lovely old towers anchored the eye, while the bridge's span split and each half angled upward. Oly wheeled up next to her, both of them tipping their heads back to watch. She took an easy breath.

"Lania, look at that boat."

"Wow." It looked a bit like a small pirate ship.

They watched while the sailboat glided under the open halves of the bridge. When it disappeared from view, she looked at the long line of waiting traffic backed up because of the bridge opening.

Oly caught her eye and tipped his head at the impatient drivers. "They're not having any fun at all."

Lania gave a mournful sigh. "I could be having more fun too."

Oly raised an eyebrow. "Yes? And how could that possibly be?"

"How about I show you?" As she leaned over and kissed him, drivers behind them started honking. Oly took her face between his hands and took over the kiss, ignoring the impatient cacophony. For once, letting him take control felt perfect.

"My first film was when I was very young. I called it 'Mom Cooks' and it was a total success in the family. My mom was rattled by having me hover around her with a camera while she prepared the stew, and she cut her finger almost to the bone. I ended up getting footage of the whole thing, from chopping block to stitches."

Lania looked dubious. "And your family loved it?"

He opened wide for an enormous bite of falafel, tahini, cucumber, and tomato wrapped in a warm crispy-soft pita. Lania waited with proper respect while he dealt with his huge mouthful.

"Okay, everyone but Mom and my grandma. People usually get off on blood and guts. You'd be surprised…"

"No, I guess I wouldn't be," Lania said. "So you've been a filmmaker all your life, eh?"

"Yeah. My mom and dad both tried to get me more interested in serious subjects in school, and I'm glad about that. My grades were good enough to get some scholarships. I needed them because out-of-state tuition for Evergreen State is no joke. The rest of my college expenses were paid a little at a time by winning competitions for my student films. I had almost unending film resources through the school, and I churned out short after short. I submitted them to everything, and all the prizes made me look good. It was a self-perpetuating cycle after a while."

Lania shook her head. "Once again, I have something to learn from you. I worked forty hours a week the whole time I was in college just to pay for my living expenses and books. My dad paid the actual tuition."

"Lucky you."

"I know, but wow. I wonder if there were scholarship contests for writing."

"I'm sure there were. You never heard about any from your counselor?"

"I only saw my counselor twice—once when I was brand new and once right before I graduated."

"You've got to be kidding me."

"No way. I signed up for classes that fulfilled the requirements and sounded interesting. It worked out."

"Don't get me wrong. I think that's amazing. But it's how people end up going for fifth and even sixth years. They get to the end and realize they didn't take enough basic courses or the right courses in their major."

"Well, it worked for me."

Oly tried to charm Lania back into good humor. "But did it work for your dad?"

Lania grimaced. "Well, I'm certainly not going to ask him at this late a date."

"My college films…they were all under fifteen minutes. They take so long to make and use up so many resources, but I also had to make sure they'd be eligible for the shorts contests. Then, I seduced Jeremy away from theater and things changed."

"I didn't know you two had that kind of relationship." Oly ignored her arch tone and stuffed more falafel in his mouth. "You've known Jeremy since college?"

"Since our freshman year. We were in a program about dissent in media together our very first quarter. We got along so well that we arranged to share a suite in mixed gender housing." Oly shook his head and swallowed another bite. "It took a while to turn him to the dark side, though. He was quite the theater purist. He wanted to be a stage manager."

Lania chewed the last warm bite of her falafel sandwich and leaned back with a sigh. "So what worked on him?"

"He tells people that Evergreen's interdisciplinary, intersection-driven approach opened him up to the idea, but that wasn't the only thing going on. Don't tell him I said this…" Oly leaned in and lowered his voice as though someone might be listening. "It was really performance anxiety. At the end of our freshman year, he put on a play with his program group. You should have seen him; he was a total wreck. Everything was smooth all the way through rehearsals. But the first night with an audience, he choked. Not badly, not enough for the audience to notice anything. But he was never the same after that, and he came back from summer vacation our sophomore year with a film production focus."

"That's so sad. Does he ever talk about getting back into theater?"

Oly leaned back and crumpled his napkin up with the falafel wrapper. "No way. That first year was hard on both of us, and we both turned corners that summer. When we got back together in the fall, there was no doubt that we were going to work together. No one, including Jeremy, has any doubt about his gift for film production at this point.

"It was easy for him to switch, since Evergreen doesn't have traditional majors. They don't even have traditional classes. He and I ended up in complementary programs for the rest of undergrad. We learned pretty much everything that school had to teach by the end."

"What about you? Why was your freshman year hard on you?"

"Well, that's when I started hormone therapy."

"Tell me more."

Oly blew out a breath. "I started transitioning young, so I was really boyish already. My parents named me Olympia, but I've gone by Oly since I was, like, eight. I went through pretty much every phase and stage of experimentation along with my guy friends. We hung out in groups, occasionally went to the movies or spent the night at each other's homes. The girls and boys would pair off, and it was weird for a while. There was a point when one of the girls kissed me. She reacted just like I was a boy she thought was cute. It was a high point of high school."

His lips pursed a bit. "That opened the flood gates. Some of the girls wanted to try me out without anyone knowing. Some would flirt with me, but they never could get over the thought that I wasn't the same kind of boy as the others. I started getting a sense of how hard it might be to get a girlfriend. The be-all-end-all of high school. When I went sailing with my uncle, no one knew my trans history but him. He never brought it up, so I didn't either. I never really decided to, but I ended up thinking of it as a time to sow my oats or whatever. I got good at getting a girl off without letting her touch me. In some important ways, it made me more of a man. But I really hated the closet and, as you know, I'm not built to be stone."

Lania frowned in sympathy.

"When I got to college, I went to the health center on campus. They hooked me up with a study on trans men that included hormone therapy. And I was ecstatic that I'd be able to fill out. They say it works better the younger you start."

"But you didn't understand what testosterone was really going to be like."

"Right." Oly shook his head at his younger self. "What a drug. I got totally obsessed with sex and jacking off. I felt driven in a way I'd never experienced. I don't know if guys who get the T for free have the same experience in adolescence, but I didn't know how to control urges so strong."

Lania sat in silence a moment. "You're so present in the moment-to-moment of life. I haven't thought about you in terms of self-control." She shook her head. "Focus, you have. I guess I would have thought that implied self-control as well."

"I had to learn that part. I figured out a balance with girls—sex, really—and film. Basically, film won. I decided that I had to keep my sex life casual. It's been like that ever since." He paused and seemed to make up his mind. "This thing we're doing—I've never made this much time for anyone. I don't know how long it can work."

Lania's heartbeat kicked at the warning, but she also frowned. "Oly, you were a kid. I know that some people devote their entire lives to their art, but I think you're being too hard on yourself."

He seemed unconvinced.

Chapter Nine

Lania pulled her phone out of her pocket to answer Oly's call.

"Have you ever been to Carkeek Park?"

"No, I haven't. Where is that?" Lania replied, cuddling the phone to her as though she could get closer to Oly that way. She set the old-fashioned oilcan on the drop cloth but remained in a crouch beside Esmeralda.

"It's north of Ballard. The trains go under a footbridge between the main park and the water. If you are on the bridge when one goes under, the bridge rumbles, and it feels like you're the one moving in the middle of all the noise. And a picnic is a wonderful thing. So how about it—Saturday afternoon?"

Lania hummed in appreciation and swayed on the balls of her feet. She replied with real regret. "Sorry, I have plans Saturday. How about Sunday?"

A moment of silence ensued, followed by Oly's too-hearty response. "Sure, I'll try to change the filming from Sunday to Saturday." Lania tried to protest, but Oly wouldn't let her finish. "No, really. I had the option of filming Saturday to begin with, but I didn't have any reason to consider either day better. I'll change that now."

"Thanks, then. Should I ride down and meet you at your loft? What time?"

"Let's meet at the loft around two. We'll work up an appetite for an early dinner."

"That sounds great."

"I'll see you then." Oly sounded a bit stilted.

Lania agreed and hung up the phone. Oly had seemed odd at the end of the conversation. She wondered for a moment what was going on with him, but let the question float away as she finished preparing Esmeralda for her next print run. When she'd cleaned everything, including her oily hands, she picked up her phone and speed-dialed her dad. While the phone rang, she poured herself a glass of water and took it to her kitchen nook. She sat on the wooden chair and, in response to his greeting, said, "Ready to hear about the boat hunt?"

She brought him up to date on the boat search, mentioning her trip to Silverwood in passing. She waxed poetic about winches and salt-water foot pumps until she realized that she was dominating the conversation. Abashed, Lania asked, "But how have you been, Dad?"

"Copacetic. You're not done, though. Sounds like there's another story in there—somebody named Oly?" After a moment of silence in which Lania felt frozen in place, he crowed with satisfaction. "I knew you were dodging! Come on, now. Give me the skinny."

"Oh, Dad." She floundered, seeking a way of putting him off. "I don't know if I'm ready to put this under the microscope."

"Can't you give me the basics?"

"Oly and I met at the Center for Wooden Boats. He's a film director doing an independent feature about the Seattle General Strike. Um, let's see. Well, he's blond, with green eyes and he's about my height. Strong and solid, but lanky rather than stocky. He's trans, but he's been on testosterone for years, and most people don't know unless he tells them."

"Trans, as in transsexual?"

"Yep."

"Male to female or female to male?"

Lania shook her head. Her dad was cool, but not that cool. "If he were male to female, I would have been saying 'she.' He was assigned female at birth but is male. That's the most appropriate way I know how to explain it without invalidating his real sex as male."

"Makes sense. So…tell me about him."

"He's really bright, and so passionate! He believes so strongly in workers' rights and art and all kinds of things that I tend to be more cynical about. He's a strong personality, very popular, with lots of friends."

"Right on. How serious are you about him?" Trust her dad to cut right to the heart of the matter.

"Here we go." Lania's throat thickened. "Too serious. I'm trying to enjoy myself with him. We've only just met, but I feel like things are on some sort of accelerated timeline. Or maybe it's me. He's so focused on his art. I'm buying a boat. Bad timing for me, and…well, I don't know what he wants." She shivered. "Besides, this feeling is scary."

"Honey, you might want to go with it. This could be good for you."

"I know, but it could also be really bad."

"You know what I think. You gotta let go and ride the flow. Maybe it's time to shoot the rapids."

"I feel like I have to stand on my own two feet, and this relationship feels like it's trying to sweep me off of them."

Her dad sighed. "You need to stop thinking about love as losing something. You don't lose your self-control, self-determination, or self-image. You can share strength and emotion without subsuming yourself to the other person."

"I don't know, Dad. It feels dangerous."

"I wanted to make sure you were a strong, independent woman, but sometimes I think I may have overdone it. Yes, you have to be able to take care of yourself. But you also need to know when to trust someone else and give them the gift of being allowed to take care of you."

Lania put her head in her hand with her elbow braced on the table. She took a drink from her glass of water to buy time. "I hear you." She couldn't give him more than that. She couldn't promise to make herself vulnerable. But maybe she could try.

She wrapped up the conversation with promises to keep in touch about the boat search. She pulled her heels up to the edge of the chair and wrapped her arms around her knees. Lania considered loving Oly. Maybe they could love each other for a while and then just move on when it was time.

She picked up an article she was editing and the *48° North*, taking them both to bed so she could work and play at the same time.

❖

Jeremy brought the peanut butter and jelly sandwiches into Oly's room in Belltown and put them down on Oly's bed. He threw himself on the bed and started munching, asking with his mouth full, "Find anything interesting?"

Oly nodded, grabbing a sandwich without looking and taking a huge bite. He scrolled further down the Web page he was reading and swallowed. "We've done it. We've scored."

Jeremy sat up. "Scored as in what? A hundred dollars, a thousand dollars? Ten thousand dollars?"

Oly stopped reading and looked at Jeremy. "More than ten thousand dollars. On this batch alone. Who knows what's left in that building."

Jeremy looked ready to weep at the idea. "You mean I could pay off my mom? And my credit card?"

"And I could pay my bill at the lighting rental shop. And pay Roshan back for the film stock." He looked over at the hefty piles of books and magazines.

"How about we plan to celebrate once this stuff sells?" Jeremy hesitated. "It sure would be good to see you more."

Oly was still thinking about selling the piles of magazines. "Yeah, when we have more money, we'll go out."

Jeremy watched while Oly started an online auction listing. "You've kind of been a stranger lately."

Oly turned in his chair and frowned at Jeremy. "What do you mean? We work together every day."

"Yeah, but we used to go out a lot too. You know, work the crowds, find extras and people with talent we need, keep ourselves and the project in people's eyes."

"True. Do you think it's a bad thing?"

"Yeah, I kinda do. Not really bad. But I'm no good at that kind of thing by myself, and you're always with Lania."

"Not always," Oly replied shortly. "Are you jealous?"

"No! Jesus, no! I just, you know, it's just that, well…people are asking about you. They're wondering if you have the flame on high for this project. There have been grumbles that you're not doing as much work as you were before. And now you've changed the filming schedule to be with her."

"I am working hard. That's my whole life, Jeremy. I've only had four real dates with Lania. Do you begrudge me my time off?" Heat filled him, a rage he didn't want to identify as defensive.

"I don't begrudge you anything. Really! Of all people, I'm glad to see you investing some emotion into a relationship." Jeremy stood halfway across the room. He put his hands in his pockets.

"Then what's this about? Why are you so threatened? It's not like Lania and I are going to stay together and live happily ever after, Jeremy."

"I don't know about that. We've been together for a long time. Except for sex, we're practically married. There's…We were facing the same direction. You'd fuck around and it was no big deal because we were more than friends. Partners, just not in a gay way."

"And?"

"Since you met Lania, you're not here anymore." Jeremy looked at his belt, hands in his pockets. "That's not right. It's like you're oriented toward her. No matter where you're standing or what you're talking about, you're facing her and not me." Oly frowned and Jeremy shook his head. "You're not on the same road as me. Fuck. I'm no good at metaphors."

"I think I get what you're saying. You and me—we've been working toward shit together. The films are good because we're tight. We can talk and build on each other's ideas, and your energy makes me better and all that." Oly hesitated. "You're right about it being different. The idea of going off alone to work is new and I get why it's weird to you. I don't know what to say about that. I don't know what that'll look like when it happens. If it happens. That's not about Lania, though."

"It is, too. You're falling in love with her. And that's changing you."

"I may be changing, but you've got it wrong. Love? You know I don't have time for that kind of thing."

"That's what you always said. A couple months ago, I would have been happy for you with the whole girlfriend thing. But now I'm scared that you'll end up losing yourself in this woman. You keep talking about simplifying and doing something by yourself next time, but it's all Lania I'm hearing."

"Seriously? You think I'm losing myself? That's a hell of a thing to say." Oly clenched his jaw. "Or is that you're losing me? It's just petty jealousy, isn't it?"

"Well, yeah. Okay, it's that too." Jeremy shook his head. "But whatever, right?"

"Fuck that. What the hell? What are we doing here, breaking up?"

"Jesus, Oly, I'm just trying to tell you how it is."

"What does that mean?" Oly gripped his knees and stared at Jeremy. Jeremy stared at his shoes.

"Whatever happens later on, right now we have a movie to make."

"You think I don't know that, Jeremy?"

"Here's what I know: the force of your personality is gonna get this film made, printed, and distributed. If you split your attention like this…we might not have a movie."

Oly sat in silence. Jeremy looked up at him, finally. "We will finish this movie." Oly stalked out of his own room then slammed out of the front door.

❖

Verona Wild stepped up to Oly, shoving one finger into his chest. "This will not continue. You will not ever, ever talk to me like that again. You will not make people cry and force me to redo makeup all day. Do you hear me? Get a hold of yourself."

Oly began with quiet control. "I don't want to fight with you, Verona…"

"Then just stop."

"…but I will get this shot, even if I have to make everyone in the state of Washington cry!"

"First of all, you won't get the shot if everyone's crying. Asshole. Second, we all busted ass to get here a day earlier than scheduled to make your life easier. Asshole. Third, you're an asshole!"

He clenched his fists. He tried to take a deep breath, but the boa constrictor around his neck wouldn't budge. His pulse pounded in his temples, and his entire cheek flexed with the desire to break something. Verona glared, toe-to-toe with him, and he turned around for some quick physical therapy before he cracked. By rolling his neck and stretching his arms over his head, he dissipated a little tension. He dropped into a crouch and hugged his knees to his chest and then bounced back to a standing position. Oly turned back around to face Verona.

"I'm an asshole. I'm also the director of this movie, and we won't have a movie if we don't get the shots we need." He turned to face the packed room. "Since we seem to have everyone's attention, let's talk. We're going to do this again. We're going to do it half speed and by the numbers. We're all, every one of us, going to do our jobs, and it is going to go smoothly. Once we've run through it slowly but while filming, we'll do it again at full speed. Got it?"

"Finally, the man of action reappears," Verona muttered. When he'd called, she'd been pissed that the filming had been changed from Sunday to Saturday, especially when he didn't explain why the change was necessary.

Guilt wormed into him and he stalked through the overcrowded room full of props and people. It was Saturday, and Lania had plans. Surely it wasn't a date. She wouldn't do that. They'd agreed.

He'd changed filming plans for a damn picnic. He couldn't get her out of his head, as much as he wanted to keep work and pleasure separate. She was a hell of a frustrating distraction, whether he was trying to set up the next day's shots or scan old footage for usable bits.

The crew came together and made the re-creation happen at half speed. The slowdown made the dialogue sound like old-fashioned oratory. Oly thought, with grim amusement, that this might be the take he'd end up using.

"Cut," Oly yelled at the end. "Now again from the top. This time, I want everyone on their marks at full speed. I want all the lighting and sound cues to come a quarter second before they're written to happen. Make this one crack, people!"

The entire crew went back to their starting positions and settings. Oly motioned for the clapperboard and cried, "Action."

After a perfect, magical, inspired performance by all hands, Oly announced that they were done a bit early for the day. He couldn't get any more work out of these people. They were all exhausted from the emotional wringer he'd put them through.

"Good work, Oly," said Verona at his elbow. "I'm sorry, but everyone was muttering behind your back, and I knew you wouldn't be able to get anything out of them until it got brought out in the open."

Oly stared at Verona. "Yeah. That was a hell of a manipulative way of pulling my head out of my ass. I was furious."

Her answering smile looked tired. "And now you have your shot, and we all get to go home. I'm not afraid of you, Oly. You'd never hurt a fly. I am afraid of what could happen to this group and this film if you don't pull your shit together and take care of business." Verona was as serious as Oly had ever seen her. "I can only provoke you when you're not expecting it. You'd better find other ways of motivating yourself from here on out." Verona started to walk away, but tossed one last teasing comment over her shoulder. "Asshole."

Oly helped hump all the gear back into their van and then rode his bike like a fiend back to his loft. He felt better, having burned off some of the nervous energy that had threatened to explode. He looked at the clock, which read four p.m., and thought about Lania. What was she doing?

Before he even realized it, he pulled his cell phone out of his pocket and was looking at her phone number. Staring at the entry on the little screen, Oly felt a bit like a stalker, but he realized that he was going to do it. He was going to call and see if she answered. He was desperate to know what plans she had.

He hit the talk button and took a deep breath before moving the phone up to his ear. It rang a couple of times, and Oly realized that Lania wasn't likely to answer if she was in the middle of something important. He panicked at the idea of leaving a message and then Lania answered. "Oly!"

Relief flooded him. "Lania!"

"What's up?" Lania panted and the sounds of traffic came through the phone, loud and clear.

"Were you riding?"

"Yep. I was running late for my appointment, but I'm about to lock up my bike and the guy isn't here."

The word appointment buoyed Oly's spirits. "What's the appointment for?" Now he felt that he could indulge his curiosity.

"I'm looking at a boat on Westlake." Lania's voiced bubbled with excitement. "I've looked at four boats this week, and it's so exciting! They're all different, even the ones that look like the most boring of production boats."

This announcement floored Oly. He hadn't realized that she was boat hunting with such dedication. "Wow. That's great! So you're going to look one over right now?"

"Now-ish, apparently. I've been checking out *48° North*. Have you read that magazine? It's fabulous, and this boat seems to be a good fit for what I think I want."

"Hey, can I come look at the boat with you? I'd love to see what you're talking about."

"Sure. That sounds great. You know, you're lucky I even answered the phone. I hate talking on my cell phone in public."

"I know how you feel. I keep thinking that I'll be able to stop answering the phone, but people keep calling me about emergency filming arrangements."

"You hardly ever answer the phone when we're together!"

"I can't really put you on hold, can I? You're more interesting than anything that could happen by phone." Oly closed his eyes as it hit him. Jeremy was right. He was putting Lania before the film. Fuck. Letting calls go to voice mail. Putting off checking his e-mail, when he used to glance at his phone every few minutes for news.

"That's the part I hate the worst—being put on hold in real life so that someone can take a phone call. I'm the one in front of you! We were talking!"

"Well, in order to save you from the horror of putting a real person on hold, let's get off the phone. I'll ride out to see this boat and we can converse without being rude."

Lania agreed and gave him directions to the marina. Oly memorized the location. He emptied a sixteen-millimeter camera, storyboards, and scripts out of his backpack before she said good-bye and hung up. He rushed out with his bike and pumped up to cruising speed.

Oly busted ass on his way down to the marina, passing the slow weekend traffic through the touristy Seattle Center area. As he rode, he turned ideas over in his head. Could he be falling in love? Could it be a real love, an adult love, one that could last? Was there any future for such a love for Lania?

What about the film? He still burned to put the story on the screen. He couldn't let it turn into an either/or situation.

Oly's sense of self-preservation whispered caution, caution, but for once, he ignored it. He decided that he would let this grow as it would and that he would be more careful to give the film its due attention. Everything felt right with the world, and he gained even more speed, flashing through intersections and around corners. Energized by joy and breathing like a bellows, Oly tore through the city toward Lania.

❖

Lania glanced around the fancy marina, taking in the same expensive boats she'd ignored only days before.

A BMW pulled up with a well-mannered purr, but the man who stepped out was brusque. He unlocked the gate for her and looked her over, seeming to find her unthreatening. "I can't stay. If you have any questions, you'll have to text me. No. Call me. I'll be on the road and I can't waste time getting another ticket."

Before she could reply, his cell phone rang and he answered it with a bark. He gestured her on ahead of him through the gate and then took the lead while yelling something incomprehensible about sourcing silicon into his cell phone. As an aside, he said to her, "Lock it up when you leave."

Again not waiting for an answer and without ever introducing himself, he strode up the dock and back to his still-running car. Lania stood next to the boat and watched as he backed out and drove away.

Quiet settled around her and the lapping of the water on the pilings brought Lania back to the task at hand. She turned, shaking her head, and eyed the boat.

This man had the money for upkeep. The boat sparkled from stem to stern, and the teak handrails and ventilation boxes gleamed with varnish. She couldn't see any rust or other kinds of leaks. No sails, though. Based on the rest of the boat, they were probably taken down to protect them from sun and weather. Surely she'd find them on board.

Once aboard, Lania did her usual walk-around of the exterior. The lines of the boat impressed her. She stepped up to the mast, thinking about the missing sails, and tried to move the main winch. Like most boat parts, it was crucial. Wrapping a line around it and using a handle made it far easier to pull heavy loads. This winch was for raising the main sail. It resisted her, and she could feel something inside grinding instead of gliding. Shocked, she stepped around the mast and tried the jib winch. It moved without effort, but she was still considering the winches when her cell phone rang.

Lania glanced to the top of the dock and sure enough, Oly stood there, waving his phone at her. She stepped off the boat and walked toward the gate without answering her phone. He put his away and locked his bike next to hers on the chain along the crushed oyster-shell walkway.

She opened the gate and welcomed Oly with a touch of her hand on his arm. He swept her into a close embrace and brushed his parted lips across her mouth, open on an "oh" of surprise. He released her, but took her hand and pulled her down the corrugated steel gangway. "Where's the seller?"

"Gone." The shift from passion to casual closeness dazed her. She swallowed and composed herself. "Speaking of cell phone etiquette…this guy didn't even introduce himself, he was so caught up in a conversation. And he left me here to look around by myself, saying that I should call with any questions." Oly's grossed out look made Lania laugh. "I'd be afraid to call him. I'm sure he'd be driving in traffic, already on one call, and he'd get in an accident trying to use call waiting."

"All the better! We don't have to worry about anyone hovering around while we look."

Lania led Oly aboard. He went to the bow, and Lania called out to him. "I'm going below. I haven't seen anything down there yet."

"Great. I'll be down in a minute!"

Lania stepped down into the boat and was struck by the dank wetness in the air. Streaks on the cabin walls looked like mold someone tried to clean away. The boat moved as Oly walked around on deck, and Lania heard him exclaim in disgust. He must have tried the bad winch.

The boat's pilot berth doubled as the navigation station's seat, and she sat there to look for maintenance logs. The cushion under her was damp, and Lania frowned as she pulled the logs out of a drawer under the nav table.

The maintenance log for the boat was a strange muddle of work done without dates attached and dates listing items like "Filters need changing." She wondered, had they been changed on that date or was that when they needed to be changed? She flipped through and realized that the first filter change entry after that was almost eighteen months later.

She'd learned the trick of looking at the logs on the last boat she'd seen. It looked kind of run-down, but the log had listed every bit of work done for the last fifteen years. That stunning batch of information told her that the weaknesses in the boat were cosmetic, not systemic. It was too bad that boat didn't fit her needs—no real galley.

Lania stood and stepped toward the bow. Oly hopped down into the cockpit and crouched there, looking at her. "I don't know; this boat gives off mixed messages. Everything out here looks clean, but the anchor windlass isn't very well attached. It's basically painted on rather than bedded properly."

"I didn't catch that. Did you notice the main winch?"

"No, is it broken?" Oly stood to look over the cabin top toward the winch.

"It's grinding when I try to move it. Might be salvageable, but the bearings might have to be replaced altogether."

"You're more knowledgeable than I expected. I thought you hadn't sailed much before."

"I've been studying up. It doesn't pay to underestimate what I can learn when I put my mind to it."

"I wouldn't dare consider anything beyond your reach, Lania. You are amazing."

She tucked a curl behind her ear. She could tell that Oly meant what he said. His face showed his admiration. She liked being seen as the strong, can-do woman she felt herself to be.

"Check this out." She handed him the log.

"Fishy." He flipped to the end. "Did you see another log? This one has empty pages, but the last entry was almost two years ago."

Lania spread her hands. "I haven't seen anything else. But look at this water damage." She pointed out the mold streaks on the cabin sides. They got down to business and started to pull the boat apart. Lania watched and learned as Oly pulled up floorboards to look into the bilge for the keel bolts and checked the deck under the loose anchor windlass for signs of leakage.

Oly in turn watched as Lania pinpointed corroded electrical connections and jerry-rigged electronics. She traced a loose wire and glanced up to catch Oly reaching out to touch her hair. Arrested by the look on his face, she accepted his kiss, then got back to work.

By the time they'd made it through the boat, they agreed that it had been ignored until recently. It seemed as though it had fallen into deep disrepair and, when the owner decided to sell the boat, he'd ordered some cosmetics fixed without touching the real problems. Without even trying the engine, Lania knew that she wasn't going to buy the boat. She made notes in her boat-hunting notebook about what she'd found, what new ways of looking Oly had shown her, and what she thought of the design itself. The boat was well laid out and seemed like a solid design, so if she found another one advertised, she'd be willing to check it out and assess its condition.

As they walked up the gangway, Lania admitted to herself that she'd be spending more time looking before she would be willing to invest in a purchase of this size. A little let down, she looked for a distraction. "Let's get a burrito. You deserve a reward."

"Not really. It was fun to get back onto a boat, even one that had been mistreated. I haven't spent much time looking at boats from the point of view of a buyer, though. Tearing through a boat like that is exciting."

They unlocked their bikes and started back toward Oly's loft. Burrito could only mean one thing—Mama's Mexican Kitchen's vegetarian Nolasco. It was the perfect food for sharing—a huge platter-sized burrito smothered with enchilada sauce and cheese, topped with sour cream, guacamole, and two olives. With Mama's calling, they made the ride in short order and burst into the restaurant like starving children.

Once seated and munching on the chips and salsa, Lania sighed with satisfaction and looked at Oly. Her heart stuttered as she watched him. He was eating chips and swinging one leg. She could see him at nine years old, endearing and mischievous.

Lania sipped from her water to clear her throat. "Did you get all your boat knowledge from your uncle?"

"Yep. He had a sixty-foot schooner and it took a crew of six to sail her. I spent a few months aboard as mate, sailing around in the Caribbean and down to Rio de Janeiro. He was a retired navy man, so his idea of the right way to do things involved a lot more cleaning and polishing than I had expected."

"You must have managed to have some fun."

"Oh, yeah. Just because he was blind to the romance of the boat and the ports doesn't mean I followed his example. The up side of coming into port in clean and pressed uniforms is a bounty of female attention."

"And I imagine you were no slouch reaping the rewards."

"No doubt. But it wasn't all bikini babes. On some of the longer trips, getting whipped by wind and salted by spray, I'd get deficient enough in vitamin C that straight lime juice tasted sweet."

The waitress whirled up and left a burrito on the table. They fell to and devoured huge portions before their first rush slowed. Oly asked Lania, "So what are you looking for in a boat?"

She twisted her fork in the cheese and sauce gathering at the bottom of the platter. "I didn't have a realistic idea about what I wanted even a couple weeks ago. None of the research I'd done has compared to looking at boats. Layouts that seem great on paper can end up feeling cramped or lack storage space. It seems to come down to this: a sailing rig that I can manage by myself while on the move, a comfortable berth, a propane stove with at least two burners, a foot pump for fresh water and one for salt water, a toilet plumbed to a small tank and overboard with a y-valve. If a boat is inexpensive enough, I can install some of that. I thought I wanted a full keel, but I've seen some fascinating modified full keels and twin keels. I didn't even know that twin keels existed."

Oly blinked. "I found out right this moment. What does that look like?"

Lania pulled a sheet of paper from her notebook. She handed it to Oly and watched as he absorbed the cutaway drawings of the split keel boat she'd seen.

"People also call them bilge keels. This one was in my price range because it had sunk and been brought back to the surface. I feel like I'm supposed to want a fixer-upper, but I just want to sail."

Oly nodded and tipped his head. "That's clear-headed of you. You can get so wrapped up in getting ready to sail that you never make it out of the boatyard." He finished the burrito and leaned back with a satisfied sigh. "My uncle worked on his boat for five years before he put it in the water. It took another two years before he went anywhere at all."

Lania scrunched up her shoulders. "Is it bad of me to want to start sailing right away?"

"Not at all. Some of the people in the boatyard with him had been there for decades. These fixer-uppers can bring you down instead of you bringing them up. It's a lot of work and money. This might be none of my business, but how are you going to pay for a boat?"

Lania grimaced and toyed with a tortilla chip. "Loan. I won't be able to leave the country until I pay the boat off, but I can always get another job as an optician. There's a lot of coast between here and foreign waters. I think I'll head up to the San Juan Islands, then maybe down to Portland or San Francisco. The sailing is supposed to be amazing down in the San Francisco Bay."

"True. Still, the less you owe, the less time you have to spend working, right? Do you have a down payment?"

"I'll be selling Esmeralda for a down payment."

"Fuck. That sucks."

"Why do I keep getting that response?"

Oly winced. "It feels unthinkable." He shook his head. "Don't get me wrong, I'm sure it's a great decision if travel is your goal. It's just strange to think about you without Esmeralda."

"I feel melancholy about selling her, but she doesn't belong on a boat. I put a few notices up about selling her. I'm already getting calls. I didn't think it would be that quick."

"Are you sure you couldn't put it in storage or something? Maybe someone would keep it for you while you traveled?"

"That wouldn't get me a down payment. I don't have any money saved up. I spend all my money on the magazine. While I was printing this week, I broke a very small part and wiped out the benefit party's take replacing it."

"Isn't there somewhere you can borrow the money? Or maybe you could lease the press rather than selling it?"

Lania shook her head and ate another tortilla chip. "Oh, but I did bring you a copy of the magazine!" She pulled it from her backpack. "You can read it later, okay?"

"Awesome." He put the magazine in his backpack. "What got you interested in sailing?"

"Restlessness. I've always been antsy, wanting to go places and not look back. I decided to take some lessons and found the Center for Wooden Boats. I'm still amazed by how quickly I took to sailing."

"You looked great coming into the dock the day we met. Total pro."

She feigned modesty. "You're too kind."

"Seriously. I've been impressed with you since the moment I first saw you."

Lania touched Oly's hand where it lay on the table. "Thanks. That was the day that I realized that sailing could be the method. The goal was travel and adventure. I was serious about exploring places I'd never been and making friends of strangers, but I wasn't attracted to the backpacking through Asia kind of thing. Suddenly, it hit me that I was a good enough sailor to move to the next step. Getting a boat of my own and starting to do bigger, longer trips. Building my chops on the water until I can head past Neah Bay and turn south down the coast. The Pacific Ocean. The world."

"You hear about people who set off and never come back. Is that your plan?"

"That's my idea. I wouldn't go so far as to call it a plan. Sailing is the perfect way to blend the freedom to move with the comforts of home. Wherever I am, the boat will be my base of operations, my security, and familiarity. I'm convinced that having my entire home with me, everywhere I go, will give me a better chance of really experiencing and absorbing everything outside my oasis."

"It was true for me in the Caribbean. Real foreignness can be overwhelming. Letting it flow around you and through you, so you really get the experience, well, it can be hard to maintain that kind of openness. I saw a lot of people looking dazed, like they couldn't smell one more unfamiliar scent or they'd go into overload."

"But the boat helped?"

"Yeah. Having a place of my own, even just a tiny bunk in a shared cabin, let me settle each night."

"Exactly. That's what I want. I'll bring my home with me, rather than making trips and then going home at the end, trying to remember it all and struggling to integrate what I learned."

He put his elbows on the table and crossed his arms in front of him. "What about a two-person boat? What do you think would be different?"

"Not much, I guess. Well, tankage. Enough water for two. Wouldn't you still need to be able to single-hand the boat, if only so that one person can be sleeping and the other person can be on watch alone?" Oly nodded. "I guess you'd need a double berth rather than a single. Even if you spend a lot of time doing watches at sea, you're sure to spend more time in port and you'd want to sleep together, right?" If she traveled with someone, it certainly would be someone with whom she would want to sleep. Someone like Oly. The thought made her nervous.

"Yep, sleeping together is non-negotiable. So no split v-berths, right?"

"Right. And you'd want enough dinette space that two people could eat together. And they'd have to be able to move around each other in case one person wanted to get into the galley or the berth while the other one was reading or cooking." The shiver of alarm she felt, thinking about traveling with Oly, drowned in warmth. It would never happen, but it didn't hurt to dream. Wasn't that what she'd decided?

Lania sketched the two-person boat of their dreams. Oly pointed out ideas she missed and they ended up with a comprehensive list of qualities they'd want in the perfect two-person boat.

Lania stowed her notebook in her backpack and paid for the inexpensive meal. "For services rendered."

Oly waggled his eyebrows. "I think I deserve more than half a burrito."

Lania ducked her head, looking left and right as though scandalized. "Shhhhh! Don't let Mama hear you say that!"

Oly put his hand to his heart. "No offence to Mama, bless her saucy soul. But I think we can celebrate a good day with a bit more goodness. Stay the night with me."

"When you put it like that…"

Side by side, they walked the short block back to Oly's loft. Lania stopped on the sidewalk and tipped her face up to catch the misty air on her cheeks. In a crystal moment, she looked at Oly from half-closed eyes, crisp air and soft streetlight mixing with his warm regard to stop time. Lania honored the reality of her feelings for Oly. As long as she didn't name the emotion, she could dwell in heightened sensation without fear, without having to plan or figure or worry at all.

How long could she maintain such a fragile state? How long could she avoid thinking?

Finally, Lania tugged Oly across the street and down the alley to his door.

She pulled him into her and backed up to the wall. She wanted to be compressed between him and something hard. She wanted him to hold her down and fuck her.

Oly must have caught the hunger in her grasping hands because he planted a foot behind and pressed into her. His other foot slid forward and his thigh angled between hers. Lania slumped onto the thick muscle, her clit sparking. The concrete wall pulled her hair, and she moaned.

Oly used his hips to hold her in place and braced his hands on her shoulders. He shoved them back against the wall, making her breasts thrust toward his chest. Lania breathed deeply to decrease the distance between them, even her nipples pushing outward for contact. When Oly rolled his torso into hers, she moaned again, then gasped when his mouth engulfed the muscle on the side of her neck.

She gripped his strong arms as he pushed back from her. "Let me get the door," he said, panting. He turned away, reaching in his pocket for his keys.

Lania couldn't release him, though. She kept one hand on his bicep and swept the other across his shoulder, which flexed as he dug in his pocket. She growled and explored the shifting muscles on both sides of his spine, down to his ass and back up.

Oly backed up a step to swing the door wide, dislodging her hands, and she reached out for him again. He wrapped an arm around her waist and danced her inside. She lost control of her momentum, a frightening feeling, but Oly was in charge of gravity. She landed on the stairs, her head supported by one of his hands and the other protecting her back from the tread. The shock to her ass wrung a cry from her, but her legs were already rising to lock around Oly's lower back.

He shoved his cock at the heat radiating from her cunt and locked her head in place for a deep, sucking kiss. Their mouths created a shared cavern filled by their tongues, dancing to the rhythm set up by their hips. The stair cut into her back, regardless of his attempt at pulling her upward, and she whimpered at the frustration caused by undesired pain.

Oly pulled back and stood. Lania gladly took his hand when he offered it. He pulled her up to stand beside him, then dragged her up the stairs.

Oly felt like every muscle was hard enough to break rocks. Lania had signaled every way possible that she wanted him to fuck her. He wanted to shove into her with his entire body, as much of it as possible. He wanted to mark her, a desire that made him howl inside and turn away from thought.

Inside his room, the cracking of the slammed door met the small scream she made when he bit the muscle of her shoulder. He bit her hard, his mouth filled and his breath snorting from his nostrils. Her hands scrabbled across his back, flinching and grasping in turn as he modulated the pressure and suction. He filled his hands with her ass and pulled her tight to him, his mouth now skating over her collarbones and the tendons of her neck. Her head fell back and tightened her skin under his lips.

Oly turned a tight curve, moving Lania when she seemed frozen. He put his hands on her waist and shoved her down onto the bed, following her down with his hands and mouth already open for her breasts. The cotton over them disguised her smell and he would not tolerate that. He dragged her shirt off so fast her arms flew over her head, then he pulled them back down with the straps of her bra. Her arms were trapped now by her sides, but Oly ignored her rocking attempts to free them while he pressed his face between the breasts he raised with hard hands.

He wished he'd packed hard. Fuck. He wished his cock was as big as it felt. He wanted to fill her up so full that she would gasp, and so he released her and rose to his feet. Lania lay sprawled, her hair a writhing mass when she shook her head back and forth in frustration.

"Don't leave me now," she demanded with hands outstretched.

"I'm going to fuck you," Oly said, substituting words for hands, giving her something while he prepared. "You are so fucking sexy there with your bra around your waist and your bike pants tight on your hips and thighs. I'm going to strip it all off and fill you up with this cock." Oly pulled open the toy drawer in his low dresser. He chose a large realistically shaped dildo made of silicone, one that had balls. He held his silicone cock to his pubic bone with one hand and stroked it with the other. The bouncing pressure on his own cock made him groan and lower his eyelids. Lania rose to her elbows, her breasts falling to each side. When she licked her lips, Oly hummed in pleasure.

"Get it on, Oly. You're driving me crazy."

She watched his hand on the cock and he felt unstoppable. The flush across her cheeks and the shifting of her legs telegraphed her arousal. The usual discomfort of stripping and putting on a harness and cock dissipated in the way she moaned at sight of his hard-on. It was smaller by far than the silicone one in his hand, but her eyes focused on him hungrily and her hand drifted between her legs.

Oly looked in the toy drawer and considered a moment. The harness that fit like briefs was most comfortable, but—Oly glanced at Lania over his shoulder and her hands were behind her back unclipping her bra—didn't give as much power and control. He'd go with the old favorite, leather in a jock-strap configuration. He stepped into the leg straps and shoved the dildo into the tight O ring at the front. He buckled the harness tight at the hips and grabbed the lube.

Before he could turn back, Lania pressed her body to his back and reached around. She drew one finger down the length of the silicone cock and Oly watched, breath caught. He pumped lube over her hand and the cock, the creamy texture making him think as always of premature ejaculation. With this cock, though, they could both come over and over without having to stop.

Lania stroked the lube over the smooth silicone. It had a head and ridges molded into the shape, and her thumb stroked delicately across them when she reached the tip. Her grip tightened and Oly groaned. The sight of her hand firming, the additional pressure of the base of the silicone cock on his own, and the press of her breasts against his back drove him wild. His hips bucked even as the silicone pulled his flesh uncomfortably.

Oly slid his fingers between his pubic bone and the harness and dildo. He spread some of the lube over his own cock and refitted the dildo to press there. Lania continued stroking the cock. Her other hand splayed over his abdomen and she pulled herself harder into his back. Thighs and hips still encased in bike pants. Belly and breasts gloriously bare. Oly let her continue, closing his eyes to enjoy the sparks of sensation over so much of his body.

"I can't wait any longer, Oly."

"You don't have to." Oly turned in Lania's arms and grabbed her head for a desperate kiss. When he moved his hands to her breasts, her head fell back and he bit at the bruise he'd made minutes ago. Little nips sufficed to make Lania squirm and gasp, shrinking away and pulling him closer in the same motion.

"I have to fuck you right now."

Lania's "Yes" flowed as air, without force, but Oly heard her. He turned her around and bent her over the dresser. Her hands scrabbled for purchase but only succeeded in knocking his change jar to the floor. Coins rang and rolled as he pulled the tight bike pants down around her thighs, trapping them together. He put his hand on the silicone cock and guided it between her ass cheeks. He slid it lower, finding her cunt with his fingertips and then pushing, shoving, thrusting the big cock into her while she panted and tilted her hips back. Her arms folded over her head, against the wall, and that gave her a little purchase. She pushed back while he worked the cock into her. She took it with a gasp and then moaned when he pulled back out a little.

Oly's hands crushed Lania's hips, the soft flesh giving and her hipbones providing anchorage. Now, with all the power of his strong thighs, Oly rammed home.

The silicone base shoved his cock, and he trembled. Lania arched her back to pull off the cock and then drove back onto it. The resistance of her cunt provided pressure from the base of the dildo to his cock, yet again, and Oly had to move.

He thought she needed to be opened up some more, so he pulled out slowly, stopping when the ridge of the head came into view. He shoved back in, more slowly still, groaning at the sight. Lania's cunt was pulled tight around his silicone cock. It disappeared under the curves of her ass as he worked his way into her. Her legs were planted, her thighs flexed, blending soft and strong in layers of muscle and fat. Her hips narrowed at her waist, and the muscles on either side of her spine mounded as she arched her back. Oly thrust slowly, and Lania moaned again, her head to one side, her face hidden in her hair.

All that hair. It slid across her shoulder blades and piled in the curve of her elbows. Somehow, it was the last straw.

Oly slid a hand up her back and into the hair at the back of her head. He grabbed a huge fistful and pulled her head back with it. Folded over her back, he could just make out the shape of her lips and the curve of her cheek. "Open up to me. Open up, Lania."

"Yes yes yes…" Lania's agreement opened the floodgates. Oly shoved her pants the rest of the way down and stepped on them so she could pull one leg free. Lania spread her legs wider, bracing herself, tipping her cunt to open it as wide as possible.

"Fuck yes," said Oly, his growl loud in his own head. One hand in her hair and the other on her shoulder, Oly pounded into Lania. He hit her hard with his hips and thighs, ramming the cock all the way into her. She quivered under his hands and held her ground.

Oly felt the fucking build in him, and he knew that he could come. Some part of him wanted to wait for her but, when he slowed a fraction, Lania reached behind and raked his hip with her short nails. Fuck it, then. He released her hair and her shoulder, standing upright and pulling her again by her hips. He angled to get the most sensation on his cock and added a circling motion to his thrusts. His motions turned frenzied and his thighs shook. Lania made encouraging sounds, and the expansion and contraction of her ribs proved that she was with him.

Oly felt the swell of tension, the internal preparation for cataclysm. "Yes, fuck, yes, fuck, yes fuck yesfuck…"

His vision blurred and his whole body shook with the force of coming. Lania took over the motion, maintaining speed when he froze and jerked with the full body release. He poured the tension, the built-up energy into her and she pressed for more, voracious.

Oly's legs weakened, and he stumbled under the demand of her hips. He guided the fall and landed in the straight-backed wooden chair next to his table, pulling Lania down on top of him so that the cock stayed buried in her cunt. He could feel her heat and her need. She never stopped moving, switching from the backward thrust to a rise-and-fall without missing a beat.

Lania's legs spanned Oly's and she braced her hands on his knees. He stroked her waist, amazed by the vivid red marks of his hands on her hips. She swayed on him, ass pressing to his abdomen and moving away, hair following the motion a half-beat behind. She was gorgeous and daunting, hungry and giving.

Oly clenched inside and marveled at the speed of his recovery. He slipped his hands around her and under her belly. He traced the tight hole, filled with cock, before rubbing three fingers across her clit. She hummed in short bursts along with her bouncing. Wrapped in cunt lips, his fingers curved to dome the tender, turgid flesh. A little tease that didn't last long.

With the direct stimulation, Lania switched her motion to a slide. Forward and back, she moved on and off the silicone cock with a horizontal motion that put the base back on Oly's cock. Oh fuck. He wanted to focus on her. He wanted her to come, and he attacked her ferociously. He pulled back her hood and rubbed her clit directly, no mediating skin, no protection. She thrust back on the cock so hard that the chair creaked, and Oly realized it must be pounding her G-spot. Would she gush when she came? He wanted to feel that. He wanted it.

He rocked forward to meet her slide, and the creak of the chair formed the beat for their music. He rubbed her clit hard and, when her back muscles clenched, he rubbed even harder. Sweat shone on her back. She fucked herself onto him, steadily, and her hands rose to her breasts. Though he couldn't see it, Oly growled at the image of her fingers on her own nipples.

"Softer," Lania said on a gasp, and Oly eased up his rubbing. He held his fingers in such a way that her thrusting provided the rub and Lania keened, high and long, tighter and tighter until she fell forward, hands on his knees again, and pulled almost all the way off the dildo. She fucked down onto it a couple inches, twitching and crying out, pulling off again. Long, low moans rolled from her throat while Oly cradled her swollen clit, focusing his rubbing to each side. Four, five times she rose as though about to dismount, but each time she tipped her hips back onto the cock. The anticipation made Oly want to squirm, but he controlled himself. He didn't want to interrupt the rough focus of her motions.

Finally, after such a long build that Oly was amazed, Lania started to shake from head to toe. She rose and fell twice more, then her hands spasmed on his knees and she pulled all the way off the cock. Ejaculate drenched the silicone, the harness, and Oly's hips and thighs in three distinct rushes. The smell and feeling pushed Oly to the edge and he worked to concentrate. He kept rubbing Lania's clit lightly and she dropped heavily back onto the cock. Her body jolted as though electricity streamed through it and she screamed.

Unstoppable now, she pounded Oly, wetness flying, thighs slapping. She jerked to a stop and moaned, only to start thrusting again. Oly shook when she stopped and grunted when she started. She brushed his hand aside and used her own, finely tuned to her need. That left his hands free to reach up and smash her nipples between his fingers. The chair screamed, moving across the floor with the force of their fucking, and Oly realized a moment late that it was a new sound.

The chair collapsed under him, cracking sharply. Lania landed on top of him, cock still firmly seated, chanting, "No no no no…"

Oly couldn't let her hang there, second—or maybe third—orgasm waiting to be unleashed. He rolled her over to the side with less wreckage and drew her ass up. Her fingers working her clit hard again, Lania's chant changed. "Yes yes yes yes…"

Pounding, pounding. Vaguely aware that Lania was taking care of her own needs, Oly fucked her hard. Her come had thinned the lube and he could see how red her flesh was. She was going to be sore, but he couldn't go easy on her. He was sure she wouldn't allow that. He braced his hands on her ass cheeks, pushing them up and separating them so he could see her take the cock so hungrily. He squeezed hard, lurid handprints appearing on her skin, and he felt it again, the rise of orgasm, starting in his calves and biceps and drawing all his focused power to his cock. Sweat dripped from his jaw. Pounding, pounding, his cock swelled behind the harness, rubbing and shoving along with the silicone cock until he shouted and came.

His frenzied thrusting must have pushed Lania over the edge because she wailed, the sound ringing for a long moment before changing to quieter sounds along with his weaker motions. She collapsed, face down on the floor, and Oly followed her down.

Breath rasped from his throat. Sweat evaporated, leaving a slight chill behind. The dildo twitched and Lania moaned. Oly smoothed her hair back. "Hold on a second. I'll pull out slowly."

The silicone stuck to Lania's flesh and Oly winced at her flinch. When he had pulled all the way out, Lania turned onto her back and looked at him. Satisfaction and amazement filled her expression, no hint of pain or reproach. Oly leaned on his elbow and brought his lips to hers gently. So gently.

He whispered. "You're going to be bruised."

"I know. You too."

"Why me?"

"You landed hard when the chair broke. I hope it wasn't some kind of heirloom."

He shifted and looked down at her. "No kind of heirloom, but you're right. I think I'm going to bruise." He brushed his hand across her damp ribs and blew on her nipple to make it tighten.

"Cold!" Lania's objection sounded lazy and satisfied.

"Let's take a shower to warm back up."

"And clean off."

"And then just hang out tonight. What do you say?"

"Yes, please. That sounds perfect."

Lania lay on her back, eyes closed so that she could picture Oly as they spoke on the phone a few days later.

"Jeremy and Joyce are getting serious. He's spending all his free time with her and it sounds like they're having a great time."

"You sound uncertain about the whole thing."

"Yeah, I guess I'm used to Jeremy being all about our work. I mean, he knows how to have fun, but he's never spent so much time on other stuff. Not that I have any right to talk. We've been seeing each other a lot too."

"I didn't expect to get this much of your time—you are such a busy guy. Is it okay? For real?"

"It's hard, sometimes, but it's what I want."

"You'll let me know if we need to back off a bit?" The sliver of pain took her by surprise.

"Right now, I'm thinking the opposite. Mama's burrito and a show at the Crocodile tonight? The Suicidekicks are playing to promote their new album. It's called *Party in the Vomitorium*."

CHAPTER TEN

Oly sat across from her at her neighborhood Indian restaurant. "That's amazing. So you spent how long in India?"

"It was basically a school year. Nine months." Lania grinned and forked up another bite of basmati rice and malai kofta. "Long enough to give birth to a whole new me."

"I wondered how people got into exchange student programs."

"It was the one thing I wanted badly enough as a teenager to figure out the system and use it. It was almost a popularity contest with all of the recommendation letters I needed, but it got me what I wanted."

"So you lived with a family?"

Lania nodded. "The smells bring it back for me. It's one of the reasons I like eating here. Not that this is what I ate most of the time. In South India, the food is a bit different." Oly cocked his head to the side in inquiry and tore off a piece of garlic naan. "North and South India differ culturally. The south is ancient and Dravidian in culture and language, while the north has had a lot more change due to invaders and changing rulers. The northern culture and language is Indo-European, based on Sanskrit, same as the languages you're used to hearing, and the northern food is also more what you're used to."

"What did you think of India?"

"Oh, I loved it. For one thing, India is foreign culturally, but a lot of people speak English. I attended an English-speaking school, and the family I lived with, they were all fluent. It was a small family by Indian standards—three kids. One of the two girls was my age, and that's why they'd sponsored me. The youngest was a son and spoiled rotten."

Oly nodded, mouth stuffed, but Lania shook her head. "Not that it means the same thing there. He was the prize kid. The girls babied him like a doll, and the parents were so proud of him. But there was no tolerance for tantrums and such. I didn't see that kind of behavior the whole time I was there. I forgot what it was like to be shopping while a kid ran screaming circles around his parents. I thought a lot about why kids were better behaved there." Lania paused to eat the last of her kofta ball.

"What did you come up with?"

"Oh, I didn't get any real answers. I hadn't been watching for it in India, so I hardly noticed how the parents controlled their kids' behavior. I think they refused to allow it from a very young age."

"I never got away with that kind of thing. My parents insisted that all adults be called by their last names, Mister or Missus So-and-so, and never let me go on for very long. I knew that there was a line, and over that line was being taken outside and whacked."

"Your parents spanked you?"

"Yeah, but I don't remember it hurting. I remember being embarrassed and missing out on whatever the good stuff was. Yeah. I guess it was more of a swat than a real spanking."

"My parents said they believed in spanking, but I was good for the most part. And when I wasn't, they seemed to find other ways of punishing me. I don't remember ever being spanked."

"What about you? Do you think you'll spank your kids?"

"I don't plan to have any kids." She had been wondering when this would come up.

"Me neither."

"Really?" Relief seemed like a strange response to that. The kid issue could make or break a relationship, but she and Oly weren't working on a lifelong love. Why was she so happy that they were on the same page?

"Yeah. My sister's going to have my share, I'm sure. I want to stay free to move, free to do whatever I want. I'm not that fond of children to begin with, and mix that up with the pressure and responsibility…"

"I know what you mean. Besides—they're expensive! My life will be uncertain financially. I can't be planning kid expenses."

"Here's to all the things we'll never have to buy. Let's pay for this meal with the diaper money!"

"It's my turn, Oly." Lania didn't back down when Oly tried to pick up the check. She kept her hand on top of the piece of paper until he shrugged and raised his hands in surrender. She picked up the check and her last bite of naan at the same time. She dipped the bread into the remains of her sauce and did the figuring again. "You took me out for a couple of drinks, which was like a pretty nice dinner, I took you out to Mama's, you paid for Thai food, so you're still ahead by about twenty dollars."

"What are you talking about, Lania? You're keeping track?"

Lania flushed. "I want to be fair." She picked at a drip of malai kofta on the tablecloth. She hadn't realized that she was still doing it—staying so carefully out of debt.

"It'll even out." She peeked at Oly and almost groaned when she saw how furious he looked. The loss of their easygoing accord made Lania's chest squeeze. His voice was tight. "Don't worry about it."

She stumbled over her words. "I'm happy to spend the money. I promise it's not that I think you'll take advantage or I'll come out behind. As a matter of fact, I'd rather pay more than less."

"Why is that?"

Lania squirmed inside, even as she froze at the new chill in his tone. She licked her lips and prevaricated. "I want to keep things even Steven. I want it to be fair."

"I know you automatically split things into even halves. You've said it's because you and your brother made such a big deal over sharing as kids. This has a different ring to it. It's not like splitting a piece of cake. And you didn't say even, you said you'd rather pay more."

"It's not a big deal!" Lania's slow anger started to burn. How dare Oly bully her like this? What right did he have to question her on being fair, of all things?

"It's a big deal when you're keeping score in your head. I don't like the idea of you knowing to the penny how much we've spent on each other. I thought that taking turns would keep us from having to split the check every time, but it sounds like that's basically what you're doing!"

Lania started to turn resentful. "I have to know that I'm doing my part." Oly tapped his knife on the table. He looked like he was going to explode.

"And more? Why is it better for you to pay more if possible? So that you can feel better than me? What kind of ego game is this?"

Lania gaped at Oly, then looked around the half-full restaurant to make sure people weren't staring. "What the fuck are you talking about?"

He grabbed the check out of her hand, cheeks taut. "If I pay this, how will you feel?"

Lania picked up her water glass and took a sip. She crossed her arms over her chest and looked away from him.

"How, Lania?"

"Indebted." It popped out, though Lania had no intention of allowing the inquisition to continue. "Okay? It's not you. I know that you wouldn't try to make me feel like I owed you." Lania tucked her hair behind her ear and then pushed the whole mass behind her shoulders. She sighed and gave in to his desire to know why. "I have to know that I don't owe anyone anything. I can't be indebted. I have to know that I'm doing this myself."

"Doing what yourself?" The edge was off his anger now that she was giving him answers. "It's not like I'm trying to be your sugar daddy. I wanted to pay for dinner. It makes me feel good to take you out to eat. The way you enjoy your food, the way you get into the sensuality of food—it turns me on. It makes me want to feed you all the time."

"See? You are trying to buy something from me. I will eat on my own terms, not to provide you with a turn-on." Oly looked at Lania in horror. She had the delayed realization that her accusation was maybe a bit unfair. She wanted to take it back, but the kernel of truth and her need to be strong held her back.

"How did I turn into the bad guy here? You're the one with a pathological need to one-up everyone!" Oly pushed his chair away from the table with a rough shove.

"Pathological?" Lania sputtered. "I don't need to be diagnosed here. And will you keep your voice down? I don't like being stared at." She looked around to see that the people in the tables near them were keeping their eyes scrupulously on their food.

"Let me tell you, lady. I think it's a problem when you can't take a gift. I would have liked to have made this dinner a gift to you." Lania's anger cracked, a tiny weakness that threatened to allow the tears behind her lids to well. "Watching you enjoy a gift is not the same as trying to buy something from you."

"I've never been good at accepting gifts. It makes me feel so vulnerable. Can't you understand?" Lania was on the razor's edge between tears and raging.

Oly took a deep breath and let it trickle out. She watched him pull together a calm that seemed too cold. Now that it was too late to take all her words back, she wanted to tell him that she loved his giving nature. She knew that she had already accepted more from Oly than she had allowed anyone else to give her. And not a bit of it involved the price of a meal or a movie.

Lania grabbed Oly's hand and pulled it to her. She looked at his knuckles and the calluses he had from holding a camera. "Please don't close me out. I'm sorry. I have to go slowly. I can't open myself up all at once." Dizzy with the chance she was taking, with the vulnerability she was exposing to him, Lania lifted her head.

Oly's face held a concerned look. She tried to project sincerity and openness and was relieved when he sighed and looked at her with a soft frown. "So I shouldn't try to give you things."

"You give me so much already. Don't you see how much happiness you've brought me?" A distant part of her looked on in fear and horror.

"Maybe I thought you were always like this. Glowing."

"No, Oly. I'm not." Try as she might, Lania couldn't open up any further. She felt more naked in the middle of the busy restaurant than she did when they fucked. When Oly gave the check back to her, Lania let out a slow breath. She tried to be calm, reassuring herself that he seemed to understand that she needed time and space. By force of will, she stood to begin the rest of their night together.

❖

Lania mopped the floor to the beat of a pop song on the University of Washington college radio station. After seeing a movie together, she and Oly had arrived at her doorstep muddy and drenched from the rain. They'd carried their bikes into her apartment, trying to be considerate of the other tenants who had to share the hallway. Once in her apartment, Oly had looked around, a lost and drowned look to him that made Lania crack up laughing and drop her bike. She wheeled it to the special patch of wall between the breakfast nook and the living room and leaned it there, gesturing for him to follow. He grimaced and carried his bike the whole way before propping it against hers. Oly frowned at the gathering mess under the bikes and the track she'd left on the hardwood floor. "It's not supposed to be raining at the end of June."

His frustration was so endearing that Lania had attacked him, stripped him bare, and thrown him into the shower—moments before joining him herself. They made slow, wet love as the chill of the rain and wind left their bones for the smoldering heat of passion. He couldn't convince her to clean up the mess afterward, either. She demanded that he join her in bed, yawning and promising that she didn't mind washing the floor in the morning.

And it was true. She didn't mind. Cleaning the floor seemed a small service.

Since their big argument, Oly had allowed her to guide their spending. They'd enjoyed sushi and saag paneer together, seen movies and plays. Lania cast her thoughts back over their last half dozen dates and realized that they had spent the night together every time they'd gone out. And they'd gone out six times in the last two weeks. She both marveled that she got anything else done and recognized the feeling that three days a week was not enough Oly for her. What a discomfiting thought.

The sex was golden. Lania used to let partners find her tender spots through trial and error, but Oly listened with such hunger to her mumbled or gasped directions that sexual heat infused the very act of telling him what she wanted. Oly pinned her down and ordered her not to move while he explored her body, licking and sucking her until she came three times in a row. She returned the favor, turning Oly into a yelping, growling animal by finding all the spots on which he could be bitten. Sometimes fucking with a strap-on, sometimes using hands and mouths, sometimes rubbing together like the first night, Lania and Oly became familiar with all the planes and hollows of each other's bodies.

Whatever had happened between Oly and that Cynthia woman from the loft party wasn't the same as what was happening between Lania and Oly. Far from avoiding her phone calls, Oly's responsiveness tempted her to believe that he loved her too. Lania's mop strokes slowed at the thought of love.

Lania grabbed the top of the mop handle and leaned her head on the back of her hand. Panic seized her muscles and shortened her breath. Inside her, something wailed, "But I had it all planned!"

She stood there for long moments, mixed ecstasy and agony roiling within her. It was too late to think of protection—she was deeply in love with him. She thought about him all the time, picked restaurants that he liked, movies she thought he'd want to see. Was she losing herself in him?

Her greatest fear—and she'd let it happen. What am I supposed to do now, she wondered. Her stomach twisted at the idea of changing her plans, changing herself, to fit into the possibility of a life with Oly. How did people do this? How did they give themselves up to another person? She couldn't do it. She couldn't lose herself.

Could she backtrack, get some of her self back? Could Oly fall in love with her? Which was scarier? Lania finished mopping the floor while considering the question of what she would do if Oly didn't fall for her. She flashed on his warnings that film came first.

Maybe she could keep seeing Oly and, when he moved on, chalk the experience up to growth. Mmm, yeah, right. Of course, she could be the one moving on—onto a boat and away.

How could it be right to keep planning to leave? How could she stop now?

Lania rubbed her socks off on the rug, dropped onto her rumpled bed, and curled up, pulling the covers over her. Her bed smelled like Oly and sex, and the idea of being without him sapped her of energy. It was too late to protect herself. She'd hurt now or she'd hurt later. No reason to bring the pain on any sooner than it needed to happen.

A boat could float her off into a new life when this phase ended. Whatever happened, however it went between them, she needed something to hold onto afterward.

A small, traitorous voice wondered if Oly would consider boat life. She almost allowed herself to picture the two of them sailing around the world, but that was one step too far into vulnerability. Boating, of all things, symbolized self-reliance to her.

Lania circled her pillow with her arms and buried her face in it. Too scared to cry, she focused on her breathing and calmed, becoming clear and empty.

Lania uncurled and lay on her back, staring at the ceiling. Oly was a blessing, an amazing man, and she should enjoy every second she had with him. She needed to have direction that was independent of him, though, and boating was the answer. She whispered to herself, "Take what you can get and sail away."

Jeremy leaned on a shovel while Oly sorted magazines in the Shit Palace. "And the distribution deal will be so good that we'll get huge chunks of money up front, plus a great percentage. Then, when the movie gets picked up and plays in indie theaters across the country, we'll be rich!"

Oly glanced up at Jeremy and looked back at the pile of magazines on the makeshift sorting table set in the middle of the mid-sized room. He leaned forward in his chair, shoving an enormous pile of moldering fan mags off the table and into the wheelbarrow.

When Jeremy picked him up that morning, it just clicked somehow, like old times. It was a relief to him, but talking about it seemed like a good way to end their unease with one another.

"I'm thinking the money will be hidden behind a wall in here somewhere…" Jeremy glanced around at the old lath and plaster walls, amusing Oly with his willingness to believe. "Or maybe you're right. We'll sell the distribution rights to the film and make a chunk of change." He pondered for a moment.

Oly contributed. "Should we go for the big up-front payment, or the long-term money?"

"This movie's gonna be huge. We'd better hold on to a solid percentage for later. Though I like money up front too. It's a good thing that the magazines are selling. I've been spending a lot more lately, since Joyce and I have been going out to dinner a couple times a week. She doesn't like peanut butter and jelly. At least, she doesn't think it's good enough for every meal."

"Especially when you're on a date."

Jeremy reddened at the implied criticism. "I haven't dated in a while. I guess I jumped in the deep end with Joyce. She's so smart that I have a hard time keeping up sometimes."

Oly knew that Jeremy could hold his own in any intellectual discussion. "I'm glad you met her."

"Me too. We went to a show at a loft downtown that was a lot of fun. A few bands and a spelling bee. Can you believe that? People are so weird! But Joyce triumphed. Her competition crumbled under the onslaught of hundred dollar words. Crystal Math played. Remember them? They play rock music but they write everything mathematically. Like this one song where the time signature starts out simple but gets more complicated at the rate of the Golden Mean. They're pretty weird, but it's a good show." Jeremy propped the shovel against the peeling wallpaper and supplied Oly with another huge stack of magazines to sort. "These are going to pay our expenses until the film's done, right?"

Oly speculated on the take. "I think it's going to do it. We sold the *Playboy*, the *Fortune Magazines* from the 1940s, and the *Cosmopolitans* from the 1890s. That got us out of the hole and a little ahead. We still have the early science fiction magazines and the *Star Wars* comics. I don't know anything about *Judge Magazine,* but they look great to me. If nothing else, the covers are great art from the beginning of the twentieth century. Plus"—he pointed with his chin—"whatever we find in the stacks we haven't sorted yet."

Jeremy nodded like his head was spinning, clowning. Oly threw a 1963 *Movie Stars Magazine* at him.

Chapter Eleven

"Wow, three calls in one year! I'm the luckiest dad in the world."

"Yeah, yeah, yuk it up."

Her dad's voice dropped to a scratchy whisper. "Who'd you kill? No, there are gangsters after you, right? No, wait, I've got it. You want your cat back."

Lania rolled her eyes and waited for her dad to stop fooling around.

"Don't roll your eyes at me, young lady!" he barked in his best drill sergeant voice.

Lania burst into giggles. His normal voice floated across the miles. "Okay, I'm done. What?'"

"Good, because I need to ask you for help."

"Trouble?"

"Oh, no, not at all. I've been looking at boats, and it seems like there are better deals in Canada. I was wondering if you mightn't be desirous of a lovely drive through the countryside of Vancouver Island, B.C."

"Well, as a matter of fact, no, I had no such thought in my head. But now that you mention it..."

"Tease." Lania addressed the question of the trip. "So you would be into it? A little bit of a father-daughter road trip? I'm thinking four nights, starting in Seattle, heading across the Olympic Peninsula to Port Townsend, and then catching the Black Ball Ferry at Port Angeles. We'd arrive in Victoria and then drive north to

Nanaimo, where the B.C. Ferries run to Vancouver. Then back south to Seattle. That makes six nights for you with one spent here on each end. What do you think?"

"Right on. I'll bring the vehicle; you plan the trip. Just tell me where to turn."

"Thanks, Dad. I was thinking mid to late July. Are there any dates that would be best for you?"

"Retirement means I'm at your service. Just give me the heads-up a couple days in advance so I can get a neighbor to feed the chickens."

"Right, the chickens." Lania shook her head. "I'll have to ask for time off, so you'll get more notice than that."

"Great. Are things rolling along with Oly?"

"Well, I've been trying to open up with him and let things go where they will. We had a huge fight about who was going to pay for a meal."

"A good fight or a bad fight?"

"Pretty good." It didn't suck to have a dad with conflict management training. "Yeah. Pretty good."

"You could be more enthusiastic."

"Well, besides that, a weird thing happened. Oly called when I was about to look at a boat, and he came down to help me tear through it. It turns out he's an experienced sailor. He went from Corpus Christi to Rio de Janeiro with his uncle once, a while back."

"Right on. What did he think of your desire to get a sailboat?"

"He seemed excited by it, actually. We went out to dinner after we looked the boat over, and he and I connected on what kinds of things we'd want out of a boat. He asked really casually about what a person might want in a boat for two people rather than one, and we went through the equipment and accommodations again. It was magical, except for the fact that he never came right out and said he was interested in boat living. I've been fighting the thought, myself." Lania wrapped a lock of her hair around a finger. "He's not the kind of guy you expect to see settling down."

"He doesn't sound like a slow-top to me, Lania, but he could be wigged out by any hints toward permanence. If you're buying a boat, planning to live there together is like planning to buy a house together. That's no joke. You two haven't been dating that long—what, five, six weeks? It might be too much to expect from him. It's kind of freaky that *you're* thinking that way, to tell you the truth."

"You know me, Dad. I never can find a perfect balance. Or maybe it's bad timing. I want to get a boat and move aboard now. I don't want to wait a year to find out whether I should look for a one- or two-person boat."

"What's the difference between boats for one or two people?"

"Not much, in the end. I can get a smaller boat if I'm living by myself, with less elaborate facilities for cooking, less storage space, and with a single sleeping berth rather than a double. And since boats get more expensive as they get larger..."

"Well, you should keep your eye out for both." He sounded so final that she agreed to take his advice. After a few more minutes of chatting, they both said good-bye and Lania sat in her kitchen, pondering her relationship with Oly. Talking to her dad always helped simplify things. Even if he didn't say anything, she felt like she made more sense phrasing things for his ears.

❖

Carla showed up in a plain, homemade dress straight out of *Little House on the Prairie*, vibrating with tension and excitement. Oly stood back and let Jeremy take the lead. "Hey, Carla. Welcome to the crew."

"I'm honored."

"No, we're honored. Come on in. We're using this studio to record the Train Track Pennies." He ushered her into a room that was empty in the middle and packed with gear along every wall. There were parts enough to create three drum kits, and microphone stands, cymbal stands, and stools for a band the size of the Gypsy Kings.

Carla took a look around, slung her banjo case into a corner, and walked past Oly, back out into the hall. "Where's the sound booth?" she asked, sounding hungry.

Oly pointed to a different door and allowed Carla to walk in there by herself. They'd hashed out a plan over dinner weeks back, and she had e-mailed periodically to clarify details. It obviously meant a lot to her to get back into being a sound engineer.

Jeremy stepped close to Oly and leaned down to mutter in his ear. "There's something about her…I noticed at dinner…"

"What do you mean?"

Jeremy looked to be sure Carla was still in the sound booth. "Do you think Carla has always been a girl?"

Oly shook his head. "Well, let's just say her parents probably thought she was a boy."

Jeremy pondered for a moment. "Oh. Do I know any other trans women? I know what it means for you, but I don't know what that means for her."

Oly shrugged. "Don't let it mean anything. Except that her voice is that much more amazing, if she's done anything to bring her range up."

Jeremy nodded. Oly decided to broach the subject of their strange fight. "Jeremy, I'm sorry that I walked out on you a few weeks ago. Hell, I have been on a hair trigger for a month now. Everything seems either to infuriate me or make me ecstatic."

"Oly, it's okay. I understand. Lania's got you all twisted up inside."

"Yeah, and I don't know what to do about it. She's so dedicated to sailing away."

"I've been thinking about that. The way you've been talking, why don't you go with her? Not right away. Surely she could get a boat and live on it here for a while? Why don't you use some of that famous charm to get this girl to stick around a while?"

Oly huffed. "I can't say I ever thought of that. Strange."

"Well, think about it. I don't see how you're going to do any better without her than with her at this point. If we were going to be able to go along like we had been, you'da had to get loose of her a while back." Jeremy's slight bitterness shocked Oly, who had never heard that tone from him before. "But I can handle it. I'm picking up loose ends on the film, and I have Joyce now." He walked into the sound booth, and Oly looked after him in some confusion and not a little concern. His relationship with Jeremy was changing so fast. Oly moved into the studio space and started setting up mike stands and mikes.

As he grabbed mikes, Carla's voice floated from the monitors with directions on which kind should go where. Within a half hour, everything was set up for the recording, and Hoss and Melody showed up with their gear. Another fifteen minutes later, the Train Track Pennies were laying down practice tracks to figure out how the room sounded and whether the mikes would need to be changed.

The rest of the crew started to show up just when Oly was starting to think they'd all forgotten this day of shooting. Since they were filming the making of the film to use in the film itself, it made sense that they should get footage of the musicians as well. Carla, warmed up and happy, took one look at the cameras and turned pale. She froze. Oly thought, oh, great, and went to calm her down.

Verona Wild beat him there. As the set designer, she had informed him that the studio was perfect and didn't need to be changed. For filming the crew, she didn't do any wardrobe work since authenticity was important. Makeup, however, was necessary regardless, to keep the unnaturally bright filming lights from turning everyone gray. The small, graceful Verona looked somehow more solid against the stick-thin, starving alley cat look of Carla. Verona took her by the arm and pulled her to the side of the room, behind the cameras.

"Hey, sweetheart." Verona kept her voice to a purr, so Oly strolled closer to hear. "You have the prettiest, silkiest hair I've ever touched." Verona petted Carla, unbinding one braid and rebraiding it more loosely. "Cameras love the shine of hair like yours."

Carla ran her fingers down the new braid. "No, it's just plain old hair." Carla looked in the mirror and turned her head so Verona could do the second braid.

"Let me get a look at your face." Verona turned Carla's face to the light, and Carla's smile faded. Verona touched Carla's cheek, turning her head a little more. "I won't need to do much makeup. You're beautiful."

Carla shook her head in emphatic denial. "I know better than that. I aim for tidy most of the time."

Verona grabbed the end of Carla's chin and held her face up so that she would meet her eyes. Oly watched, thinking that he would never dare be so physical. "I can make anyone look like processed cheerleader. Believe me when I say that you have something I can't create. I call that beauty. And I can highlight it with my paints, but don't worry that I'll try to make you look like someone you aren't." Verona applied the smallest possible amount of makeup, enough to keep Carla's delicate lashes and eyebrows from fading from visibility in the filming lights, and brought out a mirror. Carla looked up at Verona in new determination. Verona raised Carla by one arm, gave her a quick hug, and then turned her and sent her back to her place with a pat on the back.

Oly caught Verona's eye and gave a jerk of his head, and she sauntered over. "What you just did was amazing."

"Just gave her a few of the compliments she needed. She's beautiful—she just doesn't know it."

Oly looked at Carla. She didn't fit his definition of beautiful. He liked round women with lots of hair. He frowned. He loved being absorbed by Lania whenever they were together, but thoughts of her distracted him when he was working on the film. She made the film feel like a job, like something taking time away from the best part of life. Just a few short months ago, filming was the best part of his life.

That wasn't fair—she didn't make him turn to her, not on purpose. She was the one who brought up how much time they'd been spending together.

He couldn't even string three analytical thoughts together on the topic. Frustration bloomed. The band was ready and everyone was waiting on him to start the process, but all he wanted to do was toss it all aside and find Lania.

He recognized these feelings. Frustration, rage, bitterness, resentment. Wanting too much, wanting too many irreconcilable things. It reminded him of hitting puberty and going the wrong direction, getting tits and not getting facial hair. Now, he wanted to focus absolutely on the film. He wanted to deepen the partnership he had with Jeremy. He wanted to be with Lania all the time, absorbing her inspiring attitude and world view. She'd brought up his latent hunger for travel, which he'd figured he could satisfy after becoming successful as a documentarian. Once he had a good, solid movie under his belt, he'd be able to get funding for bigger productions that would involve exploring the ways that people build such differing cultures with the same clay of basic human needs and desires.

There he went again, saying that she'd done this. He wanted to own his feelings, even the ones that were new since meeting Lania, but he felt influenced by her in a way that made him think uncomfortably of control.

He'd learned in transitioning that he couldn't always have exactly what he wanted. He made the best of his male body and enjoyed the hell out of every pleasurable inch of it. Still, he had moments when the cock in his hand wasn't the right one, the perfect one—when he wanted more.

Whatever he did about Lania and travel and film, he knew with a bone-deep ache that he would end up with some of what he wanted, wanting more.

He sighed and glanced at Verona, who was still watching Carla. He blinked, catching a gleam in her eye that he hadn't expected. Was everyone pairing up, or did it just seem like that?

Oly sat on the rear fender of the empty van, talking to Lania on the phone. "Check this out. Verona and Carla look like they might get together. Unexpected, right?"

"They do seem like a bit of an odd couple—tall and short, dark and blond, skinny and curvy. More power to them!"

"Filming is coming to an end, though. I wonder if Carla is going to make a move before it's done."

"I imagine it'll be Verona doing any move-making."

He agreed. "I'll have a lot of work to do after filming is done, but it's different work. I'll be editing and either selling or distributing it but it's on my own schedule instead of a hundred people to be wrangled." He thought about the hours and hours of film he'd have to cull through, finding the perfect shots that tell the story with unblemished clarity, and the reams of paper that document exactly what they did, why, and how they'd planned to use it. If they'd done a great job—because good wouldn't be enough—they'd have a reasonable working edit after the first go-round. If there were glaring holes in the structure or story…well, he was going to believe that they'd done their jobs right and not send himself down that rabbit hole.

Lania said, "Hey, if you're going to have an easier schedule, and maybe you'll want a bit of a break, would you like to go on a trip with me? My dad and I are going to drive up north looking at boats. We'll be gone for four days and we're hoping to get up as far as Nanaimo, B.C. I'd love to get your take on the boats we'll be looking at. We haven't set a date yet, so we could be kind of flexible. Dad's retired and I can get time off with a week's notice."

The mountain of work ahead of him beckoned. Looking at boats with Lania lured. Didn't he deserve a break? "A road trip sounds great. Meeting your dad sounds a little intimidating, but I'll be on my best behavior. How about two weeks from Wednesday?"

CHAPTER TWELVE

Lania stood by herself at the end-of-filming party, watching
Oly from across the room. Being without a role, some job
to do, made her uncomfortable. She wished she had offered to serve
canapés or something instead of standing there brooding on Oly's
attitude. She'd built fragile hopes around Oly's excitement about
the boat hunting trip, but then he'd cancelled a couple of dates. She
understood that they were finishing a major part of getting the movie
done, but it hurt. He had also invited her to this party with mixed
messages—he wanted her there, but said he might not have much
time to spend with her while he was schmoozing.

Jeremy appeared next to her and handed Lania a margarita.
"Haven't seen you since your party. Carla's working out well." He
slurped down a large portion of his own margarita.

"That's what I hear." She would do her duty with Jeremy, at
least. "Congratulations." He ducked his head and nodded his thanks.
"What kind of work will you be doing now that the filming is done?"

"Same as before. A little bit of everything, including trying to
make sure we don't run out of money while we edit." He glanced
at Lania out of the corner of his eye. "You planning to stick around
for a while?"

"I'll be here all evening, I think."

"No, I mean Seattle."

"I don't know. What would you call a while?"

"I mean, when do you plan to sail away?"

Lania stiffened, sensing an undercurrent that she couldn't put her finger on. "The boat comes first. Can't sail away until I have one."

"So it'll be a while?"

"Why do you ask?" The inquisition was making her uncomfortable. It was a common question, but Jeremy didn't seem casual about it.

"Oly never gets all wrapped up in a girl—woman, I mean." He looked at Lania to make sure she wasn't insulted.

"Never?"

"Nope. It's just been him and me until now."

"But now you have Joyce."

"Yeah, that's right. And Oly has you. It's kind of hard to get him to focus lately, but he seems so happy. You guys are good for each other."

Lania was touched and annoyed by this backhanded and mixed compliment. "If it's a problem, you should be having this conversation with Oly instead of me."

"No, no, I didn't mean it like that. Oly is still doing great work; don't get me wrong. He's just not as single-minded as usual, and the movie isn't getting the same attention it was before." Jeremy seemed to realize that he was digging himself deeper into a hole, and he frowned at the glass in his hand.

Ginger strolled up to them. "Jeremy, Joyce is looking for you. She's over by the tapenade and cracker spread." Ginger patted Jeremy on the shoulder. They watched him walk away, and Ginger raised an eyebrow. "Was that as dreadful as it looked?"

Lania pursed her lips. "I think he's worried that I'm stealing Oly away from him."

Ginger arched an eyebrow. "I didn't know they were that close." Lania rolled her eyes. "Well, he'll get over it. He's hooked by Joyce now. Ah, the first flush of new love!"

Lania clutched at the opportunity to change the subject. "Who are you feeling flushed about, Ginger?"

"Oh, this is such a straight crowd. I hardly dare get flushed. I might get hit by a boyfriend." Ginger ducked an imaginary flurry of blows.

"That's not true. You're just used to women who know how to signal. I happen to know that the woman in the blue and silver dress over there likes women." When Ginger spotted the fleshy brunette and whistled, Lania blushed. "That doesn't mean she's not into men, but I can tell you for sure that she's into women."

"I thought you were all lovey-dovey with Oly lately?"

Lania blushed harder. "Well, I'm not blind. She flirted with me one night, and I had to flirt back a little. Wouldn't want to be rude, y'know. I know that you'll do a better job than I did of following up, and you can't tell me she's not your type."

Ginger murmured an offhanded good-bye to Lania as she moved away. As Ginger walked, her steps became slower and slinky. Without looking, she snatched a margarita glass from a tray as she walked. She stepped right up and offered the drink to the round brunette. Lania watched in amazement as they steamed up the air around them with their heated glances and short conversation. When they linked arms and headed toward the door, Lania shook her head in wonder.

Alone again, Lania mused on Jeremy's complaint. She hadn't realized that Oly's friends were feeling bereft, but most of the people who greeted Oly acted like they hadn't seen him in ages. Lania realized that it might be true. Between their dates and his work, he probably hadn't been to a party in a very long time.

Lania found Oly in the crowd. She caught his eye and gestured a question. Okay if I join you? He nodded and turned back to the conversation. The throngs of people milled all around her, glasses clinked, and the DJ was spinning enough energy to keep the mood up in the room. She walked up next to him and put her hand on his arm. When he didn't respond, she turned to the rest of the group looking for the source of tension. A cold knot formed in her stomach as the subject became clear—money.

"I'm not trying to be ungrateful," Oly said. "This is a great party, Madeline, but I'm more concerned about the budget for the editing studio time."

He addressed a sharp-faced woman. Her gown screamed one-off designer, and the ease with which she wore it confirmed the impression of money. She made a cutting gesture with her hand and spoke to Oly with impatience. "You understand the value of visibility. What's wrong with you, Oly? This party is absolutely necessary—as necessary as editing the film itself." A calculated blend of insult and encouragement filled her tone. "You can't sell a film nobody has heard of, and this party has press written all over it. I've put together the most exclusive crowd, the hottest talents, and the best bar in Seattle, and this party is going to sell your film as surely as the merits of the film will."

Oly's eyes tightened at the corners. "A party can't make brilliance out of shit."

"No, but the right attention can sell shit to the right people. And the fact that your film is brilliant but controversial means that having the right people behind you will be absolutely necessary." Madeline tsked in disgust. "But you know that. This is how you got your last film into the One Reel Film Fest, remember? That prize did wonders for your reputation. Now, for the first time, you have funding, significant supporters, and what do you do? You start nickel-and-diming your own operation. You know that's not how you make it in this industry."

This harangue wilted Oly. "I don't know what's wrong. I'm not on my game tonight."

A dapper man in the woman's coterie raised his eyebrow. "You've been out of the game for a while now." He looked Lania up and down. "If I were you, I'd weigh the cost of losing touch with your connections against any...benefits...you may be receiving."

Lania glared at the sneering man.

"You're the one who's so good at weighing...benefits." Oly dismissed him and drew Lania away.

When they were far enough away for privacy, Lania pulled free of Oly's grip and stopped him. "Oly! Who was that?"

"No one. Just a hustler."

Lania tried to catch Oly's eye, but he was scanning the party. "Please. That woman is hosting your wrap party. She can't be no one."

"Oh, Madeline. She's an investor. It doesn't matter, though."

"Obviously it does. What was that all about? Everyone here is acting like you've returned from the dead!"

Oly clenched his teeth and looked at her. "I used to do a lot more party-hopping. Being seen, to keep the film in people's minds while we're finishing production."

"That guy was insulting. I can't believe he said that."

"I can." Oly shifted, turning away, and took up his scan of the room again.

"Really."

"He's an ass. Don't worry about him."

"You seem upset by all this. Would it be better for the film if you went to more of the parties you're talking about?"

"Yeah." Oly turned and walked toward the drink table, leaving Lania gaping behind him. She caught up with him and reached for his arm.

"I could go to some of these parties with you."

Oly looked at her in disgust. "What good would that be? It's work."

"Do you think I could be useful?"

"How? You don't have any connections. I wouldn't be able to babysit you and make sure you have a good time."

The kick to her heart staggered her. "Well, then. Sounds like I'm useless to you. Don't worry. It doesn't matter to me if we cut back on seeing each other."

Oly looked away from her. How dare he? How dare he say something like that and then look as though she had hurt him? She wanted to tell him to go to hell. She wanted to tell him that she needed him. Lania picked up a fresh margarita and took a couple of quick drinks. She turned away and said over her shoulder, "I'll leave you to your work."

❖

Feet on the floor, Oly flopped back on his bed. What a terrible night. He covered his eyes with one arm and wished he could relax.

What was he doing? He'd spent years pulling together a crew, a real team that worked well together and understood his vision. He had Roshan Gita, a brilliant cameraman; Joyner Wright, the gaffer and grip and all-around construction wizard; Verona for aesthetics; and now Carla for sound. And Jeremy. Jeez, Jeremy.

These people would stick with him. They could be like Scorsese and his techs, working together for decades and making consistently great films. Jeremy was his best friend, and plenty of Oly's best ideas came out of talking to him, but the entire group had a vibe that elevated their work. Made it fun and satisfying and good. They were his friends as well as his crew.

Not to mention the business connections. His award from the Bumbershoot One Reel Film Festival had turned into real money for this film. Every time he put out another film, he gained more of a reputation for enjoyable films that satisfied serious-minded viewers. And he came in on budget.

Groaning, Oly kicked his shoes off, struggled out of his clothing, and curled up. Could he consider trading all of that, the whole film industry and his place in it, to sail away with a woman chasing a dream?

A beautiful dream. Was it his dream?

Feelings sucked the thoughts from his head, leaving only vacuum. He struggled to work though the emotions in some sort of reasonable way, but he couldn't get off the seesaw.

He was on his way; he could feel it. If he stuck to his guns, he could make it in film. Did he want that? He'd never aimed for pop stardom, but a solid career and recognition from audiences and his peers...

Or he could be a maverick. He could travel the world by boat, devising film projects and sailing to rarely seen locations. He could be with Lania. For now? How could he shuffle aside the possibility of a great career for a relationship with such a slim chance of enduring?

That's assuming he could make amends for his asshole comment at the party earlier. What the hell had he been thinking? Calling her useless was stupid and careless. Restlessness turned him on the bed. He wished he could unsay those words, but...she would forgive him. He avoided inspecting the knowledge or thinking about her feelings for him.

Maybe they could work together. He'd been helping her with the boat shopping. Maybe she would like helping with production in some capacity. No, he'd be a shit director with her around. He couldn't be in her presence without focusing on her. It was ridiculous, the strength of her pull on him.

Oly shoved aside the uneasy thoughts. He would continue as before. He would make his movie, and he would enjoy Lania while he could. Let the future reveal itself; he would wait for things to become clearer.

I don't know if I can do this, was his last thought before he faded into restless sleep.

When he woke to a daylit room, he reached for the phone and dialed Lania without premeditation. When she picked up, he said, "I'm sorry for what I said. I'm sure you'd find a way to enjoy the industry parties, just like you enjoy everything else you do. It's true that I am distracted when you're at parties with me. I prefer you to anyone else and it is hard for me to do the social thing when I want to focus on you. It's not your behavior that bums me out, though, it's my own inability to focus with you around."

"I appreciate the apology, but it still sounds like we have a problem here." She sounded tired but still mad.

"You're the one who's good with words. Just edit my apology like you edit any bad piece of writing. With generosity and understanding and sympathy, looking for the real meaning behind the messed up words." He gestured as he spoke into the phone, wanting the words to punch through her anger.

"Okay, Oly. I accept your apology and extend one of my own. I wish I hadn't pushed then and there. We should talk about this in person and not in the middle of an important party."

He sat up in bed, ready to face the day. "I hope I'm still invited on the boat-shopping trip."

"You're still invited, but you don't have to come if you don't want to or don't have time. It's okay. I accept your apology regardless." Her tone communicated simple truth.

"I want to go." He made sure his tone did the same.

"My dad will arrive after I get off work Tuesday at nine and he'll spend the night on my couch. I'd like to get an early start on Wednesday. What time can we pick you up?"

"Pick me up whenever. I'll be at the loft. If you want to get an early start, maybe come get me around six. We can ride the ferry to Bainbridge Island and have breakfast at this kick-ass diner called the Streamliner before we drive to Port Townsend. That'll mean we miss the commuter traffic and get to the sales docks in PT by around ten."

"Will I see you before then? I have a full schedule at work, but I'd like to."

"I'm going to be working non-stop from now through Tuesday. We'll be cleaning up, making sure all the props get back to the right people, labeling all the reels we want to work on first, and stuff like that. There's so much to do."

"Too bad. I miss you."

He savored the sound of those words. "I miss you too. By the way, what's your dad like?"

❖

"Dad! You're early!"

Her dad grabbed Lania for a big hug. "I know. That's why I came here to the shop. I didn't want to sit outside your apartment while you biked home."

"You can give me a ride, then," Lania said, holding on to her dad's arms. The rough weave of the hemp pullover brought a wave of nostalgia. He'd felt just like that every winter throughout her life. "I'm so glad you're here! Wait just a minute." Lania spun around and dashed into the back room. She found the manager in her office and got permission to leave a few minutes early. She shrugged out of her lab coat and grabbed her backpack, helmet, and bike.

"Here she is now," said her dad to one of her co-workers. "Catch you later, Hui."

Hui waved them off, closing the door behind them. Lania teased him. "I can't leave you alone for thirty seconds without you charming some woman."

"Hui is a nice young lady—emphasis on the young. You know me, though; I have to keep in practice."

They drove to her apartment, and dealt with the usual parking nightmare. They circled for a while, finally parking just two blocks from her apartment building. Lania wheeled her bike along the sidewalk, and her dad ducked around telephone poles in the yellow pools from the streetlights.

The front door of her building opened before Lania pulled her keys out. "Oh, hi, Joyce," she said. "We're coming in." He walked up the stairs and took the door, holding it open for Lania.

"I wanted to go out with Jeremy tonight, but he and Oly have a late night planned. I hear you are taking him out of town for a few days?" Joyce's rasp was crabbier than usual.

"I'm not taking him; he's coming of his own free will."

Her dad said, "We're driving up to Vancouver Island to look at boats."

"Driving to Vancouver Island is not possible. There is no bridge connecting the island to the main landmass." Joyce glared up at Lania's dad.

He stared at Joyce. "Yeah. I meant to say we were going to take a ferry to the island and then drive north a ways."

"Come on, Dad. Let's get inside."

He followed her through the door. "What was that all about?"

Lania sighed and lifted her bike by the crossbar. She started up the stairs. "That was Joyce Blockcolski. She's dating Oly's right-hand man, Jeremy. I gather she wanted to be with him tonight and he has to work because Oly's going out of town with us."

He stood by while she unlocked her door and then followed her in. "I caught most of that. I was asking more about your response." Lania blushed, embarrassed, and turned away to lean her bike against the wall. "You don't usually talk to folks like that."

"Oh, Dad! Things are so weird with Oly." Lania dropped on the couch and rubbed her hands over her face.

"What's up?" He sat next to her.

"It's stupid stuff for the most part. You know I decided to give in a little and try to go with the flow? Well, I think I love this guy, but when I started letting go, he started getting kind of moody." Lania shook her head in frustration. "Not moody, exactly. More like he's torn between wanting to be with me and working on his film. Sometimes he's focused on me, and those times are great. When he's not, though, it can be pretty hard. He doesn't seem to have any kind of halfway setting."

"How are you reacting to this?"

"With nothing but grace and tact." She grimaced. "I wish. As a matter of fact, we tore each other up pretty good at the filming wrap party. His friends upset him by talking about how he'd been out of the loop. He said…" Lania found herself unwilling to expose Oly to her dad's criticism. She hedged, feeling strange that she would keep the full details of the story from him. "He said that I wouldn't be able to help him network since I didn't have any connections. He suggested that we shouldn't see each other so often. Or maybe I suggested it." Lania growled. "I can hardly remember exactly what happened. I was in such an emotional fog! But I think I hurt his feelings."

"Why do you think that?"

"I don't know. He didn't say anything. He got a tight look on his face and turned away from me."

"But what did you say, Lania?"

"I said that I didn't need him. Or that we didn't need to see each other. Or something to that effect."

"Is it true?"

Lania closed her eyes and shook her head. "It has to be, doesn't it? I mean, I wouldn't die if Oly disappeared." She tried to imagine how she'd feel but shied away. "I don't know, Dad. He means a lot to me already. I don't want to get into this deeper than he does and get hurt."

"This sounds familiar," he said. "Weren't we just talking about letting things go? It sounds like you're still trying to control the direction your feelings slide. Maybe you should try to clear your mind, meditate for a while, and then go with the flow. It doesn't matter what you wish you felt, you know? You gotta be true to yourself."

"Yeah." It was all Lania could manage.

"Well, we have an early morning ahead of us, so let's aim for an early night." He slapped his knee and stood. He headed for the hall closet. "Blankets in the same place?"

"Yes, on the second shelf. I'll get you one of my pillows." She stepped into her bedroom and grabbed a pillow. Standing next to her press, Lania stroked the clean flywheel, thinking about selling Esmeralda. The melancholy of losing the magazine layered onto the rest of her uncertain and painful confusion. She took a couple of calming breaths and turned around to find her dad standing in the doorway, watching with sympathy.

"Do you want to talk?"

"No." Lania made an effort to smile. "You're right. I'll try to do some meditation and get some sleep. I'm just stressing myself out right now." She handed the pillow over and reached out for a hug. Her dad patted her back while she breathed his familiar scent.

Lania sniffed and blinked back tears. She pulled away and said, "I'm not sad in general, really. I'm just more emotional right now than I'm used to. It's pretty stressful for me."

"Yep, it doesn't even matter what the emotion is sometimes— you get exhausted in general." He turned to the door. "Let's go to bed now, and we'll get ready to look at boats tomorrow."

"Good night, Dad."

"G'night, Lania."

Chapter Thirteen

Lania waited with her dad for Oly to get downstairs. Nerves jangled at the thought of her dad and her lover meeting. She looked around, seeing the back-alley entrance to Oly's loft space as though for the first time. She'd seen it mostly late at night and it was less than glamorous in the pallid Seattle dawn.

They leaned against his truck, and she gave him the tour of the alley. "That door," she said, pointing at a gorgeous but rusting wrought iron gate built onto the building's entrance, "leads to Louie the Blacksmith's forge. It's mostly women working there, though. They all have great biceps." Pointing at the next door on the block, she said, "That's Dead Baby Bikes. I have no idea why they liked that name. It's a bunch of punk rock bike mechanics being assholes, I think." Her dad raised an eyebrow at the ratty, headless dolls nailed around the doorframe. "On the other side of Louie's is the entrance to the Speakeasy Café. That's the living room for the neighborhood. That and the Lava Lounge."

Oly's door opened. Happiness filled her in an unexpected rush, seeing Oly and his full backpack. She had feared he would change his mind at the last minute. She saw him afresh like she had seen the rest of the environment, and she found him wonderful yet again. He nodded at them and turned to lock the door before walking over to the truck.

"Dad, this is Oly Rasmussen. Oly, Adam Marchiol." She held her breath, willing them to like each other.

"Nice to meet you, sir. Lania speaks very highly of you." Oly offered his hand.

"Just call me Adam, and nice to meet you too. You'll have to decide for yourself if she's just partial."

So far so good.

Oly looked past them at the truck. "Are we ready to go?"

Lania jumped on the hint. "Yes, indeed. Hand me your backpack and we'll take off." She opened the passenger-side door and hit the lever to fold the seat forward. The two-door extended cab had two fold down seats facing each other behind the main seats.

Oly restrained her with a hand on her shoulder. "No, you sit up front with your dad. Let me sit back here."

Lania watched him fold himself into the rear space and pile his backpack on top of her dad's duffle bag and her backpack. He didn't look comfortable at all. "We'll take turns back here."

"We can take turns driving too." Cheered by this trick for making sure Oly didn't kill himself trying to be nice, Lania tipped the seat back and climbed in.

Her dad pulled out of the parking lot. "I think I know how to get to the ferry terminal, but let me know if I make a wrong turn."

"It's all good. I'll keep an eye on you." She reached down between the seat and the door with her right hand and groped around until she found Oly's arm. He shifted and laced their fingers together.

All the way to the ferry terminal, Lania and her dad talked about the work he was doing on his house, fencing the kitchen garden and moving an interior wall for better feng shui.

Oly was silent in the backseat, and, when Lania turned her head to look at him, she realized that he had fallen fast asleep. "I guess they did work late last night. Oly's sleeping."

Her dad glanced in the rearview mirror and saw Oly's head bobbing. "This is a good time to nap. I hope he sleeps well enough that he can take a turn driving later."

In line at the ferry terminal, Oly yawned and blinked. Lania teased in a kindergarten teacher's voice. "And how are we this morning?"

Oly yawned again and rubbed his eyes. "Did I miss anything?"

Her dad said, "Nothing at all. We drove down First Street since I hadn't been in town for a while and I wanted to look around."

"And the ferry's loading."

Once aboard, Lania removed her seat belt and turned sideways so she could see them both. "Want to go up to the seating areas, or do you want to nap some more, Oly?"

"Sleep on a boat? No way! I have to check things out up there."

They walked the deck of the ferry as it made the transit across Puget Sound, the morning air brisk and energizing. A single sailboat tacked along Alki Beach. Once the ferry entered Eagle Harbor and drew near the Bainbridge Island terminal, they returned to the truck.

After they disembarked, Oly spoke up. "The Streamliner is toward downtown, so you'll want to take a left at the light." Lania's dad nodded and got into the turn lane. "It's not far down, so you can take the first parking spot you see."

He caught sight of the diner before they reached it and pulled into a parking space right next door. Lania jumped out of the truck and bounced with excitement while Oly unfolded from the backseat. "This looks awesome!"

She scoped out the very small diner. Seven Formica-topped tables lined the windowed wall. A narrow walkway separated the tables from the counter running the length of the room. It was narrowed still more by about a dozen butts on stools. There was barely room for one cook to squeeze past another behind the counter, but three people danced while flipping omelets, pulling fresh biscuits out of the oven, and chopping ingredients. It smelled heavenly inside, like coffee, garlic, potatoes, and biscuits.

She took deep breaths and nodded to the dervish of a waitress who motioned them to a table at the back. Everything had an old but well-scrubbed kind of cleanliness. Lania loved the place already, though she hadn't eaten a bite. As Lania passed along the counter, walking toward their table, one of the cooks split an avocado in two and sliced the buttery green interior into a cheese-filled omelet.

Lania and Oly seated themselves facing the room, and her dad perforce took the chair facing the back wall. The waitress glided past with an armful of plates for another table and called to them, "Coffee?"

Lania and Oly chorused, "Yes!" but her dad called, "Diet cola!" He watched the waitress, who was now busy serving three large omelets and an ornate scramble of some sort. "I wonder if she heard that…"

A skinny teenaged boy threw waters and menus on the table and, by the time they each had a menu in hand, the waitress reappeared with two coffees, a pitcher of fresh cream, and a diet cola. "Nice to see you folks. You'll see the specials up on the board there, and everything on the menu is available today…"

And she was gone again.

Lania's appetite was wide-awake, and she started down the menu, salivating by the middle of the first omelet description. "Check this out. The ABCT omelet…avocado, bacon, cheese, tomato…"

Oly was an old pro. "I always get the green eggs and cheese." Lania hunted down the menu and groaned in delight at the scrambled pesto-egg-cheese mixture. Her dad mumbled something about huevos rancheros.

When Lania had read every word of the menu and come back to the first omelet she'd looked at, she grabbed sugar for her coffee. Oly said, "I took care of that," and winked at her.

Lania sipped. "Ahhh, perfect." She sipped again and sighed with satisfaction. She caught her dad's amused look and shrugged. "So I'm spoiled…"

He started to reply, but the waitress popped back up next to them. "What'll you have, folks?"

Oly started the ordering with the green eggs and cheese, fruit instead of potatoes, and a biscuit instead of toast. Lania requested the ABCT omelet with mushrooms instead of bacon and a biscuit. When the waitress asked if she wanted sour cream on her potatoes, Lania breathed a "yes".

Her dad teased. "I'll be special and order something the way it is on the menu—the huevos rancheros, please."

The waitress winked at him and was gone. Lania rolled her eyes, but Oly said, "You should have a bite of my biscuit, Adam. They're phenomenal."

Her dad waved away the offer. "I like biscuits okay, but they're not my favorite food."

Oly lifted his hands in front of his chest. "Hey, whatever you want, but a bite wouldn't hurt, right?" He looked over at Lania. "You'll have to back me up on this once the food arrives. You'll see."

"I'll weigh in with my opinion once I've tasted these mythical biscuits."

Her dad spoke in a dry tone. "I've never known you to be shy about weighing in with any opinion. Have you noticed that, Oly?"

"She always has an opinion, as far as I've seen, but I think they're all well-considered. Some people who have something to say about everything are grabbing an excuse for attention. I don't see Lania doing that."

"Thanks. See, Dad, Oly values my opinions." Lania nodded with mock satisfaction to hide her very real pleasure. The waitress swung by with the coffee pot and filled their cups on her way to take another order.

Her dad leaned on the table. "Oly, you got that right. But it's also true that what people say isn't necessarily what they are trying to communicate. They spout famous names and quotes when they're trying to say that they're important. They dogmatically stick to weak theories to get across the idea that they're strong-minded. You have to discount their words and pay attention to the far more infantile statements they're making non-verbally. 'I'm hungry.' 'I'm tired.' Et cetera, et cetera."

Oly nodded. "I have been in conversations that went on and on before I realized that we weren't discussing anything at all. We were bantering, trying to catch each other in mistakes rather than developing or growing ideas. It happens a lot at artsy parties."

"And feminist potlucks." Lania's contribution brought a wave of laughter.

"Then there's listening, the other communication requirement." Her dad sipped his soda. "You have good ears, Oly. Where does that come from?"

Oly shrugged. "I don't know, but it's crucial in making documentaries. Creating a whole film from the answer portion of a question-and-answer session requires the interviewer to be as quiet as possible. I have to spark others to talk rather than speaking for myself directly."

"I'd call what you do non-verbal communication. I'm sure you speak for yourself in your work, even if your voice is never heard."

Oly narrowed his eyes thoughtfully.

Lania watched Oly and her dad delve into whether non-verbal communication could be used to express complex, abstract ideas. She was impressed at how well they were getting along, and Oly held his own with her dad's philosophical style. Chitchat didn't last long around her dad.

When the waitress returned with their food, Lania thanked her with the proper enthusiasm. Lania spread the sour cream across her omelet and potatoes and then stopped to shoot Oly a significant look. "Okay, then. The moment of truth." She split her biscuit in half and spread butter and raspberry freezer jam on each side. She lifted one five-inch circle to her mouth and paused, making sure she had the attention of the men with her. Slowly, carefully, she took a single bite and set down the biscuit. Moaning, Lania allowed her eyes to roll back in her head and slumped down in her chair. "Heaven," she proclaimed, lifting the biscuit for her dad to try.

He broke a corner off the biscuit and ate it. "Damn," he said, looking at his plate. "How am I going to eat all this food, plus a biscuit?"

Oly and Lania jeered and teased him while he gestured at the waitress. With tremendous gravity, he mimed to her across the room that he wanted a biscuit and folded his hands in thanks when she winked and nodded.

Subjects flowed by like leaves on a river, each getting its share of focus and then being supplanted by the next. Lania felt a strange joy that Oly handled the conversation deftly. Most people felt that her dad was a bit much with his refusal to mouth platitudes or smooth conversations with facile agreement.

Eventually, they sat back and looked over the detritus of the meal. Oly had finished all his food; her dad had left little of his main dish and the biscuit was long gone. Lania groaned as she eyed the remaining third of her amazing omelet. "Who do they think they're feeding—King Kong? I want to eat every crumb. I just can't." She looked at Oly and then at her dad. "Want some?"

Oly scoffed and her dad patted his round stomach. When the waitress swept by to drop the check and pick up plates, she looked at Lania and teased, "A little girl like you needs to eat up. What are you doing, honey, trying to waste away?" While Lania laughed, the waitress disappeared again, taking all the evidence of their meal with her.

Her dad said, "Oly, you were right. This place is out of sight."

Lania moaned. "I've never had a better breakfast. I wish it were more accessible!"

"I'm glad it's small and out of the way," Oly admitted. "Keeps it real."

Her dad picked up the check and fended off Lania's protests. "This one is my treat."

"But this whole trip is for me. I feel like I should cover most of the expenses."

Her dad forestalled any further debate. "This is a vacation, honey. You two just gave me the best conversation I've had in months. Don't begrudge me the honor of treating you now and then on this trip or we'll end up fighting in a lot of restaurants."

Oly watched the familiar debate alertly and put in his two cents. "This has been a great conversation. I like how your mind works, Adam."

Lania gave in since she seemed to have no other choice. Her dad and Oly had gelled. The three of them would have a wonderful time wandering around, looking at boats.

Once they got moving again, her dad still in the driver's seat but Lania in the backseat of the truck, Oly twisted sideways and asked about her plans.

"Oh, I have the *48° North*, but I want to go to the sales docks in Port Townsend before we leave the Peninsula. There are a lot of wooden boats around there, though the prices seem a bit high."

Her dad asked, "Do you have some sort of guide for us to follow when we're looking at boats?"

"Kind of. I have a list of qualities I want in a boat, but how we move through one to inspect it is up for grabs. Oly and I have developed a pretty good rhythm, so maybe you should focus on getting a feel for boats in general before you take on a specific part."

"Are you interested in pilothouses? What kind of keel style are you looking for? What kind of sailing rig?"

"I didn't know you knew anything about sailing!"

"I couldn't allow myself to be relegated to the role of chauffeur, could I? I've been studying up on the Internet ever since you mentioned the boat thing to me. I didn't realize how much there was to consider."

"You're amazing. So now you're the expert, eh?"

"I'm sure I'm not," he said. "I've never been on a sailboat—only motor boats, and those were fishing vessels."

Oly looked taken aback. "You've never been sailing?"

"Never. But that's about to change."

Adam stepped off the third boat on the sales dock. "Full, modified full, or split keel, propane stove with at least two burners, lots of storage, inboard diesel engine, masthead rig—preferably cutter rigged, roller-furled headsail, plumbed-in head, and a partridge in a pear tree…" He straightened slowly.

Oly tipped an imaginary hat at him. "For having stepped off your third sailboat ever, you're getting the swing of things quickly!"

"All that reading I did was dust in the wind once I got on that first boat. It seemed like such a sensible design when I was looking at pictures and plans online, but once you're below, it's just…"

Oly waited and then provided, "Sterile? Bathtub-like? Small?"

"All of the above." Adam looked around. Lania was still aboard and out of earshot. "Do you think this will work out for her? This seems like a strange way to live."

"Yeah. I really think she can make a go of it. Most people could never live like this, but Lania doesn't need all of the luxuries most people take for granted. She'll happily, gratefully, adjust her expectations to match her environment, and she'll always find the best in the situation. I think Lania can do anything and make herself and other people happy."

"Sure, she can make the best out of anything, but will she enjoy it? Would you enjoy living on a boat?"

Oly studied the Canadian horizon across the Strait of Juan de Fuca. "I would love it. I've dreamed about living on a boat since the trip I made with my uncle." He turned to look at Adam. "You have to understand—the inside of the boat is small, but the world is large. When you live on a blue water sailboat, you're not living in the boat as much as you're living in the world. You aren't bounded by walls and streets and doors that are closed and locked. Everything is wide open."

Saying it out loud, it sounded like the perfect life. Lania was going to do something that Oly would love to be part of, though he was torn about the idea in a way that she wasn't. She never talked about leaving in terms of what would be left behind. Oly couldn't help but do the math and find the equation disturbing.

"Lania! You done down there, girl?" Adam called.

Lania popped her head up through the companionway hatch. She waved the boat's log at him. "Sorry, I got caught up in reading about this guy's sailing adventures. He took good notes of the sails he did, and he sure did hit some bad weather!"

Oly asked, "Is this boat in the running?"

"Oh, no. It's all wrong somehow. I can't even pinpoint it. It's not built for me. Everything is uncomfortable."

Adam said, "Well, come on, then. Let's blow this taco stand!"

"All right," Lania called, ducking back into the boat to replace the log. She bounced out into the cockpit and then stepped onto the dock. She shook her head and waved at the boat broker, who watched from the window in his office, before turning away with Adam and Oly to walk back to the truck.

"That's the first dock, and I've learned even more about what I want. Even if I don't find my dream boat on this trip, it's already proving to be worthwhile." She looked at them. "I hope it works out for you guys too. Thanks so much for doing this with me. It's so much more fun with you two helping!"

Adam said, "I'm enjoying myself and I've been thinking. I hope you'll start looking at boats even if they're a bit out of your price range or a little bigger than you were thinking. Looking at more boats couldn't hurt. You might find features you like. Maybe ideas for customizing whatever boat you end up with. What do you think, Oly?"

"Yeah, you're not going to see a big enough variety if you stick to your specifics. And it wouldn't hurt to look at boats that are a little bigger but can still be single-handed."

"So, did you want to stay the night here or in Port Angeles?" Adam asked, changing the subject before she could agree or disagree.

Lania said, "I had thought we'd stay here, but the hotels are fancier than we need. There are cheaper places in Port Angeles."

"Then how about we go to another dock or two and then grab a late lunch before heading over to Port Angeles?" Adam squinted in the noon sun.

Oly agreed. "That sounds great. I'm not hungry yet. That was a huge breakfast."

Lania hummed in agreement. "Huge. And delicious. God, that was good! I don't want to risk eating, since anything else is bound to be anticlimactic."

"Now I'm starving," said Oly from the backseat around four thirty that afternoon. He was ready to mutiny. They had looked at a few more boats, but they agreed that Port Townsend was too touristy and so had headed out toward Port Angeles.

"Mexican food," Lania said. "I want a burrito."

Adam said, "Hold your horses. We're almost there."

They drove through the outskirts of Port Angeles, where cheap motels lined the highway. The motel row came to an abrupt end and the water came into view. Right before the sign for the ferry, Lania pointed at a sombrero. "Dad. Park there."

After they were out of the truck, Oly ratcheted upright. "I'm glad I don't have much farther to ride today. That backseat gets old after a while."

Lania tsked. "I offered to ride back there. I fit fine."

Oly growled and grabbed her around the waist. "Your butt can't be any more comfortable on that little seat than mine."

Lania rolled her eyes at him. "Yes, but I have so much padding that my legs don't fall asleep like yours do."

Adam shooed them toward the door. "Take it inside, kiddos. Enough of this flirting!"

Between chips and salsa and a marvelous seafood burrito that Oly and Lania shared, Lania managed to make an exhaustive list of the features she liked on the boats they'd seen so far. Chattering throughout the meal, she dominated the conversation and kept them talking about boats until the check arrived. Oly nodded over his soda.

"Dad, whatever motel you drive up to is fine. Just pick one, okay?" Lania asked.

Adam agreed and herded them back to the truck. He drove straight to a decent-looking chain motel and pulled into the check-in area. Lania went in with him, but Oly sat in the truck trying to keep himself awake. They got one room with two beds, and he and Lania were to share one bed while Adam slept in the other. Oly hadn't thought about the room arrangements much, but his slight disappointment faded. He wouldn't have the energy to get sexy with Lania anyway. Oly fell onto the bed that appeared in front of him and slept.

❖

Oly awoke, alone in a dim motel room, face down on the edge of the bed with a limp arm hanging over. He closed his dry mouth and tried to swallow. He wiped his crusted eyes with a hand that tingled from being hung low. Who knew how long he had been in that position.

He heaved his legs over and levered himself into a seated position as his feet hit the floor. He felt foggy and hung over, though he'd done no drinking. He stood and walked past the vanity with the sink into the room with the toilet and shower. He shucked his boxer-briefs and stepped into the shower, eyes still half-closed.

Slouching against the wall of the shower, Oly turned the hot water knob and jumped when a stream of cold water deluged his chest. He knocked the nozzle to the side and held his hand under the flow while the water warmed. The cold water felt refreshing on his hand, and he turned the cold knob on partway once the water showed signs of losing its bitter chill. When the water was cool but not cold, he centered the nozzle and stepped under the stream, sighing.

As Oly ducked his head into the rejuvenating waterfall, his brain kicked into low gear. Boat shopping. Right.

Lania had showered already, because her soap was sitting on the tray. Oly used it, lathering himself up and rinsing away his fog and fatigue. He let the water stream over him, thinking of his accomplishments over the last two days.

Jeremy and Oly had worked hard, concentrating in order to finish organizing everything from the filming period into clumps that matched Oly's storyboard of how the film would proceed. They marked, labeled, moved, heaved, and exclaimed over lost bits and pieces all day and far into the night. When they got done, they had moved every bit of material into the editing studio's storeroom, all accessible and comprehensible. It was also four thirty in the morning, and Oly had begged a ride home from Jeremy in the van even though his loft was in the opposite direction from Jeremy's.

Oly had showered, brushed his teeth, and packed some clothing and a toothbrush into his backpack by the time Lania called from the parking lot downstairs. After they spoke, he had stood for a blank moment, swaying in the gloomy Seattle dawn, before taking a deep breath and heading downstairs.

His short nap on the way to the ferry terminal hadn't helped. The salt air on the ferry and the coffee at the Streamliner had worked much better. He had gotten through his first day with Lania's dad, and he was pretty damn proud of himself.

Oly turned off the shower when guilt for wasting water pricked. As he rubbed his body dry, he thought about Adam. He was demanding in conversation—that was for sure. It was a challenge, keeping up, but it went okay. Oly wrapped the towel around his hips and opened the door.

The room had been transformed. Adam and Lania had returned and opened the drapes. Bright sunlight flooded the mess of rumpled bedding and the jumbled pile of bagels, muffins, and Danishes on the little table. They had raided some sort of "continental buffet" and brought back the breads, a little paper bowl of cereal, and plastic cups full of milk and juices.

Lania said, "Good morning. I thought I was going to have to wake you up if we were going to make the morning ferry."

Oly walked to his backpack.

His top surgery was six years ago—or was it seven?—and he rarely felt uncomfortable going bare-chested anymore. There was always a part of him, though, that held an awareness of the reactions he got. He'd gone with the half-sleeves, in part, to give people something else to look at.

Adam did the expected by looking at his chest, but also handled himself well by leaving it at a casual checking-out. Oly didn't know if Adam knew any other trans guys, but he'd responded to Oly as a man so far. Oly knew that the developed muscles of his shoulders, chest, and belly were perceived as masculine by most people, so the scars were the thing Adam might have gotten hung up on. Being Lania's dad, it would be more than usually awkward if Oly had to school him.

Oly grabbed a change of clothes and headed back into the bathroom, nodding at Adam on the way. He heard Adam talking, but his words were muffled by the door, and Oly couldn't make them out. He wondered if it was a joke about how much he slept. If they only knew how well I'm doing, he thought.

Once clothed, Oly stepped out of the bathroom and walked to Lania, giving her a tender kiss on the lips. "Thanks for bringing breakfast, guys. I was surprised we were all sharing a room, but if it means breakfast in bed…"

Lania handed him a cup. "The coffee is terrible, as always, but we can get more when we're waiting for the ferry. Or on the ferry, for that matter."

Adam said, "What's a shared room among family? None of us are rich enough to be upset by having to listen to each other snore."

Oly sipped at the weak brown water passing as coffee. He grabbed a plate of assorted bread products and started munching, turning the idea of family in his head.

He followed Adam at the sink, brushing his teeth and feeling like a new man. He stretched and turned, working a residual stiffness out of his muscles. Lania had retrieved his boxer-briefs from the bathroom along with her soap, and Oly stuffed them into a separate pocket of his backpack along with the previous day's shirt. In short order, everyone was ready to go.

Oly tossed his backpack into the back of the truck and stepped back through the hotel room doorway. "Idiot check," he said.

"What did you call me?" Lania pretended to be insulted.

"We have to make sure we're not leaving anything." He tossed all the blankets around and checked under the beds, looked into the shower and under the sink vanity. "Got it all."

The sweet affection in Lania's look blew the last of the fog from his brain. He'd been apprehensive about being stuck with a girlfriend holding a grudge and her protective father. He'd misjudged her.

Oly climbed in the backseat of the truck before Lania could object. "It's a short ride to the terminal. You can sit back here on the other side of the ferry ride."

He wanted a little quiet time. He liked her dad, he liked her magazine, hell, he liked her toes and her hair and everything in between. Oly ignored the conversation between Adam and Lania as they drove the short distance to the terminal. This trip felt like an alternate reality, one where he and Lania were going to buy a boat together and commit to each other. One where Adam was family and the future soared out ahead into the wide blue. Fucking scary.

Focus on the film, he reminded himself.

They had forty-five minutes before the ferry would load, so they left the truck in line and walked across the street to get some real coffee at an espresso stand. Adam dragged Oly into conversation with the simple expedient of asking about his film. Oly was happy to turn his attention that direction. That conversation lasted while they returned to the truck, loaded onto the ferry, and took off, Adam asking detailed questions and Oly talking over the work, done and yet to be done.

Adam said, "It sounds like there's nothing you can't handle. The big question at this point is who's going to pay to release the film. Is that right?"

Oly nodded and glanced at Lania. He knew that she was confused by his hot and cold behavior. The whole topic of networking and distribution was a land mine to him. "But right now, we have a much different question to answer—where is Lania's boat?"

Adam allowed himself to be deflected from the sore subject, and they spent the rest of the ride talking about boats. When the ferry glided around the headland into Victoria Harbor, little water taxis zipped around the dozens of boats plying the waters. There were sailboats, fishing boats, old schooners that were floating museums, and a huge, flat boat with a sign that declared, "Glass-bottomed boat—see the sea creatures in their own environment." They watched the menagerie until the ship's captain announced that it was time to return to their vehicles and prepare to disembark.

The Victorian-era city was a fascinating mixture of touristy and homey, spiced by the cottages that graced the areas around the water. Victoria blended small town mood with a cosmopolitan aura and variety in the ethnicity of the people, food, and languages. The downtown waterfront held no sales docks, but they had a great view of the bronzed capitol building and world-famous Empress Hotel.

❖

At that night's motel in Victoria, Lania circled a dozen boat listings that looked good, some of which were bigger than she was thinking, while Oly and her dad watched a movie on cable. They had looked over two boats that day. While nice enough, neither jumped out and demanded to be purchased. The second guy had given her a copy of the local sailing magazine, and Lania read it from cover to cover.

At the knock on the door, she scrambled to her feet and pulled her wallet out. She opened the door and smelled pizza. "You're just in time! I was about to die of hunger!"

The pizza boy blinked at her exuberance and made change with fumbling fingers. She pushed a few of the bills back into his hand and thanked him before shutting the door in his face.

Oly pushed up from his reclining position against the headboard of one of the beds and teased her. "Do you know what you do to poor boys like that? Give them a glimpse of heaven and then deny them entry. You're such a heartbreaker."

"I'm friendly. What can I say?"

Oly stood and hugged her from behind as she set the pizza on the foot of the bed. He nuzzled her behind the ear and murmured, "I'd be crushed if you left me out in the cold like that."

Lania turned in his arms. "You're partial."

"That doesn't mean I'm wrong."

"Yes, you are. A heartbreaker? I would never be like that."

Her dad said, "Come on, you two, eat some pizza before I get greedy and forget to leave you any."

Lania sat next to the open pizza box and pulled a piece of pizza out of the circle. She propped the end up with her other hand and took a bite, enjoying the garlicy sauce and thick cheese. Her dad asked, "Why are you upset by the idea of being a heartbreaker?"

Lania pursed her lips and shook her head. "I think it's more about the idea of being a tease. Most of my friends in high school were guys, and a tease was the worst kind of girl in the world. I think I took that to heart." She sighed. "It's only been recently that I've been comfortable flirting at all."

Oly stared at her in surprise. "Lania, you're one of the most flirtatious women I know."

Her dad said, "Always have been."

"What do you think that felt like to that pizza boy? A beautiful woman opens a motel room door and starts calling him her savior." He lifted his hand to stop her. "I know you didn't actually say that, but I know that's what I would have heard in your tone. You're such an emotionally expressive person that people feel picked up by your mood."

"But that's not flirting. It's not like hitting on someone at a party. I like to make people happy."

Her dad said, "A straight man between the ages of eight and a hundred gets a glow when a lovely young woman broadcasts happiness his direction. And he's going to interpret it as flirting."

"So do a lot of the women you meet," Oly said. "Think of it this way. There's flirting with intent—the kind of thing you do when you're hitting on someone. That's what you seem to be thinking of as flirting. Then there's light flirting where you're interacting playfully with someone when there's a sexual undertone on one or both sides. There's no intention of doing anything but flirting."

"You've put a lot of thought into this," Lania said. "Which girlfriend did you whip that up for?"

Her dad choked on his pizza. Oly said, "I've had a jealous girlfriend or two in my time."

Lania tipped her head to one side. "You've never mentioned this before. Do you feel uncomfortable when I do that kind of flirting in front of you?"

Her dad raised his eyebrows. "Am I in the way here? Seems like this is getting personal."

Oly shook his head. "No way. This is only peripherally about me. We're still talking about Lania here." He turned back to her and said, "You're either on or off. Like at parties. One minute you're standing by yourself holding your drink and the next you're deep into conversation with someone whose head is reeling. It bothers me more when you're alone than when you're talking. I do keep an eye on folks who look like they might try to press you for more attention." When her dad nodded, Oly turned to him. "Do you watch out for her like that too?"

"Definitely. Men don't push her if they realize that I'm her dad, but I've sent warning looks a time or two through the years. I'm probably less aware when it's a woman. Hard for me to think of a woman as being threatening."

"You two are protecting me from random men who might want to flirt with me? What if I wanted to flirt back?"

Her dad shook his head. "That's the thing, honey. They interpret your behavior as flirting, but you don't realize it. Besides, I only do it when someone gives me a bad feeling, and you're onto those guys before I am."

"Well, I'm glad to hear I do something right," Lania said.

Oly said, "Really, it's you being, emotionally, the same kind of person Adam is intellectually." They both looked at him questioningly. "Naked, honest, unprotected. Adam, you don't pull punches and you don't hide your ideas in case you'll be made to rethink something. Lania, you express feelings openly in a way that most people associate with close relationships. You both encourage people to feel like they've known you for years and like they matter deeply to you. It's intimidating, but it's also exciting and attractive."

Her dad said, "I never thought of that as a similarity in us. A very good insight, Oly."

"See what I mean? You're right here, listening to what I'm saying and integrating that into yourself, real time. You're not tucking it away to chew over in private, where you won't be shamed by changing your mind or learning something."

He frowned. "It's not shameful to learn."

"But how many people act like it is?" Oly asked. "Maybe learning represents gaps in their knowledge to them. Maybe they feel like admitting to learning is admitting to ignorance."

Lania said, "And most people ignore feelings altogether." She hummed, assimilating new self-knowledge and seeing her dad and herself differently. "Wow."

Her dad looked at Oly with respect. "Good eye, Oly. Good eye."

"It's not hard for me to see. This is what I do as a documentarian. Look for the relationships, the ties between people and ideas and action. Lania's openness is one of the things I…" Oly stumbled. "…appreciate about her so much."

CHAPTER FOURTEEN

A fresh breeze stirred the hair teased from Lania's ponytail. She turned her face into the wind, allowing the loose curls to be blown back from her face. The salt tang in the air was the icing on the cake. She was sailing in the Strait of Georgia.

Since Oly had shut down the engine following the owner's directions, Lania had been immersed in the soft susurration of the water against the hull, the tug and heel from the wind in the sails. This was it. She was sailing.

Lania corrected her course a bit as a wave pushed them sideways. She felt the sails lose a fraction of their power as the boat came too far toward the wind and corrected back before they began to vibrate. A sharp, clear feeling surged through her at her deft maneuvering. She caught a look from Oly. He grinned at her as though he had felt her catch the wind.

"Belay there, matey. You'll want to be watchin' yer sass now that Capt'n Lania's at the helm."

Oly swept an imaginary hat from his head and held it to his chest. "Aye aye, sir. I mean ma'am. Put me to work!"

Lania complied with his request. "Tighten the mainsheet by one turn and bring the track over a couple of inches. Let's see if this boat has any speed in her!"

Todd, the owner of the boat, goaded Lania with a blithe challenge. "Let's see if you have the skill to squeeze some more speed out of her!"

Lania sent a mock-ferocious grimace at the young boat owner and pulled the helm a little further into the wind. Oly's laughter rang over the building sound of waves breaking on the bow as their speed increased slowly but surely. Lania concentrated on riding the very edge between luffing the sails and losing headway by falling off the wind. They raced over the choppy bay waters, the deep green-blue signifying great depth under the keel.

Lania exulted in the waves of excitement flowing through her while keeping an eye on the wind, the shoreline, and the snaking line where a lighter color signified shallower water. She felt each individual muscle in her calves flex and stretch in minute balancing adjustments as the boat surged through the water, creating momentary clouds of prismatic water droplets that burst into the air and rained onto the boat.

A determined sunbeam powered its way through the patchy clouds and lit the bay in front of them. Lania aimed for the sunny water and felt the glorious mix of control over the elements and dependency on them that exemplified sailing in her heart. She was so full of sensation and emotion that she wanted to cry, to scream, to laugh, to dance. Never had she been so fully immersed in the act of sailing—never before had the mechanics of sailing felt so automatic and embedded in her muscles that she only had to think of reacting to find that she already had reacted.

The joy that swept her was amplified by her partner in sailing, Oly. He tuned the sails, making small adjustments every few minutes. He read her mind, providing the extra bit of power she wanted in the perfect moment. Her will blended with his to speed them over the lightening waters.

Suddenly, they reached the path of the sunbeam and Oly's eyes glowed. Lania's chest tightened with a rush of emotion. She could feel herself radiating love, enhancing the connectedness she was feeling in that moment. Fear and dizziness overtook her as the strength of her emotion stole her breath.

Oly looked shaken. He sat and put a steadying hand on the cockpit coaming. Lania shook from the strength of her feelings. She struggled to bring herself back under control, and she fought a primitive desire to flee. "Dad," she yelled toward the bow. "Dad, come and take the wheel."

Todd followed her dad back to the cockpit, a crouching, stop-and-go procedure that took advantage of every handhold along the way. Her dad looked excited but serious and said to Todd, "Stick around and give me pointers, okay?"

Todd started giving him the basic lecture on steering a sailboat. Lania slipped out from behind the wheel as her dad took her place. Todd eased the sails and directed him to head off the wind a bit more for an easier point of sail. Lania and Oly had pushed the boat for all she was worth, but her dad's first stint at the helm could be made easier by changing the sail trim.

Lania gave in to her flight instinct, heading toward the bow. As she stepped out of the cockpit and made her way with care along the cabin side, she let the rolling motion of the boat ease the tension from her body. She focused on the boat—the fiberglass deck and stainless steel lifeline stanchions. She glanced at the water, looking into the pale tips of the small waves. She gained the bow and sat on the foredeck, leaning her back against the mast.

Lania allowed the boat to rock the last of her tension away. She avoided thinking about what she had experienced. Her gaze roamed the expanse of jib buoyed in the air above her.

She felt Oly's approach before she saw him. He sat next to her on the deck and took her hand in his. Palm to palm, he leaned his shoulder next to hers and sighed. Lania's slight tension eased as she realized that he wasn't going to try to talk about the communion they had shared. They sat in silence as a far more insidious, far more comfortable spell bound them inextricably close.

After some time, Lania heard Todd call from the cockpit. "We're going to tack!"

Lania waved acknowledgement and remained seated. Finally, she lowered her head and focused on their linked hands. She brought her other hand over to capture his between hers and caressed his knuckles, his fingers, his palm. She brought the back of his hand to her cheek and rubbed her softness on the long bones of his hand. He felt so strong.

Todd and her dad carried on in the cockpit, tacking time after time so that her dad could practice both at the helm and on the winches. The bobbing, darting motion dislodged Lania from her comfortable position and she lifted an eyebrow at Oly.

He replied to the silent question. "Let's rejoin the party." His undoubted strength was visible in his arms and shoulders, but his face showed vulnerability. Lania leaned into the crook of his neck for a moment before pulling away to stand. Oly followed Lania along the windward side of the boat.

As they tumbled into the cockpit and took seats on the coaming, her dad demanded, "Did you see that? I did the steering and tacked the sheets myself."

"Brilliant, for a mere swabbo."

"Right, Oly. He barely even almost killed us."

Todd said, "He picked this up fast for a life-long landlubber." He stretched and leaned back in satisfaction. "The only problem with single-handing is doing all the work. It's nice having a crew full of people who want to do the hard parts."

Lania said, "Want to? I thought we were obeying in order to avoid the lash."

Oly sat up straight. "I thought we were obeying so we'd get some rum!"

Her dad said, "You call this hard? This is a walk in the park. When I was a child, I had to walk to school, uphill both ways, barefoot in the snow!"

Lania rolled her eyes and Todd nodded, serious. "You're right, sir. I wouldn't dream of calling this work. Except, of course, when I'm by myself, it's raining, the wind is howling, the sail is jammed and won't come down, and the sheets are tangled."

Her dad held his hands up. "That might—might!—qualify as work. But I think you want to give in anyway, before I start pulling out my longer stories of hardship and struggle in the olden days."

Oly muttered at Todd, mock alarm written across his face, "Don't push this, man. He will wear you down with sheer verbiage, battering your ears until you weep and gnash your teeth in pain and desperation."

"You better believe it." Her dad smirked.

Lania rolled her eyes again. "Looks like we're headed back to Sydney?" she said with a questioning lilt.

Todd nodded. "I have a dinner date. When you came to see the boat, I was annoyed that I might not have time to go sailing today. You were so fast figuring out that you didn't want to buy it that I invited you to sail with me from plain gratitude. I'm glad I did, though. This has been fun."

"Yes, it has. Thanks for this," Oly said. Todd took the helm and directed the others in bringing down the sails. He started the motor and brought them into dock.

Lania was quiet throughout this procedure. She couldn't stop thinking about Oly's joy in sailing and her own feeling that they could do anything together. The picture of them sailing off together wouldn't be banished from her mind, though she knew that Oly was not the type to settle down—to settle for a future based on the confines of a small boat.

The image of their smooth crewing and the still-present reverberations from the day's emotional climax followed Lania though the evening like a specter.

❖

Her dad asked, "Why are you set on traveling by yourself?"

Lania's face went hot. If Oly hadn't been watching her, she would have given her dad a hurt, exasperated look. He wasn't insensitive to their tension. What was his game?

Almost blind with her awkward mortification, Lania leaned against a piling. As the static in her head receded, she pushed herself free of the piling's support and stepped away from the two men she loved. Her dad was manipulating her, but she refused to let him win.

"I'm not determined to do everything by myself, but I think it's important to be self-sufficient," she said, modulating her voice carefully. "Whether or not I were to travel with someone else, I'd need to be able to handle the boat alone. What if the other person went overboard? What about sleeping in shifts?"

He persisted. "But you keep looking at boats with tiny berths and small interiors. There are boats that are easy to handle and roomier."

"Yes, but they cost more," she replied, half-truthfully.

"There's a boat here that looks good and isn't any more money than the boats you were looking at in Port Townsend."

"Well, let's see it."

Lania wasn't surprised that Oly remained silent. If her dad had been looking for a declaration from him, he'd failed. Whatever. If she had wanted to know what Oly thought, she would have asked him herself.

Her dad led the way to a boat down the dock from the one they had ruled out. He looked around a second before opening the companionway and climbing down.

Lania moved to the bow as usual. She checked the anchor and the forestay's attachment. Oly checked the backstay and the taffrail. They made their separate ways along the boat until they passed in the middle. Oly stopped Lania, running his hand along her cheek and then kissing her before letting her pass. Shaken, she went on with her inspection. He didn't want to talk about what kind of boat she should get, but he still cared? Fuck. Guessing at what was in his mind unbalanced her.

They went below, where her dad had been reading the maintenance log. After pulling up the cabin sole in spots and looking under cushions for mold, they ended up sitting in the main saloon around the fold-down table.

"Lania tells me that she gets her work ethic from you," Oly said.

Lania looked up in surprise at the unexpected comment

"Does she?"

"Yep. That's what she says. She and I have different ideas about that kind of thing, though." Her dad cocked his head to the side while Oly paused to make sure he had their attention. "She has a job-first, art-second way of thinking that we've talked about a lot."

Lania said, "It's true. We think about that differently."

"I feel like art should be treated like the work it is. I feel like the grants, sponsorships, and such that I get for filming are simply good investments on the part of the grantors and sponsors. Lania thinks of that as dependency in a way that regular jobs avoid."

Her dad said, "I can see where she would have gotten the idea that a productive member of society is one with a job. I believe that. The first duty of a healthy adult is to provide for their own basic needs and those of any dependents. After that, creativity, satisfaction, and happiness get their turn on the list of priorities."

"Family, love, and partnership aren't on your list at all." Oly looked him in the eye.

"Well, of course I value those things. I just don't see them as something you work on in the same way. The interpersonal aspects of life are in a separate sphere."

"But you see how a person raised on your priority lists would be focused on individual success? If a person's number one duty is to provide for all their own needs, where is the place for cooperation, partnership, and community?"

"Cooperation and such are valuable when necessary, but I stand by the idea that the strongest person is the one who can do as much for himself as possible."

Lania saw Oly's point before her dad did.

"You asked why Lania is set on traveling by herself. I'd say because you've trained her all her life to think of that as the ultimate goal. Being alone and succeeding."

"I never meant that she had to be alone. Just independent."

Lania asked, "But how do you ever stop being alone if you're focused on doing everything on your own?"

"Lania!" He sounded shocked.

"Look at you, Dad. Your marriage wasn't a real partnership, even though you were together for decades. You've been alone since you and Mom split up, dating occasionally, but never getting tangled up with anyone. I have been like that too. Oly's the first person I've dated for more than a couple of months since college."

Her dad said, "I think that a deep connection with another person is an important part of life. It's not something you schedule in, though. It happens or it doesn't. It's not a job. You don't work at it."

Lania said, "No, I think you're wrong. Being in love is a lot of work, but it is joyful labor for the most part. You don't even recognize the exertion involved until you run into a snag of some sort, and suddenly, everything becomes difficult."

Oly looked at Lania with respect. "Exactly. And because you've become accustomed to the joy, the difficulty can be devastating. Love is art. When it's going well, you don't have to strain for it and so you can undervalue the time and effort you put into it. It's only when you are eking out each and every bit of creativity or joy that you realize how much energy and dedication it takes to maintain forward momentum in either one."

Lania picked up the argument. "And just because you enjoy expending the energy doesn't mean that you're not working. Work is energy expressed in calories, and I know that I burn some calories when I'm in Quasimodo mode."

Oly caught up her hand. Her dad closed the maintenance log and stood. "You two have something there. I'm going to mull it over outside. Don't hurry for my sake, though. I'll be out by the truck." He walked up the steps to the cockpit and the boat rocked as he stepped off.

"Do you think he's upset?"

"Maybe a little. Not at you, though. You opened up a door, and he's the kind of guy who can't help but walk through it. Maybe thinking about this will change things for him."

"Maybe thinking about this can change things for us, Lania." Oly squeezed her hand. "I admire your strength so much. I would never want that to change."

"I get that. But thinking of this thing we have as deserving recognition as work…well, it feels good. It's easier for me to put it into perspective and see us as…I don't know. Regardless, I like thinking that we'll work on it."

He repeated, "We'll work on it." A shadow passed across his face. "Along with a film, a magazine, a bunch of friendships, and a couple million other calorie-burners."

She nodded, acknowledging the complications. She sighed and stood, tugging him to his feet. "Come on, this boat sucks."

"It doesn't even have a place for dishes!"

Lania groaned. "Another bullet point for my features list! This thing is going to be a hundred pages long before we finish this trip."

❖

Oly stared at the screen, rolling the trackball from side to side under his fingers. Finally, he gave in and called Adam.

"Hey, you!"

"I'm glad to hear from you. The farm is a little lonelier after spending all the time with you two."

"I'm glad we did that road trip together. Intense way to meet the dad of your girlfriend but you're intense regardless. It was good."

"I thought Victoria was a great little town. It's still more people than I want to be around every day, but surprisingly relaxing for all that."

"The last day was grueling, though, eh? The hours on the Nanaimo-Vancouver ferry were too short and the hours driving from Vancouver back to Seattle were too long."

"The last leg for me was back across the pass. Good weather makes a big difference."

"Right. I had to jump right back into work on the film and haven't been able to connect with Lania in the last couple of days. Do you know if she's thought any more about that one boat she liked?"

"I haven't heard anything from Lania. I know she had to work and she had plans with her friend Ginger. I don't know of any reason you wouldn't be able to get a hold of her. Have you tried calling?"

"No, I haven't called. She usually e-mails me sooner or later but I didn't think about the fact that it's only been a couple of days. Feels like longer. I got a bunch done but I haven't been sleeping much again."

"Are you working on the editing now? What part are you working on?"

"We're finding the bits we like best of the Train Track Pennies footage. I think we're going to need to ask them to come back in because we didn't get any good shots of Hoss during their big train song. We used an old eight-millimeter camera and turns out it has a light leak. What a waste of time and film!"

"Sorry to hear it. I'm also sorry to cut you off, but I have to get back to work here. The kitchen garden won't weed itself no matter how much I try to train it."

Oly hadn't gotten what he wanted out of that conversation, but it had been a long shot. On the other hand, he'd confirmed that he had a new friend in Adam.

❖

Later that evening, Oly gripped the phone, frustrated. "What are you talking about, Jeremy?"

"The same thing we've been talking about for weeks. I thought you were going to work this shit out so we could have some hangout time, just the two of us. Can't we go for a ride or something?"

"Not tomorrow, no. I have plans," Oly said again, exasperated.

"Okay, when?" Jeremy asked.

"I don't know."

Jeremy sighed. "Whatever. It doesn't matter. Will you at least come to Miriam's party? She did all that work getting period outfits for the reenactments, and she wants to have us around for this, okay? She even wants to meet Lania, so you can bring her."

"Thanks," he said, charged with sarcasm. "When is it?"

Oly stared across the loft at Lania. She swung her long hair out of the way while she cooked up a late breakfast on the loft's shared stove.

"It's tonight, Oly. I've only told you a thousand times."

"All right, I'll make it happen."

"Great."

"Bye."

"Bye."

Oly stared at his phone for a minute, frustrated. He knocked off early one night to hang out with Lania, and Jeremy came down on him with that shit. Oly strode over to where Lania turned the potatoes in the heavy cast iron skillet. Lania covered them again and turned to him. "What was that all about?"

"Miriam's birthday party is tonight. I have to go, and you can come if you want."

Raising one eyebrow, Lania wiped her hands on a kitchen towel and leaned her hip on the sink. "Not the prettiest invitation I've ever had," she said as Oly took two mugs from the cabinet and put them on the counter.

Oly gave her a scathing look. "Look, it's a party being thrown by one of the people who helped on the film. You might or might not have fun. You are invited, though, and I'd like you to come." He poured sugar into one of the mugs and splashed a little coffee on top. He turned and slouched against the counter, swirling the coffee to dissolve the sugar.

Lania nodded. "Okay then. What do I wear?"

Oly shrugged her off. "I don't know. I don't think it's any big deal." He turned back and topped the mug up with coffee. He filled the second mug with black coffee for himself and picked up the mugs.

"Great. Let's eat." She held herself straight and tall, maintaining a clear distance between her and his bad mood.

Oly set the coffee on the table, then grabbed plates and took a few deep breaths of the garlicky potato smell. He tried to throw off his funk.

Lania slid into a chair. "I'll go home after we eat. I know you're heading to the studio, and I want to spend some time on a new article. What time should I be ready?"

"Nine." He forced the word out, but nothing else would come. In taciturn silence, Oly thought about the easy companionship of the road trip. Running away never sounded so good.

❖

Lania turned her bike south. The tension of making sure she didn't get hit at the freeway on-ramp didn't help her mood any, and when she hit the park in front of the center, she slid to a dusty stop on the gravel.

Self-conscious but satisfied by her dramatic mountain-biker's move, Lania locked her bike to the anchor chain. She assessed the park, noting the family of strangers picnicking alongside sailors familiar to her. She raised a hand in acknowledgement when they waved, but didn't slow down to chat. She strode down the ramp and along the dock to the very end, inhaling the wet wood smell and narrowing her eyes against the cloudy glare off the water.

The floating pier dipped and swayed, notifying her of someone walking her way before she heard the footsteps. Wound up inside, she kept her back turned. Why had she called Ginger? She wasn't in the mood for chitchat, and she didn't want to take out her foul mood on anyone.

A soft hand gripped her shoulder. In a split second, the iron in her spine turned to jelly and she turned to look at Ginger.

"What's wrong, Lania?"

Lania stared at Ginger's somber face, unable to speak.

"Is it Oly?"

Lania nodded. Sniffing back a sob, she leaned against Ginger.

"Tell me what's wrong. What happened?"

A shivery laugh escaped Lania. "Nothing. It's not anything that's happened. It's just everything."

"Well, then. Tell me everything."

They walked to a bench against the central houseboat section of the Center. It smelled like sawdust and water, old papers and varnish.

Ginger asked again, "What happened?

"I fell in love."

Ginger sat, waiting for more.

Lania rolled her head on her shoulders, trying to dissipate some of her tension. "I know I love Oly. What does that even mean, though? I thought love would have momentum and a direction. Lay its own road. I'm just stumbling around in the woods here, and I hate that. It's so not me."

"It's not your usual modus operandi. Is it so terrible?"

"Yes!" Lania rubbed her face with her hands. "It's good between us. He pushes me out of my comfort zones in a way I'm getting addicted to. We have great sex."

"Braggart."

Lania shook her head. "Oly's hooked into the Seattle scene. The movie business is foreign territory to me, but I can tell that he's making it. He's sophisticated, smart…he's…it's too much, Ginger."

"What's too much?"

"He's this artistic purist, but he's making films so tons of people will see it. I don't have that kind of vision. The magazine kept me from going crazy with selling glasses, but publicity freaks me out. Expanding it hasn't ever felt like an option. I'm not sophisticated like he is. I can do the party scene, but it's not my scene. "

Ginger put her hand on Lania's arm. "You can do anything you want."

"I know." Lania rolled her eyes. "I don't mean to sound like an ass, but that's not the problem."

"You say that like there's one thing. What is it?"

"Ginger, I don't know if love is enough. My best relationship before this has been with a married woman. Dating Caroline and hanging out with her and her husband was so fucking easy. They were so in love and I felt safe."

"This isn't news, Lania. We've talked about why you loved being on the edge of that duo. You said it was like a ready-made family. I still think it was the low expectations that you enjoyed."

"You're right, of course." Lania pulled on a lock of hair that had fallen over her shoulder. "I feel this great urge to commit myself to Oly in some way. It scares the shit out of me."

"Why?"

"Fuck, Ginger. If I knew that, I'd fix it!"

Ginger stared at Lania. "So what's the real problem here? Is it loving Oly? Wanting to commit to the relationship? Or is your fear the problem?"

Lania's face tightened. The muscles in her neck corded with tension. Finally, she responded. "No."

"Fear isn't the problem?"

She looked at Ginger. "It's a problem, sure, but not the big one. I'm stuck, Ginger. I want to love him and be with him, but it's impractical."

Ginger reproached her with a look. "Are you seriously beating yourself up over practicality? Like you can plan your life as though it's a question of how to get to work this morning? Bus or bike? Well, bike is more practical, so…"

"Don't act like I'm being stupid. Isn't love supposed to get rid of these problems? It doesn't, Ginger. It doesn't!"

"What problems, Lania? You're going in circles. Tell me what you're feeling."

"I…" Lania's voice clogged.

Ginger picked up Lania's hand and squeezed it. "Take your time."

She swallowed. "Loving Oly is all tangled up with living up to the heroic view he has of me. It's all tangled up with being the person I want to be. I can't, for the life of me, figure out how to be me, the best me, and stay with him."

"You're afraid that staying with him means giving up sailing?"

"He's got so much talent and so many people counting on him. He loves sailing, but he needs film." Lania's voice broke.

"What about you, Lania? What do you need?"

"I need to dream and make my dreams come true. Just dreaming isn't enough."

"Is there room in your dream for Oly?"

"On a boat, you mean?" Lania grimaced. "We've looked at a dozen boats together, and I feel like Oly and I could make it work. I think it would be beautiful. But he's got this whole other direction. That's the thing. Love isn't paving the way like I thought it would. We were heading two different directions when we met, and it looks like we'll split up or change direction. I can't give up on sailing, and he'd have to give up on film to come with me. I can't let him do that."

"You know what you want and you don't see any compromises that work. But I think you're overstepping. You're not giving Oly the respect he deserves."

"What are you talking about?"

"You can't let him give up on film? Maybe you shouldn't ask him to give it up, but you can't forbid it. What are you going to do, break up with him if he decides he'd rather sail than keep making films? No wonder you feel so hopeless."

"Would he still be Oly if he weren't pouring his passions into a film? Would he hate himself and hate me? Would I still love him?"

Ginger sighed. "If you only love the documentary filmmaker, then I'm wrong about you."

"That's not what I meant."

"I know, but be careful. He might hear that."

"Regardless."

"Regardless, you're worried about him giving up something to be with you. That's why I said you weren't giving him enough respect. He's been making shit happen for a long time now, and I don't think he'll give it all up for a lesser life. If he wants to travel with you, it will be because he thinks it's a better road than the one he was on."

"That's a big if. And I can't sit around and wait for him to make that decision. Meanwhile, we keep fighting and it's harder all the time. I don't know if we're going to last the week, let alone adapt our dreams to one another. And at the same time, I'm drawn to him so intensely that I think about staying. It tortures me to think that way, so I have to keep planning to go alone." Lania slumped, drained.

"You are an adventurer, and I believe that you will sail off into the sunset." Ginger leaned back on the creaky bench. "It's a lonely life, though, and I wouldn't wish that for you."

"I'm not afraid of being lonely."

"Maybe you should be. Love is no small thing. What is easier to change—practicalities or your heart?"

"I'm terrified of giving any more of myself away."

"If you move slowly, you might find that you get as much as you give."

❖

Jeremy spoke while watching the band set up for the new footage they needed. "Anything else that didn't turn out, we'll have to work around it."

Oly nodded. "I know. We can't call the cast back." He clapped Jeremy on the shoulder. "We're lucky it was just this scene we did on that camera."

"We lost too much money in film and studio time because of the light leak."

"And you warned me about using the old Super-8 for Hoss's shots after it got dropped at that party."

"We're lucky that the Train Track Pennies were already booked for studio time and that they're letting us film them again."

Oly agreed, paying more attention to the band's setup. Carla moped around. When she dragged a mic cable across the floor and ended up near Oly, he stepped forward. "What's up, Carla? Are you okay?"

"I guess I was surprised to see Verona didn't come with you." She swallowed hard. "I don't like cameras."

Oly controlled his first instinct, which was to tell her to deal with it. "Verona's part of this is done, Carla. She's gone on to work on another project."

Carla shrugged. "I know." She walked off listlessly.

Oly wondered what else he'd be forced to deal with. Carla was dragging herself around the room like she wanted to die. He was no better off. Tense. Irritable. He stretched his arms over his head to loosen up.

Meanwhile, Hoss touched his bells and blocks and sheets of metal, one by one. The sounds changed as he altered the way each piece hung until he liked its effect. Below this almost Oriental background, Melody gave Carla a pep talk. When she finished with Carla, Melody grabbed Jeremy and dragged him over to Oly's corner.

"All right, guys," she said, voice soothing and strong. "If we're going to do this, we need to make it happen right now. Carla's not going to get any happier today, but she'll sound great for the next hour or so. We're going to start playing. You do whatever you want to do around us."

The band started on a warm-up piece with no words, just the three of them playing their instruments. Once their fingers had limbered up, they sang along with their playing, warming their voices as well. Suddenly, the door to the studio burst open.

"What the fuck?" Melody growled from behind her marimbas, but she fell silent when she saw who was standing in the doorway.

Verona raised her bag. "I brought my makeup. Gotta take care of you, don't I?"

Carla put her banjo down with a glad cry and dashed across the room to hug Verona. They clung together for a long moment before Verona pulled back. "No one told me you were filming again until Roshan mentioned they had gotten more film from her." She shot a censorious look in Oly's direction but grabbed Carla's arm and led her to a seat. Verona fixed Carla's hair and makeup with a fast, steady hand while Oly pretended to adjust lights. "We'll make some plans when you're done here, Carla." Verona walked her back to her place and did a little touchup on Melody. She blotted Hoss's face to get rid of some of the shine.

Verona turned to walk past Oly and Jeremy, saying, "Now you may proceed."

Melody watched Carla as Hoss started the percussion solo of their signature song. By the time Melody hit the long harmonica note of the train whistle, Oly had shivers and he knew that this recording would be perfect.

Things were working out. Maybe that would spill over on him and Lania, but it didn't seem likely. He soured, sensing the chasm between the happiness around him and his own prospects.

❖

At Miriam's party that night, Oly watched from the sidelines, observing Lania's ferocious dancing. She was mad at him; so be it.

He wasn't going to pretend to be happy when he wasn't. He regained a glimmer of humor at the thought that her dancing was some very effective therapy.

After a couple of songs, Lania tracked him down, panting and taking swigs of a drink she'd picked up somewhere. She didn't look at him, just handed him the drink. "Keep track of this for me, okay?" She plunged back into the mass of moving bodies, which had gotten larger and thicker as the hour grew later.

Friends tracked him down, and Oly conversed as best he could. He was always aware, though, of Lania. She made short trips back to finish her drinks and get fresh ones. Oly realized that she'd had four or five drinks before he picked one up and sipped it. Orange juice, straight. He shook his head. She was loosening up regardless of the lack of alcohol. She danced in a small group, trading off partners with the others and doing some of the dirtiest dancing he'd ever seen her do. Instinct said to grab her and pull her out of the seething mass of sexy dancers, but Oly turned his back and tried to get into the conversation flowing around him.

Carla and Verona had come to the party together. Oly wasn't surprised after what he'd seen that afternoon. Carla walked right up to him and asked, "What do you think? Did you get what you needed today?" She was so happy that she looked drugged.

"Everything we wanted and more."

Jeremy and Joyce walked up then, and Oly felt buried in the sudden surfeit of happy couples. Joyce clung to Jeremy's arm. She seemed out of her element, and Oly wondered if Jeremy enjoyed taking the lead for once.

Finally, almost an hour after midnight, Lania made her way back to Oly, dripping wet and exhausted. She tipped her head toward the exit and raised her eyebrows in question. Oly replied with a short nod and turned for the door without further comment.

Lania rolled her eyes at Oly's bad mood and followed him out.

They walked back to her apartment in brutal silence. A desultory rain slicked the sidewalks and brought an oily glow to the blacktop streets. Lania's sweat turned cold under her hoodie. Their footsteps echoed on the empty streets as they left the more traveled streets for the neighborhoods.

The night had not gone well. Oly had barely said three words on the walk to the party, about a dozen blocks from her apartment. She was annoyed with him for broadcasting his irritation, but that annoyance built into outright anger when she realized that he was determined to sulk in a corner.

She'd decided that he could play the wounded beast on the edge of the room, but she was going to enjoy herself if it killed her. Lania's anger and the music worked well together. She had danced, shaking out the tension and frustration. She'd used up all her savage energy on the dance floor and couldn't hold on to her anger. She also couldn't make the effort to bridge the gap between them, and hot anger settled into the cold ash of resentment as they walked.

Lania couldn't quite take the step of telling Oly to ride his bike all the way back to Belltown, but she also didn't have it in her to deal with any strong feelings. Oly seemed like he was primed for a fight, and Lania avoided anything that would give him an opportunity to attack.

Without kissing good night, Oly and Lania stripped clothing off, showered separately, and went to bed. As Lania turned toward the wall, she ached to realize that they were doing a terrible job of working on the relationship so far.

CHAPTER FIFTEEN

L ania fiddled with her spoon, turning it over and over on her napkin, leaving a coffee stain. Oly hunched over his coffee cup, taking swigs now and then. She asked, uncomfortable, "Are you going to get the same thing?"

"Yes." His tone implied of course, did you think I wouldn't want to share because we're fighting?

"Okay. I'll get the usual too." She glanced left out the window at the cloud-covered morning, having exhausted the regular conversation. She sipped her coffee, grimacing at the too-sweet taste. "You make my coffee better than I do."

He grunted and she retreated, insulted and tender. After ordering, they remained quiet and ran through two more cups of coffee. They ate their food in silence, passing the plates as usual, until the check arrived. She picked it up and stood. He stood across from her and said, looking at his backpack, "I'm going home."

Her jaw clenched in the moment before she squeezed out, "Maybe that's a good idea."

Oly's hands started to move, quick and rough, packing his layers into his backpack. He started to walk out, but then turned back. "I'll wait while you pay."

She thought, don't do me any favors, and dropped the check back on the table along with some cash. "That'll do it." She turned and grabbed her backpack. She tucked her wallet back into her pocket while they walked out, bumping empty chairs with their backpacks. They rounded the corner and stopped at the bikes. Both of them leaned in to unlock their bikes, bringing them close enough to touch, but they kept a rigid distance.

"Look," Oly said. "I'm tired of feeling like things are weird. I don't know why we're so tense lately. Why is it that as soon as we talk about wanting to be together, everything goes to shit?"

She looked deep into the bushes next to the sidewalk. "Maybe we're going too fast."

"What a cliché."

"Okay, then—what's your totally original answer to the problem?"

"I don't know. Maybe you're right. Too fast, too much, too… strong." He twisted his bicycle lock in his hands.

"Maybe we should cool off. See what it feels like to actually date for a while."

"Are you kidding me? We've been dating for two months. You mean you want to be more independent, right? Almighty independence."

Lania paled. "Or maybe we should back off to make your friends feel better? Is that a better reason?"

"This is ridiculous. If you want to back off, back off."

"Live our own lives and get together now and then."

He turned and put his hands on his handlebars. He leaned forward and looked at the ground beyond his front wheel. "Yeah. We probably need to stop acting like we've already moved in together."

He doesn't seem that concerned, she thought. My heart is breaking and he looks like he wants to get out from under some kind of weight. He never mentioned love. Was this it? The moment when he moves on? She'd been trying so hard not to wait for this horrible moment. Her silence went on a bit too long. Finally, she said, "We haven't moved in together. We just see each other a lot."

Oly's shoulders bunched and he reared his head back. "Can't I say anything without you clarifying it for me? I think we should stop for a while, okay?"

As what he said sank in, she turned and maneuvered her bicycle onto the side of the street. "Bye."

He called after her. "But call me?"

"Bye." She rode off.

Oly stood in the grim gray Seattle morning, unable to move. He couldn't do anything; he could only focus on Lania, riding away from him into the dim morning light. He was stunned by his own stupidity. What kind of idiot was he? He had fought with dozens of girlfriends, but he had never seen a fight turn so wrong, so fast. When she was long out of sight, he turned, creaking like an old man, and pedaled toward Belltown. He had a long ride ahead of him.

Lania couldn't head home, to the bed they'd slept in together and the weight of her sorrow. She turned off the main road and headed for the trail, planning a ride down to the waterfront. On the way, she detoured by the sales docks in Lake Union, but every boat looked wrong. They were too glossy or too dingy, too big or too small. Lania decided that there was no better time to run away from home. She hopped back on her bike and regained the trail, taking it all the way through Myrtle Edwards Park, along the Piers, and down to the Ferry Terminal. A Bainbridge Island ferry pulled in as she approached. She paid at the booth and rode her bike up to the loading area as the ferry started to disgorge its automotive passengers. The people in the cars looked happy and satisfied. She both scoffed at and wallowed in her maudlin feelings, knowing that she'd become tired of it sooner rather than later.

Bikes boarded first, and she tied the bike to a railing on the diamond-plate deck. For the entire ride, Lania rode the bow on the car deck, dampened by mist, feet planted. The wetness on her face masked her tears. As the ferry neared the Bainbridge Island terminal, Lania wiped her face and scrubbed her hands over her hair, spreading the salt wetness and letting it absorb into the heavy mass. She untied her bike and prepared to ride up the ramp.

At the top of the terminal driveway, Lania turned left and pedaled through the kitschy "old town" with its carefully unobtrusive buildings and expensive shops. At the Streamliner Cafe, she made another left and headed back toward the water. It had been less than a week since the breakfast she'd shared with Oly and her dad there, but it seemed long ago and far away.

She rode through the park, past a small group of houses, and downhill to the waterfront. The marina had a boat sales office, and she coasted toward the front windows where they'd posted pictures of the boats for sale. Lania browsed the photos and shook her head at the overpriced, under-rigged trash for sale. The good ones were way out of her price range, of course.

She sighed—would nothing work out today?—and locked her bike to yet another anchor chain turned into a lawn protector. Lania walked the small distance down toward the boats. She sat on a concrete slab bench, set into the landscaping where the bushes and flowers were kept low. She could see the entire marina and much of Eagle Harbor behind it from her seat.

A gentle rain began to tap on the boats and buildings. While the sound eased her tense and unhappy heart, the cold wet began to seep into her thighs where they met the concrete seat. She stood with regret and lingered another moment before heading back toward shelter.

A man emerged from the companionway hatch of a beautiful little boat. His rotund form seemed a little out of scale with the boat itself. As he heaved himself out of the cockpit and onto the dock, Lania realized he held a "For Sale" sign. He attached it to the anchor. Lania stood straighter and her mind sharpened.

"Hello! Are you selling that boat?" Lania yelled.

Startled, the man nearly hit his head on the anchor. Lania waved as he looked her direction, and he hollered back. "Yeah. Let me come to the gate." She waved her agreement and stepped toward the small awning covering the gate area.

Out of the rain, Lania got a queasy feeling in her belly. This could be the one. But what about…

"Hi there. I'm Rob." The man looked even larger now that he was closer. Lania tipped her head back and looked way up at him.

"Lania. I'm looking for a boat, and I've been thinking about getting one like yours."

"Well, do you want to take a look? There's no time like the present." Laughing at his own cliché, Rob opened the gate. "It's a great boat. I'm not sure what else I should tell you, though. I've never done this before."

Lania tried to put Rob at ease as they walked down the dock. "I'm the look around type, myself. Don't worry about putting on the salesman show. I'll ask questions if I can't see the answers."

"No problem."

"First question—why are you selling?"

"It's not big enough."

"I imagine that would be so."

Rob handed Lania aboard. "Oh, no. It's great for one person, even a large one like me. My girlfriend and I can't really be on it at the same time, though, and it's gotten too hard trying to keep up the boat and her apartment. We're looking for a bigger boat."

Lania twitched at his answer, grasping at the notion that it might be better if the second person wasn't as big as Rob. He opened the hatch and waved her inside. "I'll stay out here. The rain's slowing and I want to replace the bow lines. Look around and let me know if you have any questions."

Her brief hope was futile. It's too small for two people. It's perfect for one person. Too small or perfect.

She turned to her routine of pulling a boat apart to inspect it. The boat was perfect. It had a newly rebuilt engine, new sails, and solid rigging. It was built for world travel and could be single-handed. It even had a Monitor wind vane to steer the boat under sail.

It had everything. Except room for Oly.

What was she thinking? Hadn't they decided to cool it anyway? Yeah, but this seemed so final. Their fight had been so bitter that she thought they might really be over. Even so, moving forward without him speared her lungs with frost. It was so irrevocable. Like shutting a door.

Lania sat at the small galley table and began to thumb through the maintenance logs and then the sailing log. Rob squatted in the companionway. "Everything should be there. I've owned this boat since it was new, and it's in tip-top shape."

Lania nodded. "It all looks good." She paused, considering. "What are you asking for it?"

He named a figure, and she went very still inside. It was inside the amount that she could pay off in a couple of years. She looked at him seriously. "I can afford that. I'll need a loan, which could take a little time. Do you have time?"

Rob shifted and frowned. "Well, I don't know how much time I have. I'd love to get this sold."

Lania knew that the boat would go in moments at the price Rob was asking. "Can I make an offer on this boat? I'd like to sign something saying I get first dibs."

"I listed it in *48° North* for next month, but you know, I'd like to see you get this boat. Why don't you go find a loan and we'll talk? You have a couple of weeks before it's published and I'll keep the sign off of it for now. If you can get your loan by the time the paper comes out, it's yours. If you decide you don't want it, it's no skin off my nose. Be sure to keep me up to date, now."

"I will."

She shook his hand with as much enthusiasm as she could muster while her heart felt like it was breaking.

❖

On the ferry back, Lania accepted the thought into her mind. What about Oly? He hadn't once said he'd like to take part in her journeys. She had started thinking about him as a part of her life, but who says he was thinking the same thing? He had so much going on—so many friends and plenty of women and an entire film industry that was opening up for him. She couldn't live without traveling, and Oly agreed that sailing was a beautiful, happy way to travel. But how could he live without all the people and excitement? She'd known on some level this whole time that their lives were leading in different directions.

Somehow, she hadn't thought, in all this time since meeting Oly, of what she'd do if she found the right boat. Or to be perfectly honest, she hadn't thought she would find the boat while they were having a bad time. The picture came to her, full-blown. Inspecting the boat together and sitting below, holding hands and overcome by the excitement of smart systems, comfortable settees, gleaming rigging. Oly declaring everlasting love for her and insisting that he would follow her anywhere in the world.

She snorted. Trap him into declaring his love, would she?

She didn't want to close off any chance of making herself happy, but what could she do? She felt the fork in her life like it had been created with a knife blade, slicing her destiny into two irreconcilable tracks.

On the ferry, she sat in the relative comfort of the passenger deck, watching the rain on the glass distort the city lights as they came closer and closer. Her mind emptied and she began to feel numb. She made her way back down to her bicycle, disembarked from the ferry, and rode home in the dreary afternoon light. In her apartment, Lania rubbed her hair with a towel while changing her clothes and heating a can of soup. She sat down with the soup and her damp hair and stared into the vegetable broth, not mulling over the problem, just letting it simmer in the back of her brain.

After a while, Lania dumped out the long-cold soup and rinsed the bowl. She left it in the sink to wash later, and walked over to her laptop. She checked her e-mail, hoping against hope that Oly had written.

Lania read an e-mail from Ginger. She wanted to get together and dish about all the couples, including the surprise pairing of Hideo and Melody. The last thing she felt like doing was pretend to be okay while dissecting the love lives of everyone around her. She started to reply to tell Ginger she didn't want to hang out right away, but she couldn't think of a single good way of brushing her off without bringing her charging to the rescue with food and chattering. Ginger's idea of a lovesickness remedy was lots of food, lots of alcohol, and sex with strangers. The only thing that sounded worse was her second line of attack—romantic comedy movies. What was worse than watching movies where love triumphs over all when your heart is breaking?

Lania went to bed early and dreamed of sailing.

CHAPTER SIXTEEN

Lania woke, fuzzy-headed and confused. As she returned to reality, a trickle of excitement made its way into her consciousness. A moment later, the weight of memory returned in full. Her dilemma cracked her mind along with a headache.

The excitement was real, no matter how painful the fight with Oly was. She'd been practicing for this moment. She knew what she had to do once she found a boat she liked.

And she'd done it. She'd found the boat that could take her around the world. She muted the voice that screamed at her to stop—wait—don't destroy the only hope of keeping Oly in her life. Lania threw back her covers and started making lists. Paystubs, banking statements, credit card statements. She dressed, rehearsing the list of everything she would want to bring along while she shopped banks for loans. While her coffee brewed, Lania focused on pulling her finances into a coherent format. She found a folder and placed all the documents she thought she might need into it.

She stopped a moment, thinking, and pulled the *48° North* out of her backpack. She had read every article, advertisement, and letter to the editor of each magazine within days of its publication. She remembered several ads for banks that specialized in boat loans. She took the magazine over to her little kitchen and poured herself some coffee, stirring sugar in with a repressed thought of Oly. Lania opened the magazine and started flipping through the pages.

She found the first ad and was surprised to see that they did instant loan approvals by phone. Her heart kicked in her chest. She grabbed the folder and dialed.

Forty-five minutes later, Lania sank onto her sofa. She had run through every bank in the magazine, and every one of them had turned her down, either because of her slim credit history or because of the boat's age. More than one phone operator had laughed her off the phone. The adrenaline rush had soured in her veins.

Lania did what any good American girl did when she ran into money problems—she called her father.

"Dad! I found the boat."

"Really. Well, tell me all about it."

Lania ran down the boat's features and provided a bunch of information about the state of the rigging, cushions, engine, and galley. She told him all about Rob and how easygoing he was about waiting while she found a loan.

"What's wrong with the boat, Lania?"

"What do you mean, Dad?"

"There's something you're not telling me. Why's this man selling the boat?"

Lania pursed her lips and then sighed. "It's not big enough for both him and his girlfriend."

"And what does Oly think of this?"

"Oh, Dad. He doesn't know. We had a fight." Lania's chest filled up and started hurting.

"Tell me about it, honey."

So Lania backed up and told the story of the last few days. "That was two nights ago. I can't believe how fast we fell apart."

"I don't know what I'd do in your place, but it doesn't sound like you and Oly are done yet. You have too much affection for one another. I think the biggest problem is that you are both being dishonest about your feelings."

"I haven't lied to him about anything."

"Really, Lania? Is that true? Have you been completely truthful about how you feel? I think you've been hiding from yourself as well as from him, but it's time to decide whether you're serious about him."

"Oh, Dad, I am serious. I just don't know if he is."

"The only way to find out is to ask, but I know how hard that can be. Why don't you sleep on it for a night or two and then talk about it?"

Lania wrestled the subject back to the reason she'd called—the morning's bank hunting. "What do you think? Where should I head next?"

"Have you thought about trying our bank here?"

Lania frowned and shook her head at herself. "For a boat loan? No, I haven't. Hmm. They're the only bank in the world with any real history of me as a customer." She wrote "Safest Savings" in her notebook and circled it. "I guess it was a good thing I called."

"I don't know it if would help, but I'd be happy to co-sign for the loan if they want added guarantees."

Lania blinked and her dad's fifty years of great credit history swam before her eyes. "I'm sure I can make it happen if you help. I swear I wasn't fishing for that when I called, but it might make this deal happen."

"I didn't think it was all an elaborate plot to make me offer my backup. I do think that you'll have trouble being taken seriously. You've never bought anything but a used car; I've bought and sold four houses. They like the fact that I'm unafraid of debt." Her dad's dry humor made Lania's lips quirk.

"I'm going to head over to Safest Savings now. Thanks so much, Dad. You're the best."

Lania looked around with fresh energy. He hadn't had any answers for her problems about Oly, but talking them over with him made everything easier to think about.

Lania realized that the shorts and T-shirt she had put on for her bike ride might not be the best outfit for getting someone to give her a chunk of money. She changed into one of her plain but tidy work outfits and decided that she'd better take the bus down to the ferry terminal. The only local branch of her hometown bank was about four blocks from the boat she wanted to buy.

❖

The bank manager, Steven, was nice in all senses of the word—tidy, courteous, and concerned. "I'd like to be able to loan you this money, Lania. Unfortunately, it's not up to me. I'll need to send your application past our underwriters. They'll consider your credit history and the boat itself and approve or deny the loan based on a whole slew of factors." Lania nodded. "So let's work on narrowing down the list of negative factors, shall we? Don't think of this as faultfinding. It's clearing the road so that there are as few bumps as possible."

She was amazed at what kinds of information he gathered in the moments she sat there. She filled out the loan form, and Steven obtained a copy of her credit report. He studied the report and found an old, forgotten problem involving a hospital bill that had gone to collections. It was long paid for, but it counted against her for the loan. Steven explained what parts of her history looked bad to loan officers and asked her to write letters explaining the circumstances in each case. Lania left after an intensive hour with Steven, dazed but determined.

She stopped by her boat-to-be and sat for a while. Once she realized that the sun was going down, she sighed, stood, and stretched her tense body. She walked back to the ferry terminal and arrived just in time to catch a ferry right away. She would finish some editing on the trip.

Lania sat inside with her notebook on her lap for several minutes before she gave in and pulled out her cell phone. She dialed Oly and waited, lightheaded, for him to answer. She didn't know what she was going to say.

She heard a click and then his voice mail message began. Lania laid her head back on the seat back and tried to pull her thoughts together enough to leave a message. "Hey, Oly, it's Lania. Just checking in. Wanted to see how you are." She started to feel self-conscious and panicky. "Don't worry, you don't have to call me. Never mind. Bye."

"Fuck." Lania decided that she wasn't going to call Oly again until she could speak to him calmly. No more psychotic messages on his voice mail.

Lania put her phone away and opened the notebook to work on editing an article entitled "Gender Inequity and the Trans Experience" by a guy who wanted his byline to read "Daddy's boy trevor." He was the first trans man she'd ever known, unless there'd been others who hadn't shared their trans histories with her. She knew that the article was bound to be good. He was a great writer, and he could have been a hit in academia except that he transitioned from female to male before the queer community began getting sophisticated on trans issues. Becoming a man's man in the hothouse atmosphere of women's studies feminism had roused the academics against him, from women's studies through lit crit, the psych department, and all the way into corners of academia that had no reason to be involved in the discussion.

She sighed for the trouble he'd been through, being seen as a traitor to women. It was part of what had turned her against the whole university system, because he had so much to offer in each field. What trevor had learned from his academic studies had polished a lens that he brought to bear on his experiences of gender stereotypes and how they played out in a day-to-day way. His feminist point of view, careful training in critical thinking, and thoughtful nature had given him the opportunity to contemplate, as well as experience, life lived both as a woman and as a man.

Lania dug into the work and was proved right—this was one piece that didn't require much editing. She scribbled a few suggestions and comments in her notebook so that she and trevor could talk about the way his argument flowed. The landing of the ferry took her by surprise. The article had pulled her focus away from her problems. She owed him for those moments of peace. She gathered her notebook and backpack and prepared for the bus ride home.

❖

Hoss poured hot tea into two hand-painted china cups. "Lania, the boat isn't nearly as handsome as Oly is. I think you have your priorities messed up." He offered her the sugar bowl.

Lania grimaced at him in warning. "I told you I didn't feel like talking about my love life." She glanced around Hoss' immaculate apartment. "When is your man arriving?"

Hoss sipped his tea. "Two days."

"I'm glad you could make time for me before you got all wrapped up again."

Hoss shook his head. "You know I like you, Lania. I want you to be happy."

Lania set her tea down carefully. "I don't want to talk about it. Why is it that no one can talk about anything but who's falling in love and who's fighting?"

Hoss put a hand on her arm. "What's more fun than gossiping about love?"

"It's all well and good when love is working out."

"What else is happening for you? How's work?"

"Work is as uninteresting and predictable as ever. It's good to have a trade, especially if I need income while I'm traveling, but I'm starting to think that I'd love to focus on the magazine more. I have to sell Esmeralda to get the boat, but I have a laptop and there's freeware I could use to design *Literate Life*. Maybe people really would buy the magazine and I could make my living doing what I love."

"I know you can make it work. I'll get a subscription, if you go that direction."

"Thanks, Hoss." Lania poured herself more tea. "But then I'd need to figure out a fair way of compensating the writers and research print shops that are careful about non-toxic inks and recycled paper and fair labor practices. It sounds like a big job."

"Sounds like the job of publisher."

"The part I'd really need help with is finding enough buyers to make enough sales to have enough money to pay the writers and printers while still supporting me too. A distributor, I guess, like for Oly's film."

"I bet he'd love to help you with that. He's been a good influence on you, if you're finally considering this."

"Perhaps."

"Well, I love the idea of *Literate Life* going big time."
"Let's hope lots of other people like it too."

On the Monday after finding the boat, Lania checked with Steven at the bank. He warned her that it might take a few days since he would have to send the application back with clarification if they turned her down. Lania called Rob, the owner of her boat-to-be, and let him know that the loan was progressing.

Lania called her dad too, to bring him up to date. She had asked Steven to try it without a cosigner first and she told her dad that Steven didn't have much hope of it working without him.

Then she polished Esmeralda. She flapped a clean rag around to dislodge any dust and wiped fingerprints from the flywheel, which she could never resist touching as she passed. It only took a few minutes to have Esmeralda looking as though she'd been refurbished yesterday.

When the bell rang, she went to the intercom and buzzed them in.

She opened the door and stood inside, listening to the feet treading the stairs below her. It wasn't one set of feet—there were syncopated thuds along with the expected drumbeat. She wished he'd said he'd be bringing someone with him. She couldn't get over the sense that she was getting rid of a dear pet, pain with a tinge of shame and embarrassment.

The hand that appeared on the railing was smooth and slender, dark brown on the back and rich peach on the palm. The person who followed this hand was slender as well, though he had a respectable middle-aged paunch beginning to distort the vertical lines of his body.

As the first visitor reached the top of the stairs, he turned and grasped the elbow of the elderly lady following him. She was so upright that this seemed insulting, though her bones and tendons showed everywhere her skin did. She saw Lania and nodded a hello.

Lania called down the hallway. "Hello! Are you Mr. Timmons?"

The man held his companion's arm as they made their stately progress across the wooden planking. "I am Rudolph Timmons."

Lania waited until the pair reached the door before stepping inside and gesturing for them to follow. Mr. Timmons continued. "And this is Mrs. Rosalee Grant. She is my aunt, and she is very curious about this press of yours."

Lania's resurgent nerves made her swallow. "It's right through here."

As they walked the short distance through her apartment, Lania noticed that they had taken each other's hands. Touched by this sign of affection and wondering why they felt the need to support each other so, Lania followed them into the room. Mrs. Grant stopped in front of the press and shook her head minutely. She spoke to her nephew in a voice as soft as the skin of her neck and nearly as uneven. "Oh, I don't know, Rudolph. It's been so long since I've seen even a picture."

Mr. Timmons turned to Lania. "When I read your advertisement at the community center and saw the picture of this press, I was stunned. My family never realized that the press was still operational. George Washington, the man who commissioned this press for Centralia, was like a father to my aunt's father. My grandfather was the son of George Washington's first wife, Mary Jane, by her first husband."

Lania's nerves smoothed out and she stepped forward to take Mrs. Grant's hand. "It's so nice to meet you. I love this press and the story of its early years. I've told that story so often it feels like my own."

Mrs. Grant grasped Lania's hand and nodded at Esmeralda. "My father was the original operator of this press. He would be happy to see it in use. But my father couldn't be kept in such a small town, especially after George married that other woman and had an infant son."

"I hadn't realized he left town. You don't read anything about him in the official histories."

Mrs. Grant looked pointedly at the futon and Lania jumped, embarrassed. "Let me put this up for you."

"That's not necessary," Mrs. Grant replied with dignity, "if I may sit on it as it is."

"Of course, please do." Lania found herself being more gracious, speaking more correctly in the face of such a grand dame of the old school.

"My father left Centralia rather young. Nothing scandalous, mind you, just wanted more opportunities than he saw. Of course, what he got was another job in another print shop. It wasn't until the General Strike in 1919 that his life turned a corner." Lania felt a cold knot in her stomach. Oly's hard work, the whole film. She resented that everything came back around to Oly. "He met my mother while delivering milk during the strike and they struck each other's fancies. They were married only a year later."

Lania pulled her head out of her own problems and returned her attention to her visitors. "Mr. Timmons, I thought you were interested in buying the press. Is that so, or were you just interested in seeing it?"

"No, no," he assured her. "I wouldn't come under false pretenses. We are very interested in owning this press."

"I don't want to insult you, but I'm pretty dedicated to selling her to someone who will print with her. I'm not so sure about having her end up as an exhibit or a showpiece. No offense."

Mrs. Grant's eyebrows peaked toward the middle.

Mr. Timmons jumped in as peacemaker. "I understand that desire, indeed I do. And we are very active in the community center. Perhaps we can teach teenagers to print. We can print the newsletters ourselves."

Mrs. Grant broke in. "Why do you say *her*, dear?"

Lania explained her name for the press. Mrs. Grant and Lania compared their readings of *The Hunchback of Notre Dame*. "Of course, I read it in the original French and the hunchback is not mentioned in that title." Mrs. Grant sniffed at the American publishers' alteration of the title.

In the natural pause, Mr. Timmons reentered the conversation.

"As I think about this further, I find myself unexpectedly enthusiastic about running this press. If you will teach me to use it—beg pardon, her—I will ensure that she remains a productive press as long as I have her."

Lania goggled at this quick turnaround, but Mrs. Grant clapped. "Bravo!"

Lania also cheered, though with a heavier heart. Within a half-hour, the deal was made and a schedule set. She would finish the last hand printed edition of *Literate Life* within the next week, and after that, the press would pass out of her hands forever.

With one last gentle squeeze of Mrs. Grant's delicate hand, Lania saw them out of the apartment. She watched them emerge from the front door of the building and meander sedulously through the mid-afternoon foot traffic. Amidst all the pain of giving up Esmeralda, they represented a strong shaft of joy.

Lania sighed and turned away from the window. She could use a little more joy in her life.

She called Ginger.

"Hello, stranger."

Lania winced. "Sorry I didn't call back earlier. I know I've been a hermit for the last week. I don't have the energy to deal with anyone. And before you pretend to be insulted, I know you just want to help. But trust me, being alone will help me better than anything else."

"Whatever you say. How about a little good news? Carla and Verona aren't messing around. They've moved in together because there was a room available at Oly's loft. They snatched it up—you know how hard it is to get into that artists' community. They're still getting settled in, but Carla loves the big common room. She spent yesterday evening playing and singing out there."

"I'm glad for them."

"You don't sound glad."

"I am. I'm just preoccupied. I've been sleeping a lot and editing. I e-mailed yours—let me know what you think of the changes I made. You're brilliant, Ginger, and the 'Medicinal Slavery' article is fabulous. It's so creepy to think of people going without toilet paper in order to pay for prescriptions."

"Thanks, I think. Joyce says your edits on 'Unions vs. Cooperatives—the Us/Them Experience' are incisive and persuasive."

"High praise from her. Look, I'm going to get back to work. If you decide to overrule me and visit, bring a casserole or something. I haven't been able to force myself to cook much. There's nothing in the apartment and I don't want to deal with going to the grocery store."

"Okay, then. Whatever you think is best for you. I'll leave you alone for a while. I heard through the grapevine that Oly is working too hard. Poor thing. Wait—that sounds familiar. Who else do I know like that?"

❖

Oly pulled the headphones off. He was tired of listening to bad tape. "This has got to be cleaned up. Can we get Carla in for some sound work on Friday?"

The studio was small but well equipped. Sliders and dials carried temporary labels on blue painter's tape. From his position at Oly's elbow, Jeremy said, "Yeah, she's available. We have the studio all day, and it's available all the way through the weekend if we get stuck or want to keep going."

"Perfect. We have to get just the right quality of sound."

"I know, old but not too rough."

"Yeah." Oly considered Jeremy. "You're looking tired. Is Joyce letting you get any sleep lately?"

"Her students this quarter are writing derivative spin-offs of thoroughly-explored Syndicalist theory."

Oly waited. "And that means?"

"Oh, just that her grading goes quickly. We've had a lot of time together recently." Jeremy sat back in his chair. "Joyce tells me that Lania's not feeling well and asks how you're doing."

"What do you mean Lania's not well? Is she sick or something? What's wrong with her?"

"How am I supposed to know?"

"You have to find out for me; she isn't answering my phone calls. She better be okay or I'm going to have to check on her myself and she'll hate that."

Jeremy put a hand on Oly's arm. "How are you doing, bro? Are you okay? You don't look so good yourself, and it's not just lack of sleep."

"I'm fine. Never better. I don't get sick. I'm working hard, you know. First you want me to work harder, now you're complaining that I don't look well. I'm fine."

❖

Finally, six grueling days after applying for the loan, Steven called. "Lania, you've been approved with your dad as a cosigner. We can FedEx the documents to him after you've signed them. We'll just need to wait for a title search on the boat and then we'll be able to finalize everything!"

Lania stood, frozen in her kitchen with a spoonful of clam chowder halfway to her mouth. After a moment, Steven said, "Lania?" and she snapped out of her surprise.

"Yeah!" She dropped the spoon back into the bowl of soup with a splash. "That's great, Steven. Thanks so much for all your work."

She couldn't put it off any more. She had to tell Oly.

They each had left voice mails a few times since they'd decided to slow down. She hadn't answered his calls at work because she knew she'd end up crying. She assumed that he was avoiding her calls as well.

She got as far as dialing but stopped, realizing that she couldn't tell him about the boat over the phone.

It was Thursday, the evening that marked the start of Lania's weekend, and the time stretched before her like a void that would suck her up and empty her out if she didn't stay busy. Lania picked up her notebook and the articles she had edited. It was time for a new edition of *Literate Life*. The work would keep her from thinking in circles.

Lania turned her phone off and set to. This was going to be the last hand printed issue of *Literate Life*. Lania decided to make this last issue the best one to date. She organized the material, did some final edits, and started to lay out the magazine on pasteboard.

❖

Two days later, inky and exhausted, Lania stared at the piles of magazines. She'd brought out the type plates and set the type, one set of pages at a time. When she broke each ream of double-sized, eleven by seventeen inch paper over her knee to loosen the pages from each other, the cool smell of fresh paper wafted to her. She sat on her stool and prepared to print. She ran her right fingertips across the ceramic finger-wetter and picked up the first piece of paper. She set it in place on the platen and pushed the treadle with her foot, just like she was running an old-fashioned sewing machine. As the ponderous platen tipped toward the type bed, the inky roller swept across the type and moved back over the ink disc to prepare for the next page. The paper was pressed against the type and then the platen tipped back, picking up speed as the flywheel gained momentum. Lania grabbed the printed page with her left hand and replaced it with a fresh sheet with her right hand. As the platen tipped the new page onto the type, she dropped the fresh page onto the printed stack and tapped it even. By the time the platen leaned toward her again, she had a fresh sheet of paper in her right hand and was ready to grab the new printed page with her left. She rocked the treadle at a pace that allowed her to keep the pages moving smoothly and without pause. The flywheel kept her speed regular. The purely mechanical nature of the work lulled her, and the repetitive motion grew graceful as she loosened into the sway from fresh paper to printed sheet.

When she had printed an entire ream—five hundred and sixteen sheets—of the front and back of the magazine, pages one and thirty-six, she changed the type and printed pages two and thirty-five on the backsides of the pages she'd just finished. Repeating this process again and again, adding Gillian's woodcut of her satirical cartoon on page fourteen, she worked steadily through two eighteen-hour days. Twice, she lost her stride and the inked pages made a mess of the paper-less platen, forcing her to stop printing and clean it. Without a perfectly clean platen, the backsides of the papers she printed would get smeared with ink or show a mirror image of the correct text. Finally, the stacks surrounding her were no longer clean, empty paper. She had printed her magazine.

She spent another few hours at an actual sewing machine, saddle stitching the eighteen individual pieces of paper together and folding them to make a single, thirty-six-page, eight and a half by eleven inch magazine. Because the innermost pages pushed out a little more than the outer pages, she finished the process by putting a fresh blade on her paper cutter to even up the long edge of the finished magazines. It wasn't strictly necessary, but she liked the clean-edged look.

Every time she finished a magazine run, she felt the warm, happy satisfaction of knowing that she had touched every bit of every magazine in every pile. Five hundred and sixteen copies. A physical manifestation of hard work and determination, each issue represented so much time and effort that holding the finished product usually filled her with joy. This time, she felt more empty than excited. Desperate to fill the void, she grabbed the top magazine and read the table of contents on the cover.

Literate Life

A fucking typo on the frontispiece?

Lania toppled to her side and drew her knees up. Her breathing hitched and her throat burned. When the sobs came, she quaked from head to toe from the force. When the first deluge slowed, she crawled into bed and hugged her pillow. Esmeralda. Oly. The boat. Loss opened a black hole in her chest, and she cried loudly, painfully, abandoned in a way she hadn't experienced since she was very young. Eventually, her sobs slowed, but the tears continued until she was a mess of salt and snot, her head a thick black cloud. She dumped herself into a cold shower and bathed her swollen eyes and red cheeks until the burning was less painful.

The devastation she felt wasn't about a typo. She was proud of her accuracy with the difficult, backward type, but such a total nervous breakdown could never be spawned by a wayward letter.

Lania got out of the shower, wrapped herself in a towel, and sat on the floor next to her daybed. She reached out one toe and shoved a carefully stacked pile of magazines. They teetered, but did not fall. Unreasonably cheered by this, Lania rose to her knees and tidied the stack. She sat back and rooted around in her bedding for the phone that had been off since she'd started.

Without planning what she was going to say, Lania called Oly. "Oly, I need to talk to you. Can we meet for dinner? Call me."

Lania sat with the phone in her lap. She imagined Oly holding his phone, waiting for the message waiting beep. In her head, he called his voice mail to listen to the message.

Lania's phone rang and, unsurprised, she lifted the phone and answered it.

"Are you okay?"

"Yes, but I have some news. Can we meet at Mama's for dinner?"

"I'll go over now and get in line. You know how busy they are on Saturdays."

Lania jerked with surprise. It was Saturday. She blinked and stood, creaking. "I'm on my way. It might take me a little while; I'm feeling pretty stiff."

"Lania, are you really okay?"

"Oh, yes." Lania tried to reassure him. "I didn't mean to worry you. My throat's kind of scratchy, and I spent the last two days printing. My whole body's kind of sore."

"Maybe we should meet somewhere around your place."

"No, I'm fine. I'd rather stretch out and ride a little right now."

Lania hoped the cold air would get rid of the puffiness around her eyes, but her voice was shot. Sighing, she decided not to worry about things she couldn't change. She dressed, picked up her backpack, and set out for Mama's.

CHAPTER SEVENTEEN

Oly sat, self-consciously casual. Lania hadn't been kidding when she said she might be slow tonight. He shifted in his seat and stopped worrying about looking calm and collected when Lania saw him. He blew out a large sigh and went back to hunching over his silverware. He munched dispiritedly on some chips, but he couldn't pay enough attention to enjoy them.

Oly's eyes were rimmed with red and he had a week's worth of beard. He realized he looked pretty scruffy, but when the call came through from Lania asking to meet him, he had jumped on the opportunity. She sounded terrible, and Oly worried that she was sick.

Oly glanced up to see a surprised Lania. She looked him over and he kicked himself for not taking ten minutes to clean up before he'd dashed over to Mama's. He stood and croaked. "Lania. Hey."

She slipped into the chair across from him, and the edges of her lips twitched in a halfhearted smile. Oly's heart cracked at how unsure Lania was. She looked as rough as he felt. He realized that he had been working himself to a frazzle to keep from panicking when he considered being without Lania. Was she doing the same thing?

She pulled a copy of the magazine from her backpack and handed it to Oly. The names on the frontispiece's Table of Contents were familiar to him because of her. He'd love to keep up with some of them, even if, well, even if he and Lania didn't make it as a couple.

The waitress walked up and pulled out her order pad. She recognized them and started scribbling. "Same?" she asked halfway through writing down their order.

They both nodded, and Oly realized how bittersweet it was to be eating at a restaurant they'd shared meals at a dozen times. He put the magazine in his backpack to cover his sadness.

Lania picked up a chip and turned it over in her fingers. Oly couldn't stop staring, though he could see it made her feel awkward. "How's the editing coming?" she asked.

"We'll be done in about a week. We've been working sixteen and eighteen hours a day, putting together the film and rerecording the voiceover where we change things. Carla's been priceless." Oly's heart bumped as he realized that she had missed most of the editing process. The project that he had started without her was going to be finished without her as well.

Lania looked as sad as he felt. "Distribution?"

"That's the best part. I'm getting nibbles. Nothing definite, but there are real distribution companies talking to me at this point." Chagrin tinged his pride. "That backer was right. Most of them heard about the film because of that horrible party."

The waitress returned with their burrito and winked at them before gliding off to deliver the three platters she was carrying on her other arm. Lania ate her olive and Oly did the same. Oly speared a third olive on his fork and lifted it up to Lania's soft lips. She pulled the olive off the fork with her teeth and Oly watched her enjoy the firm flesh.

Oly cleared his throat, embarrassed at the physical effect Lania's mouth had on him. It no longer seemed natural and comfortable to want her, not if she didn't want him to. Then he saw the flush on her cheeks, on her neck. She wanted him too. A little tension eased. "Did you say you were printing? I didn't know you were so close to ready."

Lania nodded while she swallowed her bite. She hesitated a moment. "I've been in avoidance mode for the last two days." She bit her lip. He saw in her serious, searching look a hint of bad news. "It happened. I found the boat."

The words were a truck crashing through the room. His head went light and his body disappeared. He heard himself speak with surprising calm. "Tell me about it."

Lania started to describe the boat, and it sounded perfect. It had all the requirements she'd developed and they'd refined while looking at boats. It was even the keel style she'd favored, the split keel that would allow her to beach the boat to clean the bottom if she needed.

Oly could feel the complex excitement in her and was happy for her, to a certain degree. The realization that she was serious, that Lania might sail off into the sunset without him, was too large for him to focus on while continuing to give her the happy, excited support that she deserved. He tried to shake off the incipient devastation and provide all the right questions and responses as Lania chattered on about the boat of her dreams. Her dreams.

Lania told the story of getting the loan. Oly couldn't believe that all this had happened since they'd last had breakfast. He continued to nod and exclaim in all the right places, but he couldn't get past the feeling that he should have been there for the whole thing.

It hit him. He loved Lania.

Oly's next realization was that he couldn't ask her to give up her dreams for him. He couldn't leave yet, and she was already gone. He was in love with someone who wouldn't be the same person if she stayed with him. Oly realized that he couldn't play the give-it-up-for-love card. He had no cards left to play.

As Lania talked, Oly beat himself up, thinking back to the opportunities her dad had created between them over and over. Adam had practically begged Oly to talk to Lania about sailing together, but he had been too proud. He had waited for her to bring it up, and now she had started down a path that excluded him.

Oly gathered his thoughts. "Lania, this is so exciting. It's what you've been dreaming of. You're going to live your dreams." Lania's smile had a frantic edge, but Oly babbled on. "It sounds like a once-in-a-lifetime find. I'd love to see it."

"Of course, I'd love you to see it. It needs the Oly seal of approval." At her words, Oly cringed, wishing he could take it back.

The torture of approving the mechanism of his loss… "Do you want to go out to Bainbridge Island with me next Saturday? I'm going to head out there to figure out with Rob what stays and what goes. He said he could leave the bedding since it was made special for the odd-shaped berth." Lania continued to talk about the things she and Rob had discussed taking and leaving. Oly felt like every detail was another link of the chain holding him anchored to his seat.

Love's a bitch.

Lania stood at the end of the meal and stretched, tired but exhilarated. Oly slid his arms around her waist while her arms were raised in the stretch and Lania started, her eyes flying open to meet Oly's.

Lania leaned into his embrace and kissed him on the lips. The tightness in Oly's body belied the softness of his expression, and Lania said, "Let's go to the loft."

They made their way to the loft with her bike. Feeling very delicate, as though she'd had the stuffing blown out of her and wasn't sure what was going to fill her up, her touches were light and her words soft. Once she'd leaned her bike in the bike rack at the top of the stairs, Lania turned to Oly and took his hand. He led her to his room, lay on his side, and pulled her down to spoon with him, kicking his shoes off the end of the bed. Lania squirmed against him, kicking her shoes off too, and then settled her back against Oly's chest, belly, and thighs. He curled his feet under hers, as though trying to touch her in as many places as possible. She tried to permeate his skin with the love that wanted to burst out of her.

Oly pressed a kiss to the back of Lania's head, burrowing closer. He smoothed his hand along her side, stroking her as though calming a nervous animal, along her hip and down the top of her thigh.

Unable to stand the tenderness, Lania stretched out onto her back and looked into Oly's eyes. He rose to his elbow and leaned over her, taking Lania's mouth in a kiss so sweet, so tender, that

Lania's poor abused eyes welled with tears again. He licked her tears up like a kitten. His hand slid up her side and over her breast to rise and cup her chin, turning her head more his direction. He sipped at her lips and coaxed her tongue into long, slow strokes with his own.

Oly wanted Lania to give in to him, just a little. He straddled her thighs and stripped his shirt off. He placed his hands on either side of her waist and forgot what he was about. Her skin was so soft that he stroked her waist again and again until she arched her back into his touch. Reaching with one hand into the curve of her lower back, he used the other hand to slide up her spine, bringing her torso up and allowing her to pull her shirt off over her head without letting go.

He felt her abdominal muscles clench, but she couldn't hold herself up. She could only drape her arms around his shoulders, quiescent. He crouched over her, holding her delicately but with great strength, encouraging her to relax into his arms with small massaging motions of his hands.

When she gave in and let her head and arms loll back, Oly felt a primal hunger he'd never experienced, along with the tenderness. She was helpless and passive in his arms, and Oly bit at the top curve of her breasts. He pulled her close enough to feel the satin of her skin against his belly and the silk of her bra against his chest and then gave in to his urge to devour her.

Oly crushed Lania to him, growling deep in his throat as he bit his way along her shoulder to the curve in her neck. He slid his upper hand higher on her back and lifted her head into a passionate kiss that left him trembling from the work of holding back his desire.

Oly laid her back down and shifted, nudging her legs open and moving his knees between her thighs. Kneeling, sitting on his heels, he pulled her hips toward him until her ass was resting high on his thighs. Lania moaned and thrust her hips even higher on his. Her head turned on the rumpled sheet and she stared up to where her legs were split by his body and thrown out behind him. She had no purchase from which to control her movements and her restless motion was transmitted to his senses as a sinuous flexing of her back and belly.

He slid one hand under her, into the curve right above her ass. He pulled her upward at the waist until her body curved like a bow from hip to shoulder and she whimpered, trying to move her hips on his body. His love burned in him like a sun going nova, searing his every nerve ending. He placed his other hand, fingers spread wide, on her belly and slid it up. Up to her neck and then back down and around each heavy breast in turn, he stroked, dipping a finger under the edge of her bra but not allowing her the release of direct contact with her nipples. He reached under and released the clasp of her bra, drawing it off the front of her body as slowly as his uncertain control would allow.

Lania allowed her arms to come forward so Oly could have her bra, and she opened her eyes to send him a look of such hunger that he leaned down and took her nipples in his mouth, one after another, using his free hand to bring her soft, abundant breasts up to his mouth again and again. He stroked over the angry red marks left by her bra and licked, kissed, and nibbled his way around each peak.

Finally unable to control himself, Oly used both hands to lift Lania's hips and thrust his soft packing cock against the seam of Lania's tight bike pants. Lania fell back on the sheet at the rhythmic pulsing of Oly's hips between her legs and brought her own hands to her breasts. "Please, Oly. Strip me." She lifted her breasts, plucking her nipples in time with his thrusts.

Oly groaned at the sight of Lania's soft, ink-stained hands on her magnificent breasts. He leaned back and slid his hands under her ass to strip her bare. Lania lifted her legs and brought them together in front of Oly's chest, allowing him to slide her pants off and toss them to the floor.

With that one gesture, Lania was nude. Oly spread her legs again and slid back so that she was no longer lying in his lap. He silenced her immediate complaining moan by drifting down her body to bring his mouth to her hipbone. He was going to steal this moment to cement her taste and smell in his memories. Stroking her closed labia with the flat of his palm and then holding her entire vulva in his hand, Oly kissed and bit his way across her belly to her other hipbone. He stroked the seam of her with the tip of one finger, asking for her to open up. Shifting restlessly, she spread for his touch.

Oly leaned down for a taste of the soft damp flesh that begged for his attentions. He slid his finger down her cleft to the entrance of her cunt and licked from his finger up and over her clit, repeating this motion again and again, until she cried out with frustration. He took the hint and dove in to suck her hard little clit into his mouth. She groaned from deep in her belly and flexed her back in time to the touch of his tongue. He slid one finger into her and allowed her to push herself down onto his hand.

She wanted him so badly. Lania ground herself down on Oly's mouth and hand, flying toward orgasm. She panted. "Too much…" Oly drove her to the peak, and she fell into the explosion that she had known was coming.

Before she was even aware of anything but the pulsing and rockets in her body, Oly had reared above her and struggled out of his jeans. She opened her dazed eyes to see Oly's face, ferocious and driven as he moved up between her legs. She stroked her belly and watched while he replaced the soft packer with her favorite of his dildos. He lubed it up and fitted his cock at her opening. He pushed the width against her still-pulsing muscles, and her entire pelvis blossomed into another set of orgasmic clenches. Lania cried out in surprise during the paroxysm that racked her. Oly's body twitched and rocked into and above her. Her next orgasm started when his pubic bone hit her clit as he seated himself all the way inside of her. He quivered and shook like a racehorse in his own orgasm.

The slow cessation of the pulsing contractions of bodily orgasm hardly brought her out of her trance.

Barely moving, sliding in and out of Lania's body, Oly continued to stroke her. She arched to him gently, wanting it to last forever. He leaned down and kissed her, making slow, lazy love to her mouth-to-mouth.

Lania moaned at the rubbing of her over-sensitized tissues and pushed her hip up to roll Oly over.

Once on top, Lania slid slowly off the big strap-on cock. The motion brought her nipples within grasp of Oly's lips, and she sighed at the warm softness. He soothed her until she pulled free and crawled down his body.

She stripped the harness off him and kissed the strap marks. His own little cock pushed out of his lower flesh, demanding. Lania took her time, squeezing and rubbing the flesh that would have been his scrotum, biting it and pulling at it. Each tug rubbed against his cock and made him quiver.

He slid a hand into her hair and cradled the back of her head. She thought he wanted to pull her mouth down onto him, so she moved that direction and stopped just before touching him. She dropped her mouth open a little and let her tongue show. She looked up to be sure she had his full attention.

"I want to suck your cock."

He shivered and the hand in her hair clenched.

She stopped teasing him and gave them both what they wanted. She lowered her head, engulfed his cock with her hot mouth, and sucked in slow pulses. She milked it with her lips and tongue in rhythm with the suction. Her cunt pulsed in sympathetic beats.

Lania pulled her mouth off Oly's cock with exquisite slowness and slid to the floor next to his bed. She tugged his legs down on either side of her and pulled his hips partway off the side of the bed. He pulled a pillow over to raise his head off the bed. Her access was better in this position, and Lania sucked down Oly's cock again. She started a slow, twisting bouncing with her head and Oly responded with an undulation of his hips. His legs fell further apart and Lania took the invitation.

Lania ran her knuckles over his front hole without interrupting the cocksucking she was doing. He was creamy, so she pressed three curved fingers into his hole.

Oly rolled his hips down onto those fingers, and closed his eyes under the barrage of sensation.

The squeezing walls pulled her fingertips together and, in a way that amazed her, aimed them for the rough spot at the front. Past being coy, past wanting to tease him or draw out the pleasure, Lania pulled hard on that spot at the same time she slid her mouth all the way down onto his cock.

The groan that ripped from Oly confirmed the feedback his body gave her. His cock swelled even harder. His legs flexed and his abs turned to rock. His hands thrust into Lania's hair and she smashed his cock against the roof of her mouth in response.

Then she set up for the ride.

She pulled with her fingers and sucked down his cock, then slid her fingers out of his hole a little and pulled off his cock until just the tip of her tongue was touching it. She waited until he opened his dazed eyes, then stared into them while she repeated the down and up.

He pulled her head down on his cock again, biceps carved with tension. He softened and tensed inside, and Lania wasn't surprised when he said, "More."

Another finger was easy. Lania stroked his cock with her lips and tongue while pressing her knuckles against the ring of his front hole. She slipped her thumb into the space created by her squeezed fingers and Oly swallowed her hand to the wrist.

Now it was the bone of her thumb that pressed on that spot inside and he cried out from the intensity. Lania met his thrusting hips with her mouth, grinding down on his cock and pulling what suction she could with his fevered movement. Pulling her hand into his tight front wall also pulled her down on his cock, and she let the violence of his motion set the pace. She pounded him inside and outside, and he responded with swelling like she'd never seen.

"I'm gonna come." He ground out the words, and she hesitated a split second, unsure of what to do. He jerked at the break in the rhythm, and his desperation rang in his voice. "Pull your hand out and milk it with your fingers again."

Lania slipped her hand out of Oly's hole, leaving three fingers to pull the knob that her stimulation had formed in the front wall. Oly moaned and pulled her head down on his cock, hard. She sucked him even harder and pulsed her tongue around his cock while pulling down along the wall of his hole.

Oly groaned, the sound vibrating from his gut, and his legs shook helplessly. Hot, salty come shot out of him between her fingers and her mouth, pouring over her chin and down her chest.

Lania shivered, made wild by the dramatic orgasm, and turned her free hand to her own clit. As Oly fucked her mouth, pulling her head onto his cock again and again, Lania used his come to lubricate her clit and rubbed it in jerky circles. He slowed and stopped, so Lania switched to long licks from his ass to his cock, the pounded, quivering flesh taking her to the edge. His eyes opened and the soaked pleasure of them pushed her over into an orgasm of her own.

She crawled up next to Oly and her body gave in to lethargy.

Oly raised himself onto his knees to turn off the light. Her body felt bereft of his warmth in the moments between hitting the switch and settling back against her and snuggling her tight against his chest. Her exhausted body drew her inexorably into sleep and she settled into the pillow and mattress and, most importantly, into Oly.

Lania woke in the deep dark of early morning, needing to pee and feeling muzzy. She became aware that she was in Oly's bed and remembered the way they'd made love. Lania lay still and treasured the sound and feeling of Oly's warm breath on her shoulder. Finally, she had to get up. Oly snuffled and then settled back into sleep. She pulled on her pants and T-shirt and padded to the communal bathroom for the loft.

Lania heard the sound of a guitar in the big room. She stopped by the doorway and saw Carla, alone in the room. She sat on a stool, crooning to herself as she finger-picked a complex melody on her guitar.

"While I watch the rolling rain
Sweep the outside sidewalk clean
I stand, alone, and think of you
Wet serpentine shines olivine
You might be closer than the rain
Or farther than the world behind
I have no way to look for you
I weep for your inside my mind"

Lania blindly turned and made her way back to Oly's room. Her emotional core spoke more clearly than it could during the day, when her defenses were up.

She slid into bed and felt the sad, resigned song beat deep within, next to the flushed and swollen heart that ached with love for this wonderful man. Her head and heart filled with the wordless knowledge that love could be a weight that held you. How could she choose a life that didn't include Oly?

CHAPTER EIGHTEEN

Lania stood across Ginger's living room from her friends. They ranged alongside one another, Ginger in the middle as befit a ringleader. Lania gripped her hands behind her back, her spine straight.

"What is this, Ginger? An intervention?"

Carla sat on the rug, leaning against Verona's leg. She looked up at Verona, who was eyeing Melody where she sat on the couch across from them. Melody looked up at Joyce, who stood beside Ginger and looked at no one at all.

Ginger's gaze never faltered. "To be brutally honest, we think you and Oly are blowing it. You got yourselves back together, but you're not clearing up any of your problems."

"And you think calling me out in front of friends is going to change my behavior?"

"I think you're too smart to hold out against truth and creativity. We've got both, and we want to put them to work to help you be happy."

"Are you ever going to learn to stop meddling?" Lania thought, *stop*. No matter how much she wanted to lay into Ginger, she, at least, had the good taste and loyalty to wait until they were alone together. Ginger wasn't going to like what she had to say then.

"Meddling is only a bad idea when you're wrong," Ginger said. "It's clear that the two of you need to sail off into the sunset together."

"Clear to whom?" Lania shifted her weight to one hip and crossed her arms in front of her. "I haven't heard any such thing from Oly. He seemed happy enough for me when we talked about the boat I offered on. And I thought I'd talked to you in confidence."

Ginger's head reared back. "I haven't told these ladies anything they didn't already know. You know me better than that."

"Okay." So much for waiting until they were alone. Shame tapped her on the shoulder. "I'm sorry. That was uncalled for."

Joyce spoke. "The point, Lania, is that your desire to be with Oly is pervasive and clear."

"Clear as mud."

"Don't be facetious, dear. It doesn't become you."

Lania raised an eyebrow at Joyce's mild chiding. She took a look around and it soaked in. She was among friends, people she could trust. If she couldn't open up to them, when could she?

"You're right. I want Oly and sailing. I've never run into a situation where my desires were so contingent on someone else's." She rubbed her hands on her upper arms and let them drop. "Help."

Carla said, "What sort of help do you want?"

"Oh, a window into Oly's heart and mind for starters."

Joyce said, "Hearsay lacks trustworthiness, but Jeremy seems certain that Oly would like to go with you."

Lania shook her head. "I'm certain that a part of him likes the idea. But his documentary work is another crucial part of him."

Ginger nodded. "Verona, what do you think? You've known Oly longer than anyone here."

Verona spread her arms. "And I've been building a fantasy of working with this group long into the future. It's hard to let go of the hope that there'd be a prizewinning future for me, Oly, Jeremy, Roshan, Joyner, Edouard, and," putting her hand on her shoulder, "Carla."

Lania sighed. "Verona, I'm not trying to take Oly away from you and that future you want. I want that for him."

Verona said, "I wasn't finished. Here's what I think. Compromise sucks. Someone is always hurting some of the time. You want sailing and Oly, right?"

"Yeah, but I also want him to have everything he wants."

"That's what I'm talking about. I can't speak for him, not really, but I know he's passionate about you, making kick ass documentaries, and sailing. If you want to be as happy as possible with Oly, you need to find a way to have it all."

Carla leaned into Verona's knee and said, "You're too zealous to live only some of your dreams. Oly's focus has turned to sailing, and I think, Lania, that you will be miserably unhappy with yourself in the long run if you don't do this."

Melody chimed in. "I second that. For your mental health, you're going to have to sail."

"I know that I need to go and I know I need Oly. That takes care of the truth portion of this evening. How about some creativity? You say that Oly's focus has changed, but he still needs to stay."

"For a while." Verona spoke with certainty. "But between projects, or between the final print and the release, he is perfectly free to do anything he wants, anywhere."

Lania ran that through her mind. "You're saying that he could meet me wherever I am?"

"Or you could stay with him and help."

"That might work." The yearning in her voice had Ginger and Melody trading looks.

"You have a boat on the line," said Ginger. "You said the loan was approved and ready to go."

"The title search is done, too. I could have signed the papers last Friday."

"Instead, you spent the whole week with Oly or at work and didn't make the appointment to finalize the deal."

Melody said, "I helped move the press to the family that's using it for the community center on Thursday, so you even had the money for the down payment. They did pay, right?"

Ginger and Joyce looked at Lania sharply. "They paid, though I'm not surprised you'd think I might give it to them. If I could do without the money, I would have."

"What's the hold up?" asked Verona.

"Nothing. I just didn't do it. Fuck. I want Oly as much as I want a boat." Lania dropped on the low couch, her legs splayed out in front of her. She dropped her head on the back. "I don't know what to do with that. How can two desires be so finely balanced?"

"You want to sail so badly?" Carla asked the question gently.

"No. No, in the end, it's not the sailing. It's the dreaming. It's living up to my picture of myself and making damn sure I don't look back on this as the moment I lost myself because of love." Lania took a cleansing breath. "It's about being the person Oly loves and I respect. I'm an adventurer, a traveler, an explorer. Sailing allows me to be all of that with a home that comes with me and the freedom to keep myself going."

"You must discuss this with Oly." Joyce's tone had never been more didactic. "You cannot develop solutions if you fail to clarify the ground conditions."

"You're right, Joyce." Lania took stock of her friends. "On the other hand, I could sweeten the pot, couldn't I?"

Ginger said, "Tell me more."

Lania pursed her lips. "High intrigue is more your style, but what if I could find a different boat? One that would suit us both?"

"I fucking love you, Lania." Ginger's glow was mirrored on her other friends' faces.

"Because I'm thinking like you?"

"Maybe." At a knock on the door, Ginger stepped away from the fireplace. "That must be Hoss. I was wondering where he was."

"You really did invite everyone! I'm surprised Jeremy's not here."

Joyce glowered. "He was not invited."

"Soooooo sorry, everyone." Hoss pulled another man into the apartment behind him. "Meet the reason I'm late—this is my boyfriend, Kylan."

Lania watched Ginger look a long, long way up to Kylan. He was four inches taller than Hoss's own six feet and wider in the shoulders. Hoss maintained a double-handed grip when Kylan got a look at the six people near-filling the living room. Ginger said, "Why don't you two get kitchen chairs?"

Once everyone was introduced and Ginger had brought Hoss and Kylan up to date, she took back the group's attention. "I'm tickled by Lania's brainstorm about finding the perfect boat because I have been thinking the same thing. I have a friend—and yes, she's a very special friend—who works at a print shop. She has supplied us with a very important tool for this plan."

"Bring your machinations to a boil, Ginger, and please reveal for us the plan." Joyce's poetic flights were overtaking her language more often than before.

"Okay." Ginger pointed to a shopping bag. "In here, I have two items which will surely get Lania and Oly on a boat together."

Verona pulled the bag over. "*48° North?*"

"And the list that Lania and Oly made about the perfect two-person boat!"

"How did you get that?" Lania looked over at her backpack in the corner.

"A boat magazine is your whole plan?" Melody slumped back on the couch.

"Oh please." Exasperated, Ginger pulled out the top copy. "The magazine won't be distributed until Monday."

"Oh, it's like getting first dibs." Verona passed around the copies. She opened hers to the loose sheet of paper slipped in toward the end. Reading it, Verona's eyebrows hovered lower and lower. "What the hell is this shit? I don't think this is going to work."

Lania looked over the list and pressed her lips together hard. Ginger wasn't fond of being laughed at.

Ginger glared at Verona and answered with great dignity. "It's a list of everything they want on their dream boat."

Kylan coughed. "Hey, I know I'm new to this whole thing, but…where did you get this list?"

"I pirated it. I borrowed Lania's notebook and memorized as many of the things on the two-person boat page as I could. I made quick notes on the measurements and wrote the rest down later."

"Ah." He considered the list gravely. "I think you'll have a problem with some of this. For example, there's no such part on a boat as a 'wandlist'. Could it have been windlass?"

Lania said, "Yes, I imagine it was." She managed to remain sober-faced.

Carla asked, "Kylan, are you a boater?"

Hoss started to answer. "Oh, he's in the Navy…"

Kylan broke in. "And I used to be a regular sort of sailor." He flashed a grin at Hoss. "I know it sounds weird to most of you young queers, but I didn't realize I was gay until I'd already married. My poor wife. She didn't know what to do. We'd done something very similar to what you have in mind, Lania, except we wanted to sail to Hawaii and live there." He bit his lip. "Something about the sail to Hawaii clarified things for me. We spent thirty-three days between Los Angeles and Hawaii, watch on watch, staring into the big, big water. Our boat was pretty basic, so we rarely saw each other. When my four-hour watch was finished, my ex would get up and take over and I would go to sleep." Shaking his head, he shrugged off the memories. "The short version is that I knew I needed to change my life by the time we hit Hawaii. Honolulu is a military place and it seemed right that I leave my ex-wife the boat and join the Navy."

Hoss said, "Of course, a straight boy who wants to find some gay sex joins the most closeted organization ever, other than the priesthood."

"Kylan," said Lania, "can I pick your brain?"

"Well, sure. I know what to avoid and what I liked. What I didn't know from my own yacht-style sailing, I've learned since. Lots of Navy people are sailors out of uniform as well as in."

"What are some of the designs you like?"

"I'll show you. Who's got a computer?" Melody, Carla, and Joyce raised their hands.

Ginger said, "You can use the laptop on the kitchen table. It's online."

"What about the rest of us?" Melody asked.

Lania went to her backpack and pulled out her notebook. She flipped to the right page and said, "Here's the original two-person boat features list."

Ginger took Lania's list and disappeared into the kitchen. Lania and Kylan followed and saw her set the notebook under the strong dining table light. She took a quick picture with her phone and then sent it to her printer. With a wink, she grabbed a bottle from the cabinet and went to the doorway. "Who else wants wine?"

Four hours later, a snuggly, wine-softened group looked at Kylan. He was looking at the *48° North* and exclaimed out loud. Lania was still on the computer, combing through online boat ads for some of the boats Kylan liked. Everyone with a computer had it out, helping with the searches. They had debated a couple of boats as a group, but she hadn't seen the one yet.

Kylan compared his hand-written notes from his conversation with Lania to the description in the magazine.

"At what are you looking?" Joyce inquired with careful boozy composure.

"It's a great boat—a little more than you talked about spending, even with two people making payments, but a sweet design. There's a website."

Lania gave up her seat at the dining table. Kylan took the chair and navigated them through all the information about the boat.

The boat was packed with gear and priced to sell.

"Don't wait until the magazine has been distributed. What if someone beats you to it?" Ginger asked.

Lania saw the ad for the Rob's boat, just as he had told her to expect. Comparing the two in the magazine—the one she'd made an offer on and the one she was starting to hope she would get—there was no contest. Kylan had found the boat for her and Oly.

Later that night, Oly sat on his bed, elbows on knees, looking up at Jeremy. "Sit down. We need to talk."

Jeremy plopped down on the replacement for the chair Oly and Lania had shattered. "Sounds serious. Are you breaking up with me?"

"I hope not."

The seriousness in his voice brought Jeremy's head up to look at him.

"Dude, I was joking. What's up?"

Oly hesitated. He hadn't gone so far as to script what he wanted to say, but he'd thought about the points to be made. It was harder than he'd thought it would be to lay it out.

"Come on, Oly, you're making me nervous."

"Sorry. Okay, so you joked about breaking up and I guess that's a pretty good lead-in to what I want to talk about. Jeremy, I don't want to lose you."

Jeremy sat straighter.

"I have to go. Lania has rubbed off on me, like you said ages ago. And I'm in love with her. I want to be with her as much as I can, without losing everything else I care about. That includes you."

Jeremy said, "So, do you mean me as a friend?"

"Definitely that, but not just that. I want to keep working with you as often as you're available. I've monopolized you, and I know there are some great producers who would love to get you on their projects. If I'm on a trip when you get a great offer, I would never expect you to turn it down."

"Seriously, man? You've monopolized me?" Oly had very rarely heard this tone from Jeremy. "It's insulting that you think you've been so completely in control all this time. You know people want to work with me? Well, I'm the one actually getting offers. And in case you think I'm a total idiot, I've considered every one of them. Maybe only for a second, but at least a little. I'm not your little brother and I'm not your slave."

"No," Oly said, shaking his head. "You're my best friend."

Jeremy stopped, then sighed. "Exactly. I've worked with you all these years because I wanted to. Because we're best friends and, well, I love you, man."

He looked so determined and uncomfortable. Oly said, "I love you too, Jeremy."

Jeremy bulled on through. "But mostly because you have great ideas. Fuck, I have great ideas. Together, we have been able to take little inspirations and build them into big achievements. And great films. If it were nothing but friendship, I would have stopped working with you ages ago. I need to make great films as badly as you do, Oly, and I'll keep doing it even if you're gone."

"Okay, then. I didn't mean to imply that you aren't as motivated or as passionate about film as I am. My feelings got in the way of seeing…who's made you offers?" Oly shook his head. "Never mind. Here's my point. You're right about the great ideas we've had. We have a list of topics we could explore in film, but there's a whole big world out there. I think there's more to explore, there are more ideas to be had, by getting out and seeing it."

"Sure. Of course there is."

Jeremy's reasonable tone frustrated Oly. He wanted enthusiasm, damn it. "Do you want to get out there and see it?"

"Not by boat."

Oly waved that away. "That's not necessary. As a matter of fact, that would ruin my idea."

Jeremy leaned back in the chair. "You have an idea, do you?"

"Oh, yeah, I have an idea. Hopefully the first of many that will give us everything we want. All of us."

"Let's hear it."

"I was letting Lania's dream color mine, after all. She needs to pare her life down, but mine can only get so small if I'm going to keep making the documentaries I want to make."

"That's what I said."

"And I had to come back to that realization myself. I can do a lot of work with small DV cameras, but to do the real deal, I need more. Turns out that I want Lania and travel, but I also want to stay productive."

"Enough build-up, Oly. I'm on the edge of my seat. What's your idea?"

"It's Kiribati, an island chain in the Pacific, about halfway between Hawaii and Australia. The Second World War displaced thousands of people in the South Pacific from fighting and atomic testing. The US responded by shipping in load after load of white rice, white flour, and white sugar. That area has enormous diabetes and dentistry problems as a result, stretching into the current moment."

"I bet there's a lot of great history there. What's the angle?"

"The angle is interference as destruction. There are tons of examples of the US doing something to help, only to have the efforts go awry or disappear altogether. In one, an earmark in some random bill gave—outright—two retired Coast Guard cutters to a faith-based organization with the idea that they would use them to bring medical and dental care to the outlying islands. Those cutters never made it farther than San Francisco Bay, according to the New York Times, but the missionaries did. I'd like to know how explicit or implicit the tie is between getting health care from them and accepting their religious ideologies."

"Hmm." Jeremy pondered. "How do the people of Kiribati feel about all this?"

Oly shrugged. "We can read other people's work, and we should. But how would you like to go find out?"

"Travel to a former Pacific paradise and expose the imported snakes in the sand?" Jeremy stood. "Love to. If we were all infinitely rich, we'd fly all over the world, meeting up and making films wherever we wanted."

Oly stood with him. "You can't fool me. I can see your teeth sinking into this idea as we speak. We can make this happen."

"Maybe." Jeremy migrated to Oly's computer. "We would fly there—the crew, I mean. We might have to bring all our own gear. Who's going to rent us equipment to be shipped to distant islands? I need more information."

"Definitely. Um, by the way, I've already floated the idea, in a general way, by Madeline."

Jeremy whistled. "She has serious juice. She liked the idea?"

"Loved it. Great visuals, from the early photos of the unspoiled islands through the atomic testing images. Also, I used the idea that Lania and I would sail there as another angle. GoPro cameras in the rigging and dolphins on the bow. That set off fireworks. Jeremy. She's talking a series by sail."

"Hell yeah." Jeremy pulled his lower lip. "We need more ideas. Where are you sailing first?"

"First is convincing Lania to get a bigger boat. Second is convincing her that we can prepare for our trip from here so I can take care of promoting *Strike!* Third is figuring out where the hell we're going to go first."

"I believe in your persuasive powers, Oly. So destinations are open?"

"She doesn't seem to have any itinerary. Just some basic places she doesn't want to miss. Thailand, New Zealand, Madagascar."

"Madagascar is fascinating, historically and politically."

They looked at each other.

"Let's do this." Oly stuck his hand out.

Jeremy walked past it and hugged him. Oly wrapped his arms around his best friend for a moment, then pounded him on the back and pushed him away.

"You get to work on shaping some rough plans and I'll get to work on Lania."

"Oh, that reminds me. Joyce gave me this magazine for you. She said you should check out the boat she circled."

"Joyce was looking at boats?"

Jeremy shrugged.

Oly flipped through until he found the boat circled in red. Of course she used a red pencil. His amusement disappeared when he read the brief ad. "Jeremy, I'm going to need the computer for a minute."

Lania rode her bike down the hill from her apartment. The weather could go either way. It was a morning of promise. Thick, heavy clouds covered most of the sky, and the ground was wet from the night's rain, but there were breaks in the clouds that could mean a nice afternoon. Like any good Seattleite, Lania was attuned to the hope of direct sunlight. She had brought all her waterproof biking gear, but she only wore her uniform of bike shorts and T-shirt.

The exhilarating downhill ride blew away the cobwebs. The speed and wind gave her mind a rest from the closed track on which it had been racing. Was she going to see that boat or wasn't she? The bottom of the hill came far too soon, and Lania turned toward the Center for Wooden Boats. After reaching the sodden, glowing park, she dropped her bike on the grass and sat at the picnic table she'd shared with Oly those short months ago. The damp bench was chill against the backs of her thighs.

She pulled the magazine out and opened it to the boat they'd found the day before. The Center's employees were working, not paying any attention to her. Lania leaned over the *48° North*. The line of the bow caught her eye again. It was high and strong, dipping a bit but maintaining a high freeboard all the way back to the cockpit. The boat was a cutter rigged sloop with a pilothouse. And it looked great, at least in the black-and-white print of the magazine.

Lania pulled her ubiquitous notebook out of her backpack and flipped to the boat search section. She flipped back and forth until she found their list of qualities for the perfect two-person boat. The ad read like a recap of their most important features list, plus some nice things they hadn't thought of, like brand new covers for everything.

Lania scoffed, yeah, and I bet this photo is ten years old. The images online had looked even better than the newsprint allowed. They could be old as well. She'd seen so many boats that read well, but showed poorly. She studied the picture and admitted to herself that new covers didn't sound like a boat that had been ignored. The owner also said in the ad that he spent every Sunday on the boat, sailing, working, or cleaning. She thought that seemed to point at a boat that was treasured, and she wondered why he was selling it.

She pondered the ad for a few more moments and then gave in to curiosity.

It was Sunday, the owner's day to work on the boat, and Lania shook her head. She was going to look at the boat. Enough waffling. Not looking at all would be irresponsible. She had to go to the Shilshole Marina and see this boat for herself.

❖

Oly unrolled the *48° North* that Jeremy had left him the night before and sat at the counter of the sparkling fifties-style diner at First and Blanchard. He nodded a greeting to Susan, the waitress, who gestured hello with her coffee pot from the other end of the expanse of green Formica. He turned the cup in front of him upright as the signal that she should fill it with coffee. After she refilled the coffees along the counter on the way toward him, she leaned on the counter and filled his cup.

"How you doing, gorgeous?" She flirted mildly and fanned herself with her order pad.

"Better now that you're in my world." Oly flirted back, the routine friendliness of it lifting his spirits.

"Oooh, honey, you better watch out with a quicksilver tongue like that." Susan ducked her head and peeked out from under her Bettie Page bangs. "A girl might get ideas for other things that tongue could do."

"Scandal!" cried the mock-horrified regular at the other end of the counter.

"Go on now. You know I'm taken." Oly growled at her playfully. He felt a sharp stab in his chest, wondering if it were true. "I'll have the waffle."

Susan took the hint and sauntered off to put in his order, leaving him to his funk. Even a hot woman like Susan in an old-fashioned waitress skirt and apron couldn't keep his attention. Oly shook his head as he flipped through the letters to the editor, glanced at the articles, and headed inexorably toward the classifieds at the back of the magazine.

Oly was well into his second cup of coffee and starting on his waffle before he looked at the boat ad circled in red pencil. He studied the photo of a boat he might have designed. He reread the ad, remembering the additional details from the Web. He closed the magazine and stared at the cover as he finished his waffle and downed a last cup of coffee. How strange to find a boat that was so right, already circled…he thought about Jeremy and Joyce reading *48° North* and shook his head.

It was a bit more than Lania had wanted to pay. He could contribute, but not significantly until he made some sort of deal for the film.

He wished that Lania had been there to share her eggs with him, and he tried to shake the thought out of his head. The boat she'd offered on didn't hold a candle to the one in the ad. If, that is, it was really as good as it sounded. He picked up the magazine after paying and rolled it back up to tuck under his arm. Maybe he should take a look.

Oly strode along First, trying to absorb as much vitamin D from the diffuse sunlight as possible. He allowed his mind to drift, emptying it and being aware of the sun's warmth.

Having the right boat on tap would make it a lot easier to talk her into waiting for him, wouldn't it? Thoughts of sailing that amazing boat with Lania crept back. Instead of snarled, though, the underlying feeling was peaceful. Yes, he would go see this boat. If it looked as though it might suit them, he would ask her to see it with him.

Oly stood at his front door a moment and then trod up the stairs. As he reached the first landing, his cell rang. It wasn't Lania's special ring, but he pulled the phone from his pocket anyway and answered it.

❖

Lania reached the salty railing that edged the marina and hopped off her bike. The ad said to call once she got there, and she pulled her phone out and dialed the local number. A gruff-voiced man answered. "Hello?"

Lania cleared her throat. "Hi there. I'm hoping to look at your boat. I'm at the marina office building now."

The man rumbled. "Well, I've already had an offer on it. The man seems serious, but he left to figure out how he could get me a down payment."

Lania leaned against the gate, sadness roiling within her. "Well, I rode my bike here from the Center for Wooden Boats. If it's no hassle, I'd love to look at it regardless."

"Sure. As far as I know, this man could have disappeared for good. Without anything in writing, I'm not going to stop showing the boat. Come on down to the gate marked 'R' and I'll be waiting to let you in."

Lania had locked her bike at the office, and she decided to walk down to the right gate rather than unlock and relock her bike to bring it closer. She looked into the water fifteen feet below and spotted a purple jellyfish. Breathing the fresh breeze off the Puget Sound, she strode down the sidewalk, amused by her own faculty for hope. Why did she want this boat to be the one? The seagulls screamed at each other and whirled around a mast before shooting off over the water. She gave in to her burgeoning excitement when she caught sight of the boat. It looked as wonderful as in the grainy picture. Her steps quickened as she neared the gate.

Lania held out her hand as she reached the older man at the gate. "I'm Lania Marchiol. Thanks for letting me look at your boat."

"I'm Rashid Khan. Please, come on down."

The cordial man charmed Lania with his firm handshake and rough hands, but she was captivated by his mix of happiness and sadness. He seemed very fit and energetic in contrast to the deep lines in his face. He could be fifty or seventy, depending on whether you believed his aged face or able body.

She led the way to the boat and stood next to it, considering the lines. Rashid cleared his throat. "I'm amazed to have had two people come look at the boat already. I thought the magazine came out tomorrow?"

She confirmed that with a nod and a shrug. "My friend has a friend at the publisher's. I don't know how the other guy got one. Same story, I bet." She walked over to the steps. "Permission to come aboard, Captain?"

"Permission granted."

Lania began her process, refined on the dozens of boats she'd seen. At the bow, she inspected the seam where the bowsprit attached and began working her way back. She couldn't hide her awe. The boat was in marvelous condition as far as she could tell. After she had rocked the wheel back and forth to feel how tight the connection to the rudder was, Lania looked at Rashid, who had gone back to polishing the stainless steel stanchions. She signaled her desire to go below, and Rashid nodded a simple agreement.

As her vision adjusted to the dimness below decks, delight grew within Lania. She recognized the hand of smart designers, builders, and owners in the tight, orderly stowage of every necessity of boat life. The maintenance log was close at hand in the navigation area, and Lania sat down to study this document. Distantly, she heard a cell phone ring and then heard Rashid's rough voice saying hello. She sat a moment, sad that she wasn't going to be the happy new owner of the boat.

Rashid called down to her. "Lania, I'm going to let this man in the gate. I'll be back in a minute."

"Okay," Lania called back, forcing a measure of cheerfulness into her voice.

Her silent mournfulness ended when voices neared the boat. Lania stiffened and her stomach jumped into her throat. She looked around in desperation and then stood. She knew that voice.

Lania left the cabin, stepped off the boat, and stopped.

Oly stared. "What are you doing here? I've been looking for you."

Rashid gestured at Oly. "Lania, this is the man I told you about. The man who made an offer on the boat."

She breathed once, twice. She took another step and then threw herself into Oly's arms.

Lania spoke into his shirt. "I'm here for the same reason you are. A one-person boat's no good when there are two people involved."

Oly's arms wrapped her up and his breathing caught in a series of near-sobs. "I can't believe you're here."

Lania repeated the words. "I can't believe that you're here. Except that somehow it seems like the most perfectly right moment of my life." She pushed back and looked Oly in the eye. She felt a small measure of shame that she had waited until the answer was so obvious to ask. "Do you want to go sailing with me? I might never stop, but we can come back here or go wherever you need to be for filming and production."

Oly caught her face in his trembling hands. "Yes, I want to sail with you. I love you. We'll make the rest work out—scheduling and planning and dreaming powerful dreams together."

Lania took his hands in hers. "What's this about making Rashid an offer?"

"This boat is so perfect. I knew you had to see it. But I'm not trying to make this decision for you. I want to give you all the room you need."

"I love you too. I know what I need now. I need you. I need for us to be together, in love and strong, taking the world on our terms."

Lania looked around Oly and caught Rashid wiping a tear from his eye. "Don't mind me, young ones. I got a little caught up in all the emotion around here. I'm still a bit fragile. I'm a widower now, just lost my wife of forty-five years."

Oly turned and wrapped an arm around Lania's shoulders as she spoke. "I'm so sorry! Have you been alone for long?"

Rashid shook his head. "No, Alana has only been gone for a month. One of the first things I did was to write the ad for this boat." He looked up at the rigging, blinking against the tears filling his eyes. "You have much to celebrate."

Oly squeezed Lania's shoulder and turned her toward him. "How about our wedding?"

Lania blinked away the quick tears and choked out a broken answer. "Yes!" She threw her arms around Oly and kissed him on the mouth. "Yes."

Rashid cheered. "Come aboard! We must share a toast." He pulled a bottle of champagne out of the icebox and began to work on the cork. He grunted as he pulled. "I stocked the boat with this in preparation for selling her. It's traditional to gift the new boat owner with a bottle of wine, and I wanted to encourage a real celebration for whomever ended up with this lovely boat."

The cork gave at that moment and Lania and Oly cheered for the smooth, soft pop that Rashid elicited from the bottle. He poured three flutes of champagne and offered a toast. "To the long and rocky road of life. May yours be more happiness than pain, more hope than despair, and more love than loneliness. You're well on your way!"

Lania and Oly lifted their glasses to tap against Rashid's and they all drank to his toast. The three of them sat in the main saloon of the boat.

Rashid spoke lovingly of his late wife and explained that the boat had been more hers than his. She had sailed all her life, and he had been pulled along into boating by his early and enduring desire to spend as much time with her as possible. "Alana was special. She had such joy in the sound of water, and the only regret she ever had was that she never anchored this boat in water warm enough to swim in." Rashid's happy memories absorbed him for a moment, and Lania took Oly's hand to reassure herself of his reality, sitting next to her on a boat that would be theirs.

Lania looked around the interior of the boat. "I barely had time to look around, and I'd like to talk everything over with Oly. When we've finished our drinks, can we finish looking around?"

Rashid assured them that he would be happy to have them around as long as they wanted to stay. Lania finished her champagne while flipping through the maintenance log. Rashid told lovely stories of some of the bigger projects. He and his wife had done most of the work on the boat themselves. Lania listened with growing respect as Rashid's stories proved that regardless of how he got into sailing, he was every inch a sailor.

Oly and Lania sat, his arm slung along the back of the settee, linking them with a light touch on her shoulders. He looked over at her, tipped his head at the forepeak, and raised an eyebrow. "Do you want to get to work on the bow?"

Lania agreed, and Rashid took himself above decks to give them some privacy. She worked her way through every inch of the boat, and she couldn't believe how wonderful it was. It wasn't just the immaculate shape of all the systems; the boat was laid out and customized in ways that fit almost all of their needs. The last few things could be added easily. Hugging in the middle of the saloon,

Oly and Lania absorbed the idea of living in this boat. They sat again, opposite each other this time, and looked around. Lania spoke. "I could live here."

"And I could travel in this boat."

"But I can't use the loan I'm approved for. This might be outside my financial limits." She ran her hand across the fabric of the settee cushion. "I sold Esmeralda for a down payment, but this is kind of a lot."

Oly shook his head and took her hands, his elbows on his knees. "Listen to me, Lania. I need you to accept a gift from me."

Lania felt a rising sense of tense anticipation. "Oh?"

"I got a phone call right after I decided to look at the boat." He stared at Lania and took a deep breath. "I sold the distribution rights to the film. It's done."

Lania's jaw dropped and she fell back against the cushion. "And you forgot this little piece of information until now?"

Oly flushed a little. "I don't know, somehow asking the woman of my dreams to marry me seemed a bit absorbing. But I figured it all out before I did the ride out here. Once the money comes through, I can buy this boat."

"You got that much in advance?"

Oly nodded, excitement running through him like electricity. "Even after the investors get their cut."

Lania sat, stunned. Oly's excitement started to turn to tension. "What are you thinking, Lania?"

"Well, I guess I'm thinking that we had better nail Rashid down to our offer before someone else comes to look at the boat."

Oly jumped to his feet. He swept Lania into his arms. "Really? You'll let me do that?"

Lania's giddy laughter spilled from her as Oly swung her in abbreviated circles in the main saloon of her dream boat. She grasped his biceps and let him sweep her away. When he put her down, she calmed enough to reply. "I have the down payment and you'll pay the rest of the purchase price. And I promise, this will be the last time I split the expenses in my head. From here on out, we're partners."

Oly pressed a firm kiss to her lips. "It might take a little while for the money to come through. I'm afraid it'll be too late to set off this fall. And I have some obligations."

"That's okay. We'll explore the San Juan Islands and the Sunshine Coast and Vancouver Island. We should probably spend some time in familiar waters making sure we know everything about the boat before we take off on the ocean."

Oly gusted a sigh. "I'm so glad to hear you say that. If we leave next summer, I'll be able to be around for promoting the film."

"Well, I have plans for an online magazine, and you'll need a computer of your own for digital editing. Getting that set up, plus supplying this boat for the trip with a watermaker…everything we might need…I'm sure we'll both have plenty to do. And then we'll leave."

"Wherever we want to go. Speaking of which, I've got a great idea for a documentary."

"Of course you do." Lania stroked Oly's jaw. "You're perfect for me."

"We're perfect for each other."

EPILOGUE

Oly watched Lania stretch, twisting her arms in the air to work out the weight of the heavy grocery bags. She adjusted her halter top and sarong, and stooped to grab the bags again.

"Want me to take one or two of those?"

Lania squinted in the bright Hawaiian sun and shook her head. "I've got it. I just needed a break." She squared her shoulders under the load. "Besides, we're almost there."

Lania had proven herself strong. The sail from Seattle to the San Francisco Bay had been exciting and exhausting, a feeling that had continued in the first part of the sail to Hawaii. Once they hit the Tropic of Cancer, life had become easy and comfortable. The memory of saltwater bathing nude on deck reminded him to put more sunscreen on when they reached the boat.

Through lava rock and lush growth, Oly followed Lania down the lane to the boat launch. They both dumped their loads into the dingy and then climbed in. Lania took up the oars and moaned at the stretch and work of her abused shoulder muscles. "Oh, that feels good." He now knew how the large muscle movements of rowing could work out the knots created by other kinds of stress.

When they reached their anchored boat, Oly clambered up into the cockpit and took the groceries Lania lifted from the bottom of the boat. She followed him up and they brought the dingy on board and flipped it over on the bow of the boat.

Lania stretched again and gazed about at the paradise of the sheltered cove. She stepped over the anchor windlass and wrapped her arms around Oly from the back. She snuggled up and then patted his belly. "Sunscreen."

Oly rubbed the backs of her hands. "You want to put it on for me?" Lania agreed and they spent a delightful hour in the distraction of gliding their hands over each other. One thing led to another, and when they came to, sweating and satisfied, they both jumped, hollering, off the boat into the warm water of the island of Hawaii. Oly wiped his hand over his much cooler chest while treading water. "We got an e-mail from Rashid. He sent well-wishes and thanked me for sending him the pictures of you diving off the bow into the bay." Oly chuckled. "Dirty old man. He just liked seeing you in your bathing suit."

Lania laughed and dove to check their anchor. She came up fast, bursting through the surface of the water like a whale breeching, then dove again. On her next trip to the surface, she climbed up Oly's body until she wrapped her legs around his waist and helped tread water by waving her arms slowly. Her mouth close to his, Lania sighed. "It's time."

She and Oly disengaged, then climbed the rope ladder onto the boat and pulled it up after them. Lania turned on the navigation instruments.

She touched her super-fast laptop. Before they left, Lania had worked out the kinks on bringing *Literate Life* into the twenty-first century. She now published the magazine online and in a subscription e-mail newsletter. People paid better for the e-mail subscription than they had for the physical magazine. Her dad produced a printed version that he mailed to the few people who preferred the old way. He and Lania e-mailed a couple of times a week, staying in better contact by e-mail than they had since she left for college.

Lania had given Oly a compact, feature-filled digital video camera that traveled in a special waterproof case. The documentary about Kiribati would need more equipment, but she knew Jeremy would take care of that. She'd gotten into the planning of the new film, from the conception forward, and found that traveling for a purpose was highly rewarding. Lania hauled the main sail up with the main sheet slacked while Oly winched the anchor out of the sand of the bay. When he yelled the all clear, Lania took in the sheet until the boat began to catch wind. They began sailing.

Lania stood, exhilarated, behind the wheel. Oly finished hauling in the anchor and then stood at the bow, legs spread. They both absorbed the increasing rush of the wind and water and watched the point begin to fall behind them. Lania cheered when they were clear of land. "On to Kiribati!"

Oly made his way back to the cockpit and hauled out the roller-furling jib. They picked up more speed and made some small adjustments before setting up the Monitor wind vane to mind the wheel for them. After watching the Big Island fall back toward the horizon, Oly and Lania settled in for a sail that would last the rest of their lives.

About the Author

Dena Hankins writes aboard her boat, whether on the high seas or in a quiet anchorage. She spent eight years as a sexpert at Babeland, soaking up the most stimulating stories of human sexuality, and is honored to provide some tales in return. Being a military brat, wanderlust is deep in her, and she has been sailing since 1999, covering waters from Seattle to San Francisco, across to Hawaii, and from Virginia to Maine. Her first three publications are erotic short stories with far-flung settings—India, North Carolina, and deep space. Whether traveling in the physical world or ranging far in her imagination, she is happiest accompanied by her partner of eighteen years.

Visit Dena at denahankins.net
or email her at dena@denahankins.net.

Books Available from Bold Strokes Books

Edge of Awareness by C.A. Popovich. When Maria, a woman in the middle of her third divorce, meets Dana, an out lesbian, awareness of her feelings bring up reservations about the teachings of her church. (978-1-62639-188-8)

Taken by Storm by Kim Baldwin. Lives depend on two women when a train derails high in the remote Alps, but an unforgiving mountain, avalanches, crevasses, and other perils stand between them and safety. (978-1-62639-189-5)

The Common Thread by Jaime Maddox. Dr. Nicole Coussart's life is falling apart, but fortunately, DEA Attorney Rae Rhodes is there to pick up the pieces and help Nic put them back together. (978-1-62639-190-1)

Jolt by Kris Bryant. Mystery writer Bethany Lange wasn't prepared for the twisting emotions that left her breathless the moment she laid eyes on folk singer sensation Ali Hart. (978-1-62639-191-8)

Searching For Forever by Emily Smith. Dr. Natalie Jenner's life has always been about saving others, until young paramedic Charlie Thompson comes along and shows her maybe she's the one who needs saving. (978-1-62639-186-4)

A Queer Sort of Justice: Prison Tales Across Time by Rebecca S. Buck. When liberty is only a memory, and all seems lost, what freedoms and hopes can be found within us? (978-1-62639-195-6E)

Blue Water Dreams by Dena Hankins. Lania Marchiol keeps her wary sailor's gaze trained on the horizon until Oly Rassmussen, a wickedly handsome trans man, sends her trusty compass spinning off course. (978-1-62639-192-5)

Rest Home Runaways by Clifford Henderson. Baby boomer Morgan Ronzio's troubled marriage is the least of her worries when she gets the call that her addled, eighty-six-year-old, half-blind dad has escaped the rest home. (978-1-62639-169-7)

Charm City by Mason Dixon. Raq Overstreet's loyalty to her drug kingpin boss is put to the test when she begins to fall for Bathsheba Morris, the undercover cop assigned to bring him down. (978-1-62639-198-7)

Let the Lover Be by Sheree Greer. Kiana Lewis, a functional alcoholic on the verge of destruction, finally faces the demons of her past while finding love and earning redemption in New Orleans. (978-1-62639-077-5)

Blindsided by Karis Walsh. Blindsided by love, guide dog trainer Lenae McIntyre and media personality Cara Bradley learn to trust what they see with their hearts. (978-1-62639-078-2)

About Face by VK Powell. Forensic artist Macy Sheridan and Detective Leigh Monroe work on a case that has troubled them both for years, but they're hampered by the past and their unlikely yet undeniable attraction. (978-1-62639-079-9)

Blackstone by Shea Godfrey. For Darry and Jessa, their chance at a life of freedom is stolen by the arrival of war and an ancient prophecy that just might destroy their love. (978-1-62639-080-5)

Out of This World by Maggie Morton. Iris decided to cross an ocean to get over her ex. But instead, she ends up traveling much farther, all the way to another world. Once there, only a mysterious, sexy, and magical woman can help her return home. (978-1-62639-083-6)

Kiss The Girl by Melissa Brayden. Sleeping with the enemy has never been so complicated. Brooklyn Campbell and Jessica Lennox face off in love and advertising in fast-paced New York City. (978-1-62639-071-3)

Taking Fire: A First Responders Novel by Radclyffe. Hunted by extremists and under siege by nature's most virulent weapons, Navy medic Max de Milles and Red Cross worker Rachel Winslow join forces to survive and discover something far more lasting. (978-1-62639-072-0)

First Tango in Paris by Shelley Thrasher. When French law student Eva Laroche meets American call girl Brigitte Green in 1970s Paris, they have no idea how their pasts and futures will intersect. (978-1-62639-073-7)

The War Within by Yolanda Wallace. Army nurse Meredith Moser went to Vietnam in 1967 looking to help those in need; she didn't expect to meet the love of her life along the way. (978-1-62639-074-4)

Escapades by MJ Williamz. Two women, afraid to love again, must overcome their fears to find the happiness that awaits them. (978-1-62639-182-6)

Desire at Dawn by Fiona Zedde. For Kylie, love had always come armed with sharp teeth and claws. But with the human, Olivia, she bares her vampire heart for the very first time, sharing passion, lust, and a tenderness she'd never dared dream of before. (978-1-62639-064-5)

Visions by Larkin Rose. Sometimes the mysteries of love reveal themselves when you least expect it. Other times they hide behind a black satin mask. Can Paige unveil her masked stranger this time? (978-1-62639-065-2)

All In by Nell Stark. Internet poker champion Annie Navarro loses everything when the Feds shut down online gambling, and she turns to experienced casino host Vesper Blake for advice—but can Nova convince Vesper to take a gamble on romance? (978-1-62639-066-9)

Vermilion Justice by Sheri Lewis Wohl. What's a vampire to do when Dracula is no longer just a character in a novel? (978-1-62639-067-6)

Switchblade by Carsen Taite. Lines were meant to be crossed. Third in the Luca Bennett Bounty Hunter Series. (978-1-62639-058-4)

Nightingale by Andrea Bramhall. Culture, faith, and duty conspire to tear two young lovers apart, yet fate seems to have different plans for them both. (978-1-62639-059-1)

No Boundaries by Donna K. Ford. A chance meeting and a nightmare from the past threaten more than Andi Massey's solitude as she and Gwen Palmer struggle to understand the complexity of love without boundaries. (978-1-62639-060-7)

Timeless by Rachel Spangler. When Stevie Geller returns to her hometown, will she do things differently the second time around or will she be in such a hurry to leave her past that she misses out on a better future? (978-1-62639-050-8)

Second to None by L.T. Marie. Can a physical therapist and a custom motorcycle designer conquer their pasts and build a future with one another? (978-1-62639-051-5)

Seneca Falls by Jesse Thoma. Together, two women discover love truly can conquer all evil. (978-1-62639-052-2)

A Kingdom Lost by Barbara Ann Wright. Without knowing each other's fates, Princess Katya and her consort Starbride seek to reclaim their kingdom from the magic-wielding madman who seized the throne and is murdering their people. (978-1-62639-053-9)

Season of the Wolf by Robin Summers. Two women running from their pasts are thrust together by an unimaginable evil. Can they overcome the horrors that haunt them in time to save each other? (978-1-62639-043-0)

The Heat of Angels by Lisa Girolami. Fires burn in more than one place in Los Angeles. (978-1-62639-042-3)

Desperate Measures by P. J. Trebelhorn. Homicide detective Kay Griffith and contractor Brenda Jansen meet amidst turmoil neither of them is aware of until murder suspect Tommy Rayne makes his move to exact revenge on Kay. (978-1-62639-044-7)

The Magic Hunt by L.L. Raand. With her Pack being hunted by human extremists and beset by enemies masquerading as friends, can Sylvan protect them and her mate, or will she succumb to the feral rage that threatens to turn her rogue, destroying them all? A Midnight Hunters novel. (978-1-62639-045-4)

Wingspan by Karis Walsh. Wildlife biologist Bailey Chase is content to live at the wild bird sanctuary she has created on Washington's Olympic Peninsula until she is lured beyond the safety of isolation by architect Kendall Pearson. (978-1-60282-983-1)

Windigo Thrall by Cate Culpepper. Six women trapped in a mountain cabin by a blizzard, stalked by an ancient cannibal demon bent on stealing their sanity—and their lives. (978-1-60282-950-3)

The Blush Factor by Gun Brooke. Ice-cold business tycoon Eleanor Ashcroft only cares about the three Ps—Power, Profit, and Prosperity—until young Addison Garr makes her doubt both that and the state of her frostbitten heart. (978-1-60282-985-5)

Slash and Burn by Valerie Bronwen. The murder of a roundly despised author at an LGBT writers' conference in New Orleans turns Winter Lovelace's relaxing weekend hobnobbing with her peers into a nightmare of suspense—especially when her ex turns up. (978-1-60282-986-2)

The Quickening: A Sisters of Spirits Novel by Yvonne Heidt. Ghosts, visions, and demons are all in a day's work for Tiffany. But when Kat asks for help on a serial killer case, life takes on another dimension altogether. (978-1-60282-975-6)

Smoke and Fire by Julie Cannon. Oil and water, passion and desire, a combustible combination. Can two women fight the fire that draws them together and threatens to keep them apart? (978-1-60282-977-0)